1

He couldn't resist the urge any longer.

He lay awake in bed, unable to sleep, clenching his pillow as he felt that familiar urge making its final push to overtake him once again. It was pounding on his senses, demanding to be set free and allowed to feed.

He used to have more control. He used to be able to hold it back longer. Six whole years separated his first time from his second. Then, four more years had passed before he gave in to the urge again. But now, faster than ever before, it had resurfaced. Despite trying everything to distract himself, more work, heavy reading, hours of prayer, after only eighteen short months that horrible, wonderful desire was back. And now it was stronger.

Much too strong to deny.

He squeezed his eyes tight, took a deep breath, and whispered his secret to the darkness. "Yes. Okay."

With those words his body eased and a calming warmth filled him. The fight was over for now. He had given in entirely to his longing and all that was left was to enjoy where it took him this time.

He drew a sharp breath as the fantasies that would soon be realities flooded in. The smells, the sensations, the squeals, the squirming.

"Yesssss."

He couldn't wait.

Why should he wait?

He'd do it tomorrow.

He rifled his schedule in his head. There was nothing he couldn't cancel or postpone. Nothing more important than this. Not even close.

Tomorrow.

The thought made him moan and squeeze his pillow tighter.

Yesssss.

He fought the urge to touch himself and relieve the pressure growing down there.

No. Save it.

He turned to the glowing clock at his bedside.

3:12 AM

Tomorrow was Saturday. No school. They'd be out and about no earlier than nine. Ten to be safe.

He rechecked the clock.

He'd have to wait seven long hours.

He took a deep breath and told himself to be calm. He was too excited to sleep, so he decided to fill the time by coming up with a plan. After all, the last thing he wanted to do was get caught.

He rolled onto his back, stared up at the ceiling, and set his mind to the task.

Somewhere a dog barked, a truck rumbled by, and he heard a bird that sings at night.

He'd gotten away with it several times before, so it shouldn't be too hard. Still, when he made his move, he had to be careful.

THE UNKIND HOURS

DWAYNE ALEXANDER SMITH

DAMN GOOD BOOKS

To the memory of my dad Albert James Strother.
He taught me how to survive and he always had my back.

The parents weren't his only worry. No.
There were always so many eyes watching the little ones.

His fingertips were only inches from the ball.

Steven Burns was lying belly down in the gutter, his right arm extended shoulder deep into a storm drain, every muscle of his upper body straining to reach an errant sponge rubber baseball.

The ball rested three feet below street level at the bottom of the drain's catch basin. Due to California's recent drought, the accumulation of dead leaves and litter, upon which the ball sat, was dry and dusty. Kissed by sunlight filtered through steel grating, the white ball almost seemed to glow in the subterranean gloom. If not for the scuffed Rawlings logo on its surface, Steven thought the ball could easily be mistaken for an egg left unattended in a nest of trash.

The ball was right there. He just had to get a little closer.

Steven wedged his right shoulder against the steel-lined curb inlet and groaned as he struggled to telescope his arm just a bit further. He stretched and stretched and-- "Dammit!"

It was no use.

"Be careful, Daddy."

Steven glanced up and flashed a reassuring smile at his five-year-old daughter, Luna.

Sporting her glitter pink Boston Red Sox baseball cap and kid-sized fielder's glove, the same gear she wore every time they played catch, Luna stood on the front lawn monitoring her dad's efforts with a fretful pout.

"Daddy's okay, sweetheart," Steven said. "No need to worry. I almost got it."

"But we don't need that one," Luna said with a head shake that caused her twisted pigtails to dance on her shoulders. "We got lots of baseballs in the garage."

In Steven's eyes, Luna's anxious expression somehow made her look even more adorable. Often he caught himself watching her, baffled at how something so pretty and sweet could be his offspring.

Steven was six-foot-two, golden brown, and lean and muscular thanks to a well-equipped home gym. He kept his short cropped hair perfectly trimmed, and his strong jaw was darkened by a groomed stubble beard. He always imagined he'd father a boy, a miniature version of himself that he could chisel into a brick of a man. As things turned out, Luna was surprisingly robust for a five-year-old girl, even tougher than most of the boys in her preschool class. But Luna, with her honey-dipped skin and bright, innocent smile, was also so damn cute. A little angel. So be it. Steven saw no reason why a brick couldn't also be beautiful.

"You're right, baby," Steven said. "I know we have more in the garage, but Daddy wants to get this one."

Luna's brow curled. "But what about the cars?"

From his awkward position on the ground, Steven craned his neck to glance up and down their quiet, tree-lined street.

Big homes separated by sprawling lawns, a gardener clipping hedges, a couple jogging, but not a vehicle in sight.

"I don't see any," Steven said to Luna, "but you be my lookout. Just give me one more minute, okay?"

After a pause, Luna nodded, but her light brown eyes still brimmed with apprehension.

Before his daughter could protest further, Steven returned his attention to the elusive baseball. He reassessed the distance to the ball relative to the storm drain's inlet. Quickly he realized there was only one solution, and the narrow rectangular cavity appeared just wide enough for his plan to work.

Like Luna, Steven also wore a Red Sox baseball cap, but his was the real deal. Custom fitted, navy blue with the trademarked red B, and broken-in to perfection. The ball cap was a keepsake from twelve years ago when Steven played third base for the Boston Red Sox. He only lasted three years in the majors, but they were magical years. How many people get to live their truest heartfelt dream, even for a second, never mind three whole years? Despite moving on from baseball long ago, Steven rarely took off his BoSox cap. Whenever asked about his ever-present headgear, he liked to joke he only removed it to sleep, bathe, and make love to his wife. Anyone who knew him knew that he was only partly joking.

Steven yanked off his Red Sox cap and set it carefully on the curb's edge.

The significance of this action was not lost on his daughter. Luna's eyes went wide. "Daddy, what are you doing?"

Steven pressed a finger to his lips. "Shhhhhh. Watch this." Dropping completely flat, he turned his head sideways and pressed his cheek to the cold steel grating; then he snaked head-first into the mouth of the storm drain. Steven wriggled forward, deeper and deeper into the inlet until half of his body was swallowed by the sidewalk.

"Daddy, no!"

Luna's exclamation was muffled by the surrounding concrete slab walls.

Supported by his lower half, that still lay in the street, Steven dangled over a subterranean chamber about the shape and size of a standard washing machine. His body now blocked most of the daylight, requiring him to squint to make out his surroundings. A crisp, moldy musk thickened the still air. He could taste each gritty breath. The smell was bearable, but not for long.

The baseball lay directly below him, now within easy reach.

He heard Luna's faraway voice again. "Daddy, a van is coming."

Steven could hear the rising muffled hush of a passing vehicle.

"Daddy, come out."

Steven grabbed the ball, but before retreating, he paused to scan the remaining debris for any other lost item in need of rescue. A cell phone? A set of keys? Money?

He found nothing.

"Daddyyy."

Steven quickly wormed himself backward out of the storm drain.

Moments later, after brushing himself off, Steven's cap was back on his head, and he was kneeling before Luna.

He flipped the ball into her glove. "Here ya go."

"Thank you." Luna flung her arms around him and gave him a big hug.

"You're welcome, but I want you to make me a promise."

"Okay."

Steven gestured towards the drain. "What I just did. You don't do that. Never, okay? Promise me."

Luna giggled. "Oh, brother. No way. I'm not crazy like you."

Steven laughed. "Good. Stay that way."

"Okay, Luna. Time to get ready." Steven's wife, Nichole, stood in the arched double doorway of their French country-style home, beckoning Luna with a wave. Wearing her usual day-off ensemble of kente print yoga pants, clingy tank top, and Nike running shoes, Nichole looked ready to hit the gym, not endure a little girl's birthday party.

"Coming," Luna cried.

Before Luna could take off Steven whispered to her, "Hey, listen. No need to mention this to your mom either, okay?" He sealed his request with a wink.

Luna gave a quick nod, "Okay." Then she whirled with a gangly grace only capable by a five-year-old and bolted toward the house.

"Aww, man, she snitched on me."

"It's not every day her father crawls down into a filthy sewer. Of course, she told me."

Steven stood with Nichole at the foot of their elegant curved staircase, waiting for Luna to make an appearance. Nichole now had her favorite Coach bag slung over her shoulder, and a birthday present tucked under arm that looked as if it was meticulously wrapped by Martha Stewart. In the last year alone, Nichole had escorted their daughter to an average of two parties a month, most requiring a ribbon-adorned tribute. Toss in Nichole's amazing creativity, and Steven was not at all surprised that she had become a gift-wrapping ninja.

Another superpower his wife of nine years possessed was a particular cool narrow stare, exclusive to black women, that made Steven feel like a busted ten-year-old. At the moment her dark hazel eyes were dialed up to about an eight.

"I didn't actually climb all the way in," Steven said. "I just stuck my head in a bit and reached for it."

Nichole shook her head. "That's not the point, and you know it."

"Okay. Did she also tell you I made her promise never to do that?"

Nichole sighed. "Still not the point." She checked the time on her iPhone then called upstairs, "Luna, hurry up. We're going to be late."

"Okay, I'm coming," Luna shouted back. Her tiny disembodied voice reverberated off the walls and tall windows of the two-story high foyer. With antique wood floors, exposed beam ceiling, and a looming hand-forged wrought iron chandelier, the palatial entryway never failed to impress anyone entering the Burns' home. Occasionally first-time visitors would even gasp as they crossed the threshold. That was precisely the reaction Steven and Nichole hoped for when they designed and constructed their five-thousand-square-foot dream house three years ago.

"Okay. You're right," Steven said, and he meant it. "I get it. I set a bad example."

His confession doused Nichole's irritation. Her brown eyes softened with understanding. "Luna's getting older. We both have to be more careful around her, but especially you. She's just like you, you know? Stubborn, messy, thinks she knows everything--"

"Hey."

"And we won't even go into the whole baseball obsession thing."

"Come on. I wouldn't call it an obsession."

"Really? Have you seen that dugout she calls a bedroom?"

Steven laughed. He couldn't help but laugh. From the moment her little hands could grip a baseball, Steven had shared his passion for America's pastime with his daughter. Sure, Luna owned her share of baby dolls and stuffed animals, but her bedroom was cluttered with the relics of this loving indoctrination. Topps cards, posters, signed baseballs and bats,

T-Ball trophies and prize medals, and, of course, a big framed photo of her dad in his Boston Red Sox uniform. Luna's room reminded Steven of his bedroom, back when he fantasized about baseball stardom. But there was one major difference; Luna had way more stuff.

Maybe Nichole had a point.

"You see," Nichole said as if she were psychic, "You know I'm right." Rechecking the time, she groaned then shouted upstairs. "Luna Elizabeth Burns, if you don't get your butt down here right now--"

"'kay, 'kay. I'm coming."

Nichole adjusted her bag on her shoulder. "What could be taking that girl so long?"

Steven gently pivoted Nichole to face him. "You know what? I just thought of something pretty amazing."

She gave him a sideways look. "Oh, yeah? And what's that?"

"Think about it. Luna got all the quirky stuff from me, and from you she got the good stuff."

"The good stuff?"

Steven nodded. "Brains and beauty."

Nichole's attempt to resist smiling lasted less than a second. She was always susceptible to his clumsy charm. She beamed, warm and affectionate. It was the same alluring smile Steven fell in love with when he first met Nichole, almost a decade ago, in a city thousands of miles away from where they now called home.

Nichole leaned in and planted a sweet kiss on his lips. "She gets that from you too, you know?"

"What?"

"The corny sweet talk." She plucked the brim of his baseball cap and Steven laughed.

Luna's high-pitched voice filled the foyer again. "Okay. I'm ready now. Are you ready?"

Steven and Nichole traded smiles then lifted their attention to the top of the stairs as if waiting for a performer to take the stage.

"Yup, we're ready," Steven called up. "Let's see. Come on."

The instant their daughter stepped into view, Steven and Nichole erupted with laughter.

Luna stood at the top of the stairs adorned in a beautiful pink fairy princess costume. Elegant butterfly-like wings and a glittery silver baton whimsically enhanced the outfit, but it was the mismatched pink baseball cap atop Luna's head that caused her parents to crack up. In the immediate wake of Steven and Nichole's conversation about Luna's possible baseball obsession, the timing was just too perfect.

As Luna bounced down the stairs, Steven and Nichole finessed their outburst into a chorus of awe and delight at the sight of Luna in her costume. The last thing they wanted was for Luna to misinterpret their laughter.

Reaching the bottom of the stairs, Luna twirled proudly.

"Wow," Steven said. "You look great, baby."

Nichole crouched down to Luna's eye level. "Good job of dressing yourself," she said, "but don't you want to wear the pretty tiara that came with it?"

Luna made a face. "Uh uh, I like my hat better."

"But it's a fairy princess party. Fairy princesses wear tiaras, not baseball caps."

"I know that. But I'm a baseball princess fairy, so it's okay. Anyway it's only make believe, right?"

Steven and Nichole laughed.

"She's got a point," Steven said. He wasn't kidding when he said Luna got her brains from her mom. Nichole had a knack for getting to the heart of an issue, and clearly their daughter inherited that gene.

Nichole said to Luna, "Sure you don't want to bring it in case you change your mind?"

Luna shook her head. "Nope. I'm super sure."

Nichole smiled. "Okay." She checked the time on her phone again as she rose to her feet. "We gotta go."

"Wait, wait." Stephen pulled out his iPhone which protected by a Boston Red Sox case. "Family selfie."

"Okay, but quick," Nichole said.

The Burns family gathered into a pose with routine ease, mom and dad crouching behind their daughter, then Steven snapped the picture.

Pausing to check the photo, Steven experienced a gratified buzz. He had a wonderful family, a big beautiful home, and those wide smiles captured in the photo were genuine. The Burns family was truly happy. He literally had it all.

Stop it.

Steven was struck with an irrational pang of fear. He wasn't superstitious, but it somehow felt perilous to luxuriate in his own good fortune. As if cheering too loudly for oneself would draw unwanted attention from some unseen force charged with keeping humanity humble. Offend said gods and your fortunes would be reversed, or worse. Pure nonsense, he knew that. Still, at that instant, Steven felt a powerful urge to knock on wood.

Did that idiom apply to thoughts as well, or only to immodesty spoken aloud?

"Okay, say goodbye," Nichole said to Luna.

"Bye, Daddy."

"Have fun, baby." As Steven hugged Luna he heard Nichole's phone ring.

The grimace on his wife's face as she answered told Steven that it was a work call.

Steven and Nichole owned and operated Burns Home Remodeling LLC. They started the business seven years ago with a loan from Nichole's father, Dr. Walter Gilliam, a wealthy Boston neurosurgeon. Although divorced from her mother, it was Nichole's father who paid for her master's degree in design from the Florence Institute of Design International. Steven's construction skills were drilled into him by his father, a successful general contractor, who thought it wise his son learn to swing a hammer as well as a baseball bat, just in case. Combining their skills, Steven and Nichole worked hard to grow, what began as a two-man operation into an exclusive remodeling firm, with thirteen full-time employees, and an annual revenue of over six point five million dollars.

Steven and Nichole split the work down the middle. They both had their own team of workers which enabled them to provide full service to separate clients simultaneously. Nichole's current project was a full remodel of a eight-thousand-square-foot gated property on Lombardy Road in Pasadena, near Caltech. The house was beautiful, but also very old. As a result, several unexpected problems had arisen causing the job to fall three weeks behind schedule. Nichole had a crew working weekends to make up lost time, but new problems kept popping up, causing yet more delays.

After less than a minute Nichole ended the call with a sigh, and Steven knew exactly what she would say next.

"A problem at the Lombardy house. Surprise, surprise."

"No, just fill me in," Steven said. "I'll take care of it."

Nichole looked puzzled. "I thought you were going to the office to meet the software people?"

"Linton's supervising the install. I'm really just dropping off a check. I can do that, then shoot out to Pasadena. No problem."

Nichole pondered the offer a second then groaned. "No. Won't work. It's the restoration subcontractor. He's driving me nuts. It would take forever to catch you up. It's better if I go."

"But Mommy," Luna tugged at her leg. "What about the party?"

"Well, I could call Sharon," Nichole said to Luna. "Or, since Daddy doesn't have to work, maybe he'll take you."

Luna bounced up and down, tugging at Steven's hand. "Yes, you take me. Please."

Nichole flashed a guilty smile at Steven, and he returned a playful glare. Nichole knew he didn't love attending kid's parties. The last one she dragged him to, over a year ago, was a Hello Kitty themed scream-fest that left his eardrums ringing for days. Their deal was she'd do the parties and he'd handle doctor and dental appointments. True, this was an emergency situation, but that's why they kept a short list of sitters, like Sharon, that they could call at a moment's notice.

"Please, please, please, Daddy," Luna continued. "It'll be really, really fun."

Nichole also knew that he would do almost anything to avoid disappointing their daughter. "Of course I'll take you, baby," Steven said to Luna.

"Yay!"

As Luna celebrated, Steven took the birthday present from Nichole, then leaned in and whispered suggestively into her ear, "You owe me."

Wearing a naughty smile Nichole whispered back, "Remind me tonight. It'll be really, really fun."

P*atience.*

Not too slow to draw nosy stares. Not too fast either.

That's how he drove through town. That's how he cruised past all the places where busy parents sometimes leave their little ones alone.

The video game store, the comic book shop, Lucy's Pets, that store on Oak Street that sold nothing but candy.

Little ones loved candy.

He had some in his glove compartment now. Hershey's Kisses. Little ones loved chocolate, especially Hershey's Kisses. They were so shiny and fun looking. He liked to place them in their delicate little hands. He liked to watch them peel away the aluminum wrapper and pop the chocolate past their pouty lips. He loved to watch them chew, their cheeks churning, drool seeping from the corners of their mouths.

These wonderful thoughts made him tingle down there.

Focus.

He squeezed the steering wheel and kept driving. Kept scanning the sidewalks.

He cruised past Mario's Pizzeria, Penguin's Frozen Yogurt,

then that McDonald's on State with the big playground out back.

Most of the little ones he spotted were accompanied by an adult or with a friend.

Earlier, there was one girl, about six years old, walking a small dog on her front lawn. She was all alone and she was so perfect. But as he slowed his car, a man exited the house. The girl's stupid father most likely. So he kept driving. Kept searching.

Patience.

Focus.

He turned onto Simpson Street and drove toward the north side of town. Toward more places where little ones are allowed to run free.

He knew he'd eventually succeed because all he needed to find was just one.

Just one sweet child left alone for a few short minutes.

And just think... he hadn't even tried the parks and playgrounds yet.

He drew a sharp breath and squeezed the steering wheel tighter.

Patience.

Focus.

Be ready.

L a Canada Flintridge is an affluent Los Angeles suburb, nestled at the base of the Angeles Crest Mountains. With charming multimillion-dollar homes, set against a backdrop of breathtaking greenery, it was almost impossible to take a bad photograph anywhere within city limits.

A decent number of the houses in the area actually belonged to former clients of Burns Home Remodeling. Most of Steven and Nichole's contracts involved kitchens or bathrooms, but occasionally they'd score a full remodel, like Nichole's current job in Pasadena.

As Steven drove Luna toward town in his Dodge Ram pickup truck he passed several residences that he and his wife had labored on for weeks or even months. From relatively modest ranch houses to gated mansions, all now worth significantly more, thanks to Nichole's imagination and Steven's toolbelt.

Not so long ago, whenever they went for a drive, Steven would proudly point out Mommy's and Daddy's handiwork to their daughter. "Look, Mommy redesigned that house," he used to say. Or, "See that brick wall. Daddy built that." But that was before Luna got her hands on an iPad mini. Now every car trip looked the same. Mommy or Daddy played chauffeur, while Luna, strapped into a high-back booster seat in the rear, played video games. Her current favorite was called Flick Baseball HD. The recommended age was seven and up but Luna swiped and poked the screen with a sureness and dexterity that seemed exceptional for fingers so tiny. Steven tried the app himself, and it was crazy fun, so he understood how Luna could become completely absorbed. What Steven could do without was the game's audio track, a mix of corny music, cartoon sound effects, a zany loudmouth announcer, and a constantly cheering crowd. Besides great schools, a low crime rate, and affable citizens, one of the things Steven loved most about his home town was its light traffic. No such thing as gridlock on the pristine streets of Flintridge. This was a major perk when driving with a five-year-old blasting video games.

Steven turned onto Foothill Boulevard, the busiest street in Flintridge, and headed north through the center of town. The pleasing ratio of franchises and independent shops that lined this quaint commercial district was closely regulated by city hall to ward off chain store blight.

As they cruised past Penguin's Frozen Yogurt, Luna's head popped up from her game as if signaled by snack-radar. "Ooh, Daddy, can we get some yogurt?"

Steven glanced at Luna in the rear view mirror. "You're going to a party, remember? I'm sure there'll be plenty of ice cream."

"Oh, yeah," Luna said, then her attention snapped back to the iPad on her lap.

Although Luna's downturned face was obscured by the bill of her Red Sox cap, Steven still saw how focused she was on beating the game. Her dangling feet bounced and her head bobbed while her fingers danced across the iPad. Actually Luna's ball cap wasn't a bad match for the fairy costume. Both were almost the same shade of pink, and the glitter decorating the cap could easily be interpreted as a sprinkling of fairy dust.

Yup, the kid definitely had her mother's creativity.

The seat beside Luna was occupied by the strap-on wings that went with her costume, and the wrapped birthday present. The gift was rectangular and flat, and Steven assumed it was some sort of board game, but he didn't really know.

"Hey," he called back to Luna. "What'd you get your friend for her birthday?"

Luna replied without ever looking up from her game. "It's a puzzle. A 3D puzzle. Guess what animal."

"Hmmm." Steven made a show of noodling it out. "I'm gonna guess a turtle."

"Heyyyy." Luna scrunched her face at him. "How'd you know?"

Steven laughed. "Because I know you love turtles, silly." Steven winked at her in the rearview mirror.

"Yup," Luna confirmed with a giggle, then she lost herself in the video game again.

Luna didn't resurface until she noticed the pickup truck turning into a parking lot adjacent to a squat one-story building. The sign over the building's store front entrance read BURNS HOME REMODELING.

"Daddy, this is your office," Luna said. "The party's in the big park."

"I know. I told you I had to drop something off first. Remember?"

"Oh. Right."

On a typical work day the narrow lot would be crowded with cars, but the office was closed on weekends, so currently only two vehicles were parked there. One, a black Dodge Ram pickup, nearly identical to Steven's truck except for a Jamaican flag bumper sticker, belonged to Steven's construction chief,

Linton Clarke. The other was a large work van with a slick logo emblazoned on its side panels. SOFTWARE SOLUTIONS SPECIALISTS.

Steven wheeled into a spot, killed the engine, then pivoted in his seat to face Luna. "You want to come in or you want to wait here?"

Luna pinned him with concerned eyes. "How long?"

"I'm just going in and out. Five minutes."

Luna nodded. "Okay. I'll wait."

"Awesome," Steven said. That was the answer he hoped for. Getting Luna in and out of the booster seat wasn't really that big a deal, but considering how quickly he planned to return, the effort seemed like a waste of time.

He powered down both back windows then hopped out and thumbed his key fob.

The doors locked with a sturdy *clack*.

He smiled at Luna through the open rear window, "Okay. Be right back."

Luna waved and smiled at him then dove back into the game.

Steven crossed the parking lot to a side door with a sign that read EMPLOYEES ONLY. He fished out a set of keys, but tried the knob first.

The door swung open.

Steven glanced over his shoulder and waved to his daughter one last time.

Luna, riveted to the lights and colors at her fingertips, did not see her father's final gesture before he disappeared into the building.

7

The headquarters of Burns Home Remodeling employed an open office concept that somehow appeared larger inside than out. There was a small, two-chair waiting area near the front entrance that saw little use because most clients were met at their homes. The main workspace was split down the middle, with a dozen cluttered cubicles lining a central walkway. Enlarged photographs of past kitchen and bathroom remodels shared the walls with framed business permits and licenses. At the very rear, a glass dividing wall isolated Steven and Nichole's spacious, shared private office, while preserving the feel of an open workplace.

Approaching his office door, Steven could see Linton inside, working with a software technician at Nichole's desk. The bespectacled technician poked the keyboard of Nichole's twenty-seven-inch iMac desktop while Linton watched over the man's shoulder.

Linton grew up in Jamaica, but at eighteen, while visiting an uncle in Brooklyn, he decided to stay and become a U.S. citizen. Steven and Linton differed in age by only a year, and were about the same height, but Linton was huskier, built more like an NFL player, opposed to Steven's lean Major League form. Linton always wore his shoulder-length dreadlocks tied back into a thick pony tail, a hairstyle that presented a challenge whenever wearing a hard hat was required.

The two met seventeen years ago on a house construction site. Steven, a high school senior, split his time between baseball practice and working part time for his dad's contracting firm. Linton, fresh off the boat, worked as an apprentice for a flooring and tile subcontractor. By far, the youngest laborers on the worksite, Steven and Linton formed an instant bond that quickly grew into a genuine friendship. Linton cheered for Steven at many high school games, and when Steven got drafted by the Red Sox, Linton was in the Burns' living room, trading hoots and high fives with Steven's parents.

When Steven left baseball and strapped on a tool belt again for his dad's company, Linton was still there, but now a highly skilled and licensed subcontractor. Hanging drywall side-by-side again, their friendship grew even stronger. When Steven and his new wife decided to form their own company, Linton was the only subcontractor they took on full time. Now Linton Clarke was an integral part of the business, game to handle anything, from leasing a massive one hundred and fifty foot crane, to coming in on his day off to supervise the installation of new software.

"Hey, how's it looking?" Steven said to Linton as he pushed through the door.

Linton greeted him with a handshake and big smile. "Nice and smooth, mon," he said in heavy Jamaican patois. The thickness of Linton's accent was directly related to the degree of formality. When pitching new clients, Linton's West Indies origin was practically undetectable.

The software technician pivoted in his chair and shook Steven's hand. "I'm Ron. It's going good, sir. BRU should be up and running in another hour or so." Then he pivoted back, adjusted his glasses, and resumed typing.

The software was called Build Real Unlimited. It would enable them to turn Nichole's designs into photo realistic virtual 3D environments. BRU was also shockingly expensive, but any tool that helped clients visualize the finished product was sure to boost sales.

"Once he's done he'll give us an hour of hands on training," Linton said to Steven. "Good thing, too. Check it out." Linton held up a thick user's manual. "It's like a freaking phonebook."

Steven laughed then patted his partner on the shoulder. "Unfortunately, you'll have to catch me up later. Nicky got called out to Pasadena, something to do with the restoration, so I gotta take Luna to a party."

"No worries," Linton said. That phrase was practically his motto. "I got it all under control." Then he glanced over Steven's shoulder. "So where is my little peanut?"

"She's waiting in the truck."

Linton looked surprise. "Are you crazy, mon? You can't leave that child in the truck."

"It's just for a minute. She's fine."

"I don't know," Linton said with a chuckle. "That girl's got spirit. She might drive off to Disney or something."

Steven laughed. "Not for a few years yet... I hope." He pulled out an envelope and handed it to Linton. "This is a cashier's check. Just make sure everything works before he leaves."

"No worries. Go have fun. And tell peanut Uncle Linton said hey."

"Will do."

~

Moments later Steven emerged from the building's side door and crossed the parking lot toward his truck.

He stopped short when he saw it.

The truck's back door was cracked open.

"Luna?"

Steven hurried over and opened the door.

The booster seat was empty, safety straps hanging loose.

Luna was gone.

Atop the back seat, the birthday gift and Luna's fairy wings were now joined by Luna's iPad mini. The device was still on, the video game flashing on screen. The cheers and music filling the cab seemed to mock Steven's distress.

"Luna?"

Steven scanned the parking lot. Positioned himself to peer around the other parked vehicles.

Nothing.

He turned to the lot's wide open front gate. His heart raced as he stared at the two-way traffic in the street beyond. Rushing cars and trucks.

No. Steven shook his head as if he could fling away the thought. Luna knew better. She wouldn't go anywhere near the street.

Steven's eyes swept the small parking lot again.

"Luna!"

The creak of the side door opening spun him around. Steven sighed when he saw Linton exit, leading Luna by the hand.

"Look who I found," Linton said.

Steven frowned down at his daughter. "I told you to stay in the truck. What were you doing in there?"

Reading his irritation, Luna fidgeted with her dress and gnawed her lower lip. "I had to go to the bathroom."

"Then why didn't you say something when I got out of the truck?"

Luna shrugged. "I don't know. I didn't have to go then. I'm sorry."

"Don't be so grumpy," Linton said to Steven. "She's fine."

Steven shot him a look, then sank to one knee and extended his hands to Luna. "Come here."

Luna left Linton's side and tottered into her father's waiting arms.

Steven leaned in until the bills of their ball caps touched, shrinking the world to just father and daughter. His worldly eyes fixed on her sad eyes. "I'm not mad," he whispered. "I was just worried. You can't just run off like that. I always have to know where you are, okay?"

Luna nodded. "Okay."

"Good," Steven said with a smile and a playful tug on her cap. "Now say goodbye to Uncle Linton and let's get to that party."

8

The squeals and laughter of young girls filled Memorial Park.

Steven cupped his ears as a blindfolded five year old fairy princess attacked a dragon-shaped piñata with a long stick. After three awkward swings and misses, her turn was over and the next fairy princess stepped up.

In all, there were eleven costumed girls waiting in line, ranging in age from four to eight, each eager to beat the sweet stuffing out of that dragon.

Mrs. Waters, the party's host and the birthday girl's mom, did a good job of keeping the game moving. She blindfolded each girl, spun them around, cheered loudest as each took three swings, then removed the blindfold and moved on to the next girl.

Steven watched from the sidelines, flanked by moms shouting words of encouragement to their flailing daughters. Many of the women he knew from events at Luna's preschool, but a few were complete strangers.

"Hold on, my girl only got two swings. She gets one more." It was one of the moms Steven didn't recognize. With her designer accessories and entitled air, she looked out of place at a kid's party. Her complaint was directed at Mrs. Waters, who had just removed the blindfold from a raven-haired girl, whose ornate fairy costume looked worthy of a Broadway production.

Mrs. Waters smiled diplomatically at the entitled mom. "No, it was three. Just like everyone else." Supported by nods and utterances from the other moms, Mrs. Waters ignored the woman's eye rolling, and moved on to the next girl.

Luna was second in line now, just behind her friend Dylan, who lived on their same block. Luna cheered for the other girls but Steven could tell by how Luna bounced in place that she was itching for her chance. When Luna shot him an anxious glance, Steven gestured for her to calm down. Like a base runner receiving a signal from a sideline coach, Luna nodded, then settled herself.

Steven felt a friendly slap on the shoulder accommpanied by a familiar voice.

"How'd you get dragged into this?"

Steven turned and saw Mitchell Canning at his side, sipping a Coke Zero. Up until a second ago Steven was the only dad at the party, so Mitchell must have just arrived. This was confirmed when Steven noticed Mitchell's six-year-old daughter Abbey joining the end of the piñata line. Mitchell, who had more hair on his arms than his head, and a slight gut, owned two Toyota dealerships. Nichole was friends with Mitchell's wife, and Luna and Abbey enjoyed regular playdates, so by default the two men became acquaintances.

"Nichole had to work," Steven said. "A last-minute thing. You?"

Mitchell downed a gulp of Coke, then said, "Vicky's sick. Just a cough, really. Figured it best she stay away from the kids. So here I am on a Saturday doing fairy duty. Good times." Mitchell burped.

An explosion of cheers, squeals, and shouts from moms as Dylan began her assault on the dragon.

Steven covered his ears again and chuckled when, all around the park, he spotted joggers and dog walkers and teens playing basketball, pausing to find the cause of the commotion.

Memorial Park, located two blocks from city hall, was a one-and-a-half-acre patch of tranquility right in the heart of Flintridge. With sprawling green lawns, a historic gazebo, and a picnic area convenient to restrooms, the quaint little park was a popular spot for outdoor children's parties.

As Mrs. Waters freed Dylan of the blindfold, the entitled mom snorted, "I see you gave that girl an extra swing."

Mrs. Waters shot the woman a weary look. "That isn't true. Now, please, it's just a game." Then Mrs. Waters returned her attention to the waiting girls. "Okay, who's next?"

Luna raised her hand and skipped forward. "Me, me, me."

Steven gave Luna two thumbs up just before the blindfold went on.

Mitchell leaned in to Steven and whispered, "You still training her to be the first woman in the majors?"

Steven nodded. "That's the plan."

Mitchell frowned. "So basically, my kid's just wasting her time on line. Luna's gonna crush this."

"Yup."

As Mrs. Waters twirled Luna round and round, Steven clapped and called out, "You can do it, baby."

When Luna stopped spinning she faced away from the hanging dragon. But unlike the other girls, who immediately began swinging, Luna extended the stick in an attempt to pinpoint the target.

"Oh, she's good," Mitchell said with a chuckle.

"It's right behind you," Steven shouted. "Turn around."

Still probing the air, Luna pivoted 180 degrees.

The stick's tip grazed the dragon, causing it to sway gently.

"You found it, baby," Steven called, "Now knock it out of the park."

Luna dropped into a batter's stance, cocking the stick like a baseball bat, and *slam*. One beautiful swing and the paper mache dragon burst open. A shower of candy spilled to the grass.

"YES." Steven slapped Mitchell a high five.

Squeals and giggles as all the girls dived in, grabbing as much candy as their tiny hands could hold. Luna snatched off the blindfold and joined the mad scramble. When fairy wings, magic batons, and tiaras began to fly, Mrs. Waters and several moms called for calm.

Suddenly two girls were fighting. The entitled mom's daughter was yanking the birthday girl's hair.

"Stop it! stop it!" Mrs. Waters pleaded, struggling to pry the two girls apart.

The entitled mom hurtled forward, pushing Mrs. Waters back. "Get your hands off my daughter!"

Suddenly the two mothers squared off, trading insults at the top of their lungs.

Other moms joined the shouting, kids began to bawl, and a crowd quickly gathered around the partygoers.

The two woman exchanged pokes and hard shoves. A few brave moms tried to pull them apart, but the intrusion just aggravated the combatants, threatening to draw more women into the fight.

Realizing the situation called for stronger hands, Steven shot Mitchell a glance. "Come on." Mitchell nodded and the two men pushed forward into the fray. Steven reverse bear-hugged the entitled woman, and Mitchell did the same to Mrs. Waters.

"Enough," Steven said. "It's over. You're both scaring the kids."

After a good deal of fitful squirming, both women settled

down enough to be released. Mrs. Waters declared the party over. The two women grabbed their daughters and went their separate ways, and the surrounding onlookers began to disperse.

Steven shook Mitchell's hand. "Thanks for your help."

"Not a problem."

As moms packed up and collected their daughters, Steven scanned for Luna... but couldn't spot her.

Abbey ran over and clung onto Mitchell's leg, peered up at him with worried eyes. "Are you okay, Daddy?"

Mitchell stroked her brown hair. "I'm fine." Then he gestured to Steven. "Say hi to Mr. Burns."

Abbey waved at Steven. "Hello."

"Hi, Abbey." Steven replied with a smile. The sight of the little girl clutching her father's leg increased Steven's eagerness to reunite with his own daughter.

A few girls in fairy costumes were still on the ground, gutting the slain dragon of its last bits of candy. But when Steven moved closer he saw that Luna wasn't among them.

He felt a pulse of anxiety begin to rise, but Steven forced it back. Everything was fine. There were a lot of people in the park. So many kids running around. He just hadn't spotted her yet. He felt an urge to call out her name, but stopped himself. That would make him appear inept, even silly. He'd look like a typical clueless dad who couldn't handle his kid. He'd look the way he was beginning to feel, frightened.

Maintaining calm, he carefully scanned the busy picnic area again.

He saw Mrs. Waters and a few moms taking down decorations.

Girls posing for pictures.

Girls being lead away by their moms.

But where was Luna?

"Hey, you okay?" Mitchell, holding Abbey's hand, was back at Steven's side.

Steven still scanned the park as he answered. "I don't know. I can't find Luna."

Mitchell's face clouded. "Are you serious?" He gave the area a cursory glance, then shouted, "Luna! Hey, anybody seen Luna?"

Initially embarrassed, Steven shot Mitchell a look, but as concerned neighbors turned and began to converge, fear burgeoning on panic took hold.

This was really happening.

"LUNAAAA!" His daughter's name erupted from his gut and carried across the entire park. "LUNA, LUNA!"

More voices joined his. Mitchell, several moms, and even some kids. All shouting at the top of their lungs. "LUNA! LUNA!"

Steven was breathing faster now. His heart racing. His sweaty hands, clenching, open and close.

Why wasn't she answering?

A hand grabbed his arm. It was Mrs. Waters, her eyes brimming with concern. "Steven, where was the last place you saw her?"

Steven looked down at the candy wrappers at his feet. "Here. She was right here picking up candy, then-- then the fight, and--"

"LUNA, LUNA!" Cries from every direction. It seemed like everyone in the park was shouting now, some fanning out to search.

"LUNA, LUNA!"

Steven blinked, and when he opened his eyes he was staring across an open field at a squat structure. A sight that instantly swelled him with hope.

The bathroom.

Steven broke into a run. He heard confused voices shouting after him, but quickly the sound of his pounding gait and huffing breaths drowned them out.

Please be there. Please.

Reaching the building, Steven nearly collided with an Asian woman exiting the woman's restroom. Panting, he asked, "Did you see a little girl in there?"

Confused and slightly frightened, the woman tried to distance herself.

"Wait," Steven said. "Please. I'm just trying to find my daughter. Is there a little girl in the bathroom?"

The woman's face brightened. "Oh, yes. A girl. Yes, she's in there."

The jolt of relief Steven felt almost made him laugh. "Please," he said to her, "could you go in there and--"

Steven's heart seized when an African American girl strolled out of the bathroom.

"There she is." The Asian woman pointed. "That's her."

The girl, who looked about ten, stopped short when she saw two adults staring at her. "What did I do?"

Wasting no time, Steven brushed past the startled girl and ran into the woman's restroom. "Luna, are you in here?"

The public bathroom was cold and damp and reeked of too much disinfectant.

And it was also deserted.

There were four stalls, their doors wide open. Each stall, empty.

Luna was not there.

Steven slumped against the sink. Fought the impulse to drive his fist into the mirror, or curl up and cry.

He had to find Luna.

When Steven emerged from the bathroom, Mitchell, flanked by concerned parents and passersby, had just reached the building.

"She's not in there," Steven said to Mitchell. "I- I thought she might be because-- well--"

Distant shouts interrupted, "LUNA, LUNA."

Beyond the gathered group Steven saw people still searching the park, still calling his daughter's name.

Steven's throat tightened and he squeezed back tears. "Where is she? Where's my daughter?"

Mitchell laid a hand on Steven's shoulder. "The police are on their way. Mrs. Waters is talking to them now."

Steven spotted Mrs. Waters speaking with alarm into her cell phone. He shook his head and said to Mitchell, "I can't believe this is happening."

"There's a lot of people looking for her," Mitchell said with an even voice. "They're checking the playground, the gazebo. She's probably still in the park somewhere."

Steven barely heard Mitchell's last words. His eyes had settled on a distant object lying on the sidewalk, just outside of the park. He couldn't make out exactly what it was, but it was small, and pink, and glittered in the sun.

When Steven started walking toward the object, Mitchell and the others followed. Perhaps it was the look of dread on his face, or Steven's hesitant, hopeless stride, but no one uttered a word.

It lay just inches from the curb, just footsteps from the passing traffic on Flintridge's busiest avenue, and only one block from the nearest highway onramp.

It weighed no more than a few ounces, but it was the heaviest object Steven had ever lifted.

It was Luna's pink baseball cap.

"...Noooo..." The mournful whisper escaped Steven's lips like a dying man's last breath.

9

"It looks like a magical castle, Mommy."

Those were Luna's words the first time she laid eyes on the Lombardy house.

It was exactly two weeks ago. Nichole was out shopping with Luna when she received a call from her crew leader in Pasadena. There was yet another problem involving the restoration portion of the job, requiring Nichole's immediate hands-on attention. With Steven out of town courting a new client, and Luna's sitter out of reach, Nichole had no choice but to bring her daughter along to the job site. When Nichole's Porsche Cayenne wheeled through the tall wrought-iron gate and rounded the circular driveway, Luna looked up from her iPad and gasped at the enormous house.

And Luna's whimsical description was absolutely right.

The design of the Lombardy house was based on an actual seventeenth century Scottish castle. Built in 1933, the construction was relatively modern, but key features, like flooring, doors, and fireplaces, were genuinely ancient, salvaged from some European ruin and shipped to Pasadena. Burns Home Remodeling specialized in modern styling and finishes, not rotting wood and eroding stonework, so Nichole brought in an expert.

Muhler Restorations was famous in the industry for two reasons; their international resume of exceptional work, and Frank Muhler's monumental stubbornness. Wanting the best for her client, despite warnings about the company's owner, Nichole awarded them the contract.

Now, as Nichole stood at the front steps of the Lombardy house arguing with Mr. Muhler for the umpteenth time, Luna's words from two weeks ago echoed in her mind.

"It looks like a magical castle, Mommy."

The irony was too perfect.

With its cone-roofed corner towers and crenellated brick walls the Lombardy house did resemble something from a fairy tale, but to Nichole the problem-ridden old building had become her own personal hell house. Over budget, behind schedule, and a battleground for her and Frank Muhler to engage in frequent shouting matches.

Muhler was bald and slender, with round glasses and a stark white goatee. His professorial guise was underscored by an infuriating superior manner and tone that constantly tested Nichole's patience.

Today's fight concerned the type of bricks used to reconstruct the curving steps that rose from the circular driveway to the arched front entrance. Muhler's specifications called for reclaimed Chicago bricks, but due to a mixup, reclaimed New York bricks were delivered instead. Because the two brick types were virtually identical, Nichole's bricklayers had already completed half the job before Muhler discovered the mistake. Now Muhler was demanding the bricklayer demolish everything and start over.

After a prolonged heated debate that drew stares from the workers, Nichole was about to pull rank and end it when she spotted a black and white police cruiser rounding the driveway. The vehicle carried the seal of the Los Angeles County Sheriff's Department, which seemed odd because Pasadena, a sovereign municipality, had its own police force. In Flintridge, a County Sheriff's car was a common sight, but here it was out of place, and even more so on her construction site.

As Nichole watched the cruiser creep to a stop and a uniformed officer climb out, she was at a loss for any explanation for this unexpected visit.

Muhler sighed and made a face at Nichole. "Goodness sake. Don't tell me you've allowed your permits to lapse."

Nichole shot him a look. "Of course not."

The officer rounded his cruiser and started straight toward Nichole. Average build, average height, nothing to distinguish him from most uniformed cops, except that look on his face. In fact, she couldn't recall ever seeing a cop with that particular expression.

He looked uncomfortable.

"Ma'am, are you Nichole Burns?" He made an effort to keep his tone flat. Unreadable.

Hearing her name, and realizing a police officer had reason to seek her out, caused her to tense. "Um, yes. Is there something I can help you with?"

The officer's eyes flicked to Muhler, then back to her. "Could we speak privately, please?"

Alarm bells went off in Nichole's head. Her immediate assumption was that the officer's presence was worksite related, but that was wrong. The fact that he knew her name and wanted to speak privately, suggested a personal matter. Nichole's heart began to race. "What's this about," Nichole said. "What's wrong?"

"Let's just move over here, Ma'am." The officer took a few steps back, moving closer to his cruiser, and Nichole hesitantly followed.

"What is going on?" Muhler called after them.

"Please remain where you are, sir," the officer said, then he took a breath and returned his attention to Nichole.

The way the officer paused to center himself and put on a professional face, sent a chill through Nichole. He was about to tell her something bad. Something about her-- *Oh, no.* "What is it?" Nichole demanded. "Did something happen to my family? To Steven and Luna?"

"It's about your daughter, Ma'am---"

"What about my daughter?" Nichole's heart was pounding now. "What happened to Luna?"

The officer swallowed. "It appears... she's missing."

Nichole blinked. The words not taking hold. She shook her head. "No. Luna's with my husband. They're at a party in--"

"Memorial Park. Yes, I know. That's where I just came from. They sent me to get you. Your daughter's missing and a detective is--"

Nichole pulled out her phone and began dialing.

"Ma'am, if you're calling your husband, he won't answer. He's being questioned. Ma'am, please."

Steven's voicemail recording filled Nichole's ear. Its cheerful, oblivious tone causing a knot of emotion in her throat.

"Ma'am, please," the officer said. "If you'd just come with me. I'll take you to him."

"No. I need to speak to him." Nichole killed the call and hit speed dial again. There was an unwritten rule between Steven and Nichole. Two phone calls back-to-back signaled an emergency. Steven always picked up on the second call. Always.

After a single ring the sound of Steven's voice made her

heart leap. "Steven, it's me. What's going--" Nichole broke off when she realized it was the recording again. The fact that it cut in so soon meant only one thing. Steven's phone was turned off.

Nichole winced as her insides went hollow. She turned to the officer, regarding him with new eyes. The awful message he delivered couldn't be denied any longer. It was real. This was really happening. Her baby was in trouble, and she was here, so far away, unable to do anything.

Nichole brushed tears from her eyes and rushed past the officer, toward the cruiser. "Take me."

10

"Did anyone speak to you or your daughter when you first entered the park?"

Steven shook his head. "No."

"Did you notice any strangers watching the party?"

"No. I mean... maybe. I'm not sure. I can't remember."

Steven was seated on a bench in the large gazebo that served as a centerpiece for Memorial Park. His body slumped forward. His face buried in his hands.

All around him was the commotion of heavy police presence. Sirens, flashing emergency lights, the squawk of police walkie talkies, loudspeakered commands to evacuate the area, a helicopter circling overhead. But Steven found it hard to watch any longer. Seeing all those vehicles and uniforms, all that urgent scrambling, only served to emphasize the direness of Luna's disappearance, and also feed his panic.

"Try to remember, Mr. Burns. I know it is difficult, but please try."

Steven lifted his head and stared up at the man standing over him.

Despite his well groomed full beard, and his professional

jacket and tie attire, Lieutenant Detective Adeel Ahmad still appeared too young for the position he held. Late twenties was Steven's guess, and at first that troubled him. People of Middle Eastern descent tended to look younger to Steven, so that might be a factor, but he didn't care. Only the gold shield clipped to Detective Ahmad's belt, and his confident and methodical command of the surrounding chaos, reassured Steven that the man peering down at him was qualified to find his daughter.

Detective Ahmad was flanked by two uniformed police sergeants. While Ahmad questioned Steven, the sergeants only listened, occasionally turning aside to bark orders into their walkie talkies.

"I am trying," Steven said to Detective Ahmad, "It's just--"

"I know it is hard, sir," Detective Ahmad said. "But we need to do this while the details are still fresh in your--"

"Lieutenant, do you copy?"

It was a static charged voice from the walkie talkie in detective Ahmad's hand. He gestured for Steven to 'hold on,' then raised the radio to his mouth. "Go for Ahmad."

While the detective engaged in a brief exchange concerning the search, Steven couldn't resist turning his gaze, once again, to the park. The level of activity had increased significantly. There were now more police in the park than civilians. He saw barricades going up, canine units scouring the picnic area, police officers questioning parkgoers, a KTLA news van pulling up, just outside the park.

As Steven's pained eyes took it all in, one dreaded thought took root.

When Nichole sees this, she'll be terrified.

"Sorry about that," Detective Ahmad said, his walkie talkie back at his side. "As I was saying, I know this seems like the worst time to bombard you with questions but--"

"Where's my wife?" Steven interrupted. "You said you sent someone. Where is she?"

With a nod, Detective Ahmad deferred to the officer on his left. The overweight sergeant was clearly older than Ahmad, but displayed unhesitant respect for his superior. To Steven the sergeant said, "Your wife has been picked up and is on her way, Mr. Burns. We expect them to arrive any minute."

"Did they-- Does she know yet?" Steven barely got the words out.

A glance from the sergeant passed the question back to his lieutenant.

Detective Ahmad spoke in an even, almost soothing tone. "The officer I sent was instructed to notify her... tactfully. So, yes, she knows."

Steven winced and cupped his face again. An image of Nichole being crushed by the news flashed in his mind.

"Mr. Burns, please. Just a few more--"

"Okay." Steven nodded. He drew a steadying breath. "What was the question again?"

"Did you notice any strangers watching the party?"

"There were other people around. The girls were making a lot of noise so- people were watching. But nobody nearby. I mean... nobody stood out."

"Did you notice anyone familiar in the park, who wasn't at the party?"

Steven rubbed the top of his ball cap. "What do you mean?"

"A friend or maybe a neighbor? Someone probably without a kid."

"Why?" Steven straightened up on the bench. "You think someone I know might've taken Luna?"

"In cases like this, often it is someone close. And that would explain how she could be lured away from--"

A disturbance at the edge of the park drew both men's attention.

Steven shot to his feet when he saw Nichole exit a police car and head into the park. She was escorted by a tall uniformed officer, who waved a reporter and cameraman aside as they quickly made their way toward the gazebo.

A moment later, Nichole, her features wrought with sorrow and fear, topped the steps of the gazebo.

Steven wanted to rush to her and pull her into his arms but her stare froze him.

It was as if Detective Ahmad and the other officers were not present. Nichole's devastated eyes only saw Steven. When she spoke, her accusing tone struck Steven like a thrown spear. "Where's my daughter?"

Steven searched for words, but before he could speak, Detective Ahmad took a step forward. "Mrs. Burns, I'm--"

"Steven," Nichole said, ignoring the young detective. "What happened to my daughter?"

The way she said "my daughter" wrenched his heart.

Why is she saying it like that?

Steven swallowed in a dry throat. "I'm sorry. I-"

Detective Ahmad ventured another cautious step toward Nichole, as if inching toward a coiled tiger. "Mrs. Burns, please."

"Shut up!" Nichole glared at the detective, then whipped back to her husband. "Steven, tell me what happened to Luna."

She hasn't accepted it yet.

Steven realized that, despite the world coming apart around them, Nichole wouldn't accept Luna's predicament until it came from him. Steven swallowed again and said, "There was a fight. I went to break it up. I got distracted and--" His voice broke. He pushed back tears and continued. "I took my eyes off of her for a minute and-- she was gone. I'm so sorry."

Nichole squeezed her eyes tight and shuddered.

"Mrs. Burns," Detective Ahmad said, "I assure you, we are doing everything possible to find your daughter."

Nichole wheeled on him, "Doing what exactly? All I see is you standing here. Why aren't you out there searching?"

Displaying practiced patience, Detective Ahmad, in a calm, assured voice, began to run off a list. "A countywide Amber alert has been activated. A photo of Luna in her costume, taken from your husband's cell phone, is being distributed to every police department in a five-hundred-mile radius. Video footage from all nearby surveillance cameras is being collected and reviewed. Anybody within fifty yards of that party is being detained for questioning. And if you look around you'll see about three dozen officers searching the park as we speak. As I said, we are doing everything possible to find Luna. That said, if you have more suggestions, of course, I will listen."

"My baby." Nichole muttered the words as tears coursed down her face. She collapsed back onto a bench and folded into a sobbing ball. Steven rushed to her, pulled her into his arms, and held on tight. Nichole's fingers clawed into his upper arms as her entire body trembled.

Peering over Nichole's shoulder, Steven stared up at Detective Ahmad. Time stretched as their eyes remained locked, a frozen moment underscored by the sounds of Nichole's doleful weeping.

Detective Ahmad maintained his professional poise, until he could no longer. When Steven saw the young detective's chest heave with emotion, he knew Ahmad would do his best.

"You have to find her," Steven whispered to the detective. "Please."

Detective Ahmad nodded. "I will."

D etective Adeel Ahmad was down on his knees, in the Sujud position, upon his prayer rug. His forehead, nose, and palms all touching the intricately patterned fabric, while facing northeast toward the Qibla in Mecca. His silent prayers were accompanied by the soothing sounds of Allah's marvelous creation. Bird song, the buzz of insects, trees rustled by the gentlest breeze, and the soft gurgle of flowing water.

"Sorry to disturb you, sir."

The officers in Ahmad's charge knew better than to interrupt his afternoon prayer. Even in police work, it was rare to encounter a situation that couldn't wait the ten minutes required for Ahmad to perform the Salat ritual. The fact that a voice other than that of Allah's was now beckoning him could only mean one thing. The awful search he'd been leading for the last two weeks had come to an end.

Suddenly, the warm inner calm Ahmad enjoyed during his daily conversations with Allah was replaced by a cold tingle along his spine.

"Sir, they're waiting."

Detective Ahmad rose from his prostate position to sit on his heels. He peeled open his eyes. He blinked at the surrounding sunlit greenery, waiting for his eyes to adjust.

He was on a rocky patch of dirt, near a small stream, deep in the southwest region of the Angeles National Forest. A short walk from his current position, two dozen men and women, a combination of police officers and volunteers, were busy conducting a slow and methodical search for human remains.

In the six days since Luna's abduction, search crews had worked dawn to dusk, scouring various sections of the wilderness. No actual evidence suggested that the unfortunate girl had been killed and buried in the forest; in fact there were no leads at all, but Luna's case did fit a disturbing pattern. In the past six years, two other girls from the region, one age five like Luna, the other seven, had been abducted, and days later their bodies were found buried in the forest. While every member of the search crew held out hope that Luna's disappearance was not connected, the glaring precedent was impossible to ignore.

Angeles National Forest was vast, covering seven hundred thousand acres, so to search it all was literally impossible. To narrow the search, focus was put on previous burial locations, and not just where the other young girls were found. Because of the isolation it offered and its close proximity to Los Angeles, the national forest was a popular choice to dump murder victims. In the last ten years alone, twenty-three bodies had been discovered in the forest, usually in shallow graves. Depending on convenience to roads, or the softness of the earth, some spots were more popular than others.

Working from a list, Detective Ahmad devoted his allotted manpower and budget to a single location per day. And every day at noon, while the search party worked, he'd slip away briefly to find a quiet spot for the Dhuhr prayer. While seeking the blessings of Allah, he always included a plea for the search party to find nothing. Failure left the possibility that this case wouldn't end like the others, and that Luna was still alive.

But now his prayers had been interrupted.

Ahmad stood up, brushed off his slacks, and turned to face the uniformed officer sent to fetch him. The absence of a service weapon on the man's hip marked him as an auxiliary officer. Detective Ahmad recognized him as a member of the search party, but didn't know his name.

"Well?" Detective Ahmad asked, an edge of hesitation in his voice. "Is it her?"

"I don't know, sir," the auxiliary cop said. "I wasn't close enough. The sergeant just told me to get you fast."

The tension at the base of Detective Ahmad's neck eased a bit. Maybe it wasn't Luna after all, he thought. It wouldn't be the first time a search party had mistaken the bones of an animal for human remains.

"One second," Ahmad said. He slipped on his shoes, then rolled up his prayer rug and tucked it under his arm. "Okay, let's go."

Detective Ahmad followed the auxiliary cop up a brief rise, then through a dense stand of bushes and trees, before emerging into a broad overgrown clearing. The sight that greeted the detective caused him to stop in his tracks.

Only minutes ago, when he left, the entire search crew was stretched across the width of the field, in a single line. They were inching forward in unison through tall grass, heads down, eyes scanning the ground for anything that might be a clue. But now the entire search crew was gathered at the far side of the field, both uniformed officers and volunteers, all standing in a tight circle around one spot.

Spotting Detective Ahmad, a few waved and shouted for him to hurry.

It must truly be her, Ahmad thought.

As he started across the open field, that cold tingle revisited his spine. His steps felt sluggish, as if the tall grass pulled at his legs, trying to keep him from reaching that awful spot. As each heavy step carried him closer, Ahmad's thoughts projected into the future, to a moment all policemen dreaded.

It would be his duty to tell them.

Detective Ahmad liked Mr. and Mrs. Burns. He admired their bravery and kindness for coming out on the sixth day, along with their parents, to meet the search party. Not only did they thank each officer and civilian volunteer personally, they even handed out bottled water.

Where did they find the strength?

Detective Ahmad and his wife, Ceyda, had a daughter of their own. Yasemine was only two years older than Luna. If something happened to his little girl, he couldn't imagine having the courage to visit the field where her body might be found at any moment. He couldn't imagine being able to drum up the spirit to put on a smile and shake strangers' hands. Mr. and Mrs. Burns were good people, and he had no desire to deliver the news that would surely crush them.

Ahmad was just a few yards away from the circle, and the entire search party was staring at him. A crowd of hopeless and tragic eyes, all relaying the same message.

Brace yourself.

Ahmad briefly shut his eyes and whispered to himself, "Merciful Allah, please do not let it be the girl."

Without a single word uttered, the search crew parted and Detective Ahmad passed through, stopping at the edge of a shallow hole.

The hole was about four feet in length, its contents draped over by a carefully placed police officer's jacket.

This sight wrenched Detective Ahmad's heart.

Found evidence is never touched before the CSU can do

their job. The fact that this tenet of police work had been ignored by all these officers, in favor of preserving the dignity of what lay in that hole, shouted to Ahmad that their grim search was indeed over.

But still, he wanted to believe they could be mistaken. It could be someone else. Hikers die in these woods all the time. Drug dealers bury their enemies here. He knew it was wrong, but at that moment Detective Ahmad wanted whoever was under that jacket to be anyone but the daughter of those two nice people.

Anyone but Luna Burns.

Detective Ahmad took a deep breath, then nodded to the officer nearest the hole, the only officer not wearing his uniform jacket.

"Go on," Detective Ahmad said. "Show me."

12

Steven watched a bead of moisture trail down his water glass.

Lately, he'd occasionally catch himself riveted to some meaningless detail around him. A leaf jostled by a breeze. A passing cloud outside the window. A stray curl of Nichole's hair. These distractions lasted just a few heartbeats, but were a fleeting escape from the racket of despair inside his head.

Steven was seated at the head of his dining table, waiting for Nichole to bring out lunch. With him were his parents Verna and Robert, and across from them, Nichole's mother, Evelyn.

After learning of their granddaughter's abduction, Steven and Nichole's parents immediately jumped on a plane. Even Nichole's father, who was notoriously unavailable for family events, made an appearance for two entire days. In truth, Steven was thankful to have them all there, especially during those interminable first few days, when everything seemed to transpire in a black fog. And after watching his wife weep in her mother's arms for hours, Steven knew that Nichole felt the same way.

With six bedrooms and bathrooms, the house was easily

spacious enough to accommodate everyone, even without the use of Luna's bedroom.

"It doesn't feel right," Verna said, "letting Nicky cook for us." Steven's mother fidgeted with her rings. She always wore three gold rings of various design on each hand, that she twisted and tugged whenever anxious. "I really should go help." She began to rise, but Steven waved a hand.

"Mom, no. We talked about this. She likes keeping busy. It helps her. Really."

Verna deflated with a sigh.

Robert patted his wife's hand in support. Steven's dad was a burly man with the thick calloused hands of a manual laborer. He turned to his son. "I think it's more that Nichole's in there alone. Maybe one of us should keep her company."

"I promise you, Dad, she's fine," Steven said. "I am a little concerned that she hasn't slept much but otherwise-- she's holding up."

"And what about yourself?" Nichole's mother asked, her voice laced with the prim tone of an Ivy League education. She peered at Steven over delicate wireframe glasses.

Steven gave a feeble shrug. "My sleep hasn't been great either but-"

"I'm not referring to sleep," Evelyn said. "Nichole tells me you haven't cried yet. Is that true?"

Steven blinked at his mother-in-law, uncertain how to respond. During those first few days, he was so upside down that he couldn't remember if he had cried or not. And now he refused to let himself cry. Crying now would feel like giving up, like all hope for Luna's safe return was pouring out of him. When his baby girl is back home, safe in his arms, that's when he'd cry, and they'll be tears of joy.

"Bottling up your emotions isn't healthy," Evelyn continued, shaking her head. "My therapist says it's better to just let it out.

I'm sure she wouldn't mind chatting with you. Would you like her number?"

Steven was spared the delicate task of refusing politely, when Nichole emerged from the kitchen carrying a tray of sandwiches and a tossed salad. She set the tray down and took the seat at the opposite end of the table.

As everyone complimented the meal and reached for sandwiches, Verna's face warmed with a reminiscent smile. "You know, Luna used to love my tuna fish sandwiches."

Steven shot his mother a look as an awkward pause seized the group.

Realizing her mistake, Verna gasped and said to Nichole, "My goodness. I meant they ARE her favorite. I'm sorry."

Nichole reached out and squeezed Verna's hand. "It's okay." Then to everyone she said, "It makes no sense to try to tiptoe around this. I mean-- It's just stupid, right?" She chuckled and brushed away tears.

Steven rose from his seat, but Nichole shook her head and waved him off.

"Don't," She said. "I'm fine. Please."

Reluctantly, Steven dropped back into his chair.

Nichole dried her eyes, then put on a smile and grabbed the salad bowl. "Come on. Everyone eat."

Steven stared as Nichole transferred salad to her plate. His wife was one of the strongest people he knew. Practical, decisive, organized. It troubled him to see her so brittle, teetering between holding it together and falling to pieces.

"I think we could all use a little distraction," Robert said as he reached for another sandwich. "Maybe we could watch a movie or something."

Evelyn made a face at him. "We said no more TV, you know that. All those news stories... it's too much. Anyway, who can focus on a movie now?"

"I don't think it's a bad idea," Nichole said with a shrug. "We could watch a DVD." A small smile appeared on her lips. "One of Luna's favorites might be nice."

Steven stared down the length of the table at his wife, his eyes searching hers. For an instant, it was as if they were alone in the room, and only inches apart. He whispered, "Are you sure?"

Nichole gave a little nod, but the tears brimming in her eyes said different.

Steven was about to veto his father's well-intentioned suggestion when, from outside, came the rumble of engines and squealing brakes. Sounds that made Steven's heart stop.

Several vehicles had pulled fast into his driveway.

The police. It had to be.

The faces of his parents and Evelyn mirrored his dread.

Nichole was already on her feet, rounding the table, hurrying to the nearest window.

"No, wait." Steven called after her.

Nichole flung the curtains apart and flashing blue and red lights flooded the dining room.

When Nichole finally glanced back at Steven, her fearful eyes were more alarming than the police lights. "Something's happened," she said.

Everyone at the table rose quickly, but with a gesture, Steven pleaded with them to remain seated.

Steven joined Nichole at the window, and took her trembling hand into his.

Two vehicles idled in the driveway. A police cruiser and an unmarked car.

Steven and Nichole watched a uniformed officer climb out of the cruiser, and Detective Ahmad emerge from the other. Ahmad directed the officer to remain with the vehicles, then the detective started toward the front door. Detective Ahmad's expression was professionally unreadable... until he reached for the doorbell. He paused before touching the button to draw a deep calming breath. In that instant, sorrow darkened his features like a passing shadow, then was gone again.

What transpired in a blink of an eye felt like an eternity to the parents watching.

Nichole whimpered and squeezed Steven's hand as tight as she could.

Steven's legs suddenly felt hollow. He gripped the window frame for support.

When the doorbell chimed, Nichole flinched.

"I'll go," Steven said. "You go back to the table."

Steven tried to move but Nichole held his hand tight.

"No," She said, shaking her head. "Don't answer it."

Steven watched tears stream down Nichole's face.

The doorbell chimed again, intrusive and deafening.

"I'm so tired," She said, her voice cracking. "I just want to go to bed. Please."

Steven pulled her into his arms and held on. "Okay."

As the doorbell chimed for a third time, Steven and Nichole walked hand-in-hand up the stairs.

13

The press conference was held the next day, at one in the afternoon, in the rear parking lot of the Los Angeles County Sheriff's Department's Crescenta Valley Station. The sky was cloudless and the air clear, allowing a perfect view of the looming San Gabriel Mountains.

A beautiful day for ugly business.

Detective Ahmad, flanked by the area commander, the division chief, and a half dozen other uniformed superiors, addressed a large crowd of reporters. The cluster of microphones sprouting from the podium carried the logos of over a dozen network and local news agencies. The staccato click of cameras competed with Detective Ahmad's loudspeakered voice.

To Detective Ahmad's left, Steven and Nichole stood, hand-in-hand, both doing their best to remain composed before the swarm of eyes and lenses.

Speaking in a clear and deliberate manner, Detective Ahmad informed the press that the couple would not be present for the entire press conference. He explained that Stephen and Nichole had requested a few minutes to speak about their daughter.

Once they were done, they would depart, then he would give an update on the ongoing search for the killer. He also made it clear that the couple would not take any questions. No exceptions. Detective Ahmad concluded this preamble with a plea for the couple's request for privacy to be respected.

Steven couldn't move.

When Ahmad stepped back from the podium and gestured for them to step forward, Steven's legs refused to work.

Last night, when Nichole mentioned she wanted to speak to the press about Luna, he loved the idea. To the media, Luna was just another victim, just another tragic tale to feed the news cycle. Maybe if Steven and Nichole told an amusing story, or talked about her silly sense of humor, or held up a few of Luna's beautiful photographs, the reporters might see their daughter as more than just the latest headline. Steven wasn't sure if any of this would change how the story was reported, but he hoped sharing memories of Luna might ease their pain, even just a bit.

But now, watching the hoard of reporters wave and point their gadgets, leering at him and Nichole like eager groupies, caused Steven's spine to tense. Suddenly, the last thing he wanted was to be a part of this show.

Steven winced as realization sank deeper. He'd seen this same stupid show on TV a thousand times. The players were always different but the starring roles remained the same. The innocent victim, the grieving loved ones, frantic reporters, and the determined police department. The plot rarely varied as well. The loved ones always looked pathetic, the police paraded about and beat their chests, the reporters asked asinine questions, and meanwhile the killer continued to run free.

What are we doing here, wasting time?

Steven's free hand squeezed into a tight fist. Luna was dead and the person responsible was still out there. Still sleeping, still eating, still watching TV. He could even be watching now, steven pondered, or even--

His next thought sent a chill rippling through him.

The man who killed my daughter could be standing in this crowd.

Steven scanned the sea of faces before him, as if he could recognize the man on sight. Something told him he would. Steven felt certain that when he looked his daughter's killer in the eye, he'd know it.

"Steven," Nichole tugged his hand.

Steven turned to Nichole and was surprised to see her staring at him with concern.

Detective Ahmad and the other officers were staring also.

"You okay?" Nichole asked.

Steven nodded stiffly, but in truth, he wasn't okay at all. Every fiber of his body was taut, as if he were wrapped head to toe with thick rope. His jaw was clenched tight enough to crack a molar. And if he squeezed his fist any tighter his fingers would break.

It took a firm yank from Nichole and an encouraging nod to get him to the podium. They had planned to take turns at the mic, but all Steven could manage was to hold up Luna's kindergarten graduation photo while Nichole spoke through tears.

Nichole concluded by thanking everyone present, but as they both stepped back from the podium, a shout from the crowd froze them.

The question came from a bearded, heavyset man at the very rear. In his upraised hand he held a mini digital recorder.

"Is there anything you'd like to say, in case the killer is watching?"

For an instant the question lingered, held aloft by Steven's sudden glare, and the crowd's stunned silence.

High pitched feedback from a microphone as Detective Ahmad lunged to the podium, shattered the moment. "I want that man removed," Ahmad said, pointing. Immediately two uniformed officers pushed through the crowd toward the guilty reporter.

"Wait." Steven's voice carried over the disturbance. Ignoring Nichole's stare and her resistant tug on his hand, Steven stepped back to the podium, leaned over the bank of microphones, and said, "I'll answer that."

Using both hands, Detective Ahmad did his best to smother the mics as he whispered, "Please, Mr. Burns. Not a good idea."

"I don't care," Steven said, dipping lower and raising his voice. He wanted the reporters to hear him. "I really want to answer that question. Please."

Just as Steven had hoped, the reporters sided with him and began flinging comments at Detective Ahmad.

"Let him speak."

"Let him answer one question."

"He has a right to speak."

Detective Ahmad leveled a frown at Steven, then stepped back, allowing Steven to square off with the podium.

All chatter dropped away, leaving only the nonstop click of cameras and the woosh of passing traffic on a nearby street.

Steven paused to take in his audience and gather his thoughts. From the multitude of pointed lenses, he focused on just one, peering into it as if it served as a single set of eyes for the entire world. In an even, dead-certain tone, he said, "Five minutes. I'd give anything to spend five minutes alone with the monster who killed my little girl. That's all I want, just five minutes."

The crowd of reporters flew into a frenzy, surging toward the podium while shouting questions at both Steven and Nichole.

As Detective Ahmad, uniformed officers, and department brass, rushed forward to stem the charge, Steven grabbed Nichole's hand and hurried away.

A t 3:22 AM Steven's cell phone vibrated on the night stand, causing a prescription bottle of Ambien to rattle.

Roused from sleep, Steven yawned and groped for his phone in the dark. First noticing the time onscreen, he glanced over at Nichole and was relieved to see the noise had not disturbed her drug-induced slumber.

As the phone buzzed for attention in his hand, Steven stared, puzzled, at the caller ID message.

BLOCKED CALL.

Luna's funeral was in just a few hours. He couldn't imagine who would be thoughtless enough to call so early, especially from a blocked number. He considered simply shutting off the phone and trying to return to sleep, but when the phone trembled in his grip again, curiosity won out.

"Hello?" Steven whispered into the phone.

A raspy but oddly pleasant voice replied, "Mr. Burns, I apologize for calling at such an unkind hour but I must ask a question."

"Who is this?" Steven asked.

"Did you mean what you said at the press conference today?"

"What? Is this a reporter?"

"Did you mean what you said or not? Just answer me, please."

"Listen, I don't know how you got this number but if you call here again I'm calling the police."

"We will speak again. Good night, Mr. Burns."

The call went dead and the screen flashed, CONNECTION LOST.

Paused by a wave of uneasiness, Steven just stared at the dead phone in his hand. Deciding the caller had to be a pushy reporter, he powered off the phone and returned it to the night stand.

After glancing over once more to check on Nichole, Steven buried his head in his pillow and shut his eyes. He tried to clear his mind and let sleep pull him under, but he couldn't get that soft raspy voice out of his head.

W*ho is that?*
While close friends and family watched Luna's small casket descend into the ground, Steven riveted his attention to a man lurking just outside the circle of mourners. Wearing a black hat and black overcoat, the man lurked about fifty yards away, seated upon an old, weathered tombstone with his legs crossed.

The burial ceremony was intimate and private. Steven knew every individual standing over the open grave, personally. But the man using a tombstone for a bench was a complete stranger.

Steven could make out something metallic in the stranger's right hand, but he was too far away to identify it.

Maybe it's a camera.

Maybe the man's a reporter.

No, that didn't make sense.

Out of respect, members of the press had agreed to wait with the cars and limos, along with the drivers and groundskeepers. But the stranger hovered nowhere near the parked vehicles or drivers. He was alone, just sitting there, watching.

A suspicion lingering in the darkest corner of Steven's mind, began to push to the forefront. With it came the memory of that odd phone call he received last night. That strange rasping voice. Steven cocked his head, as if doing so would give him a better view of the stranger.

Could that really be him?

Would he dare come here?

Steven felt tendons tightening. His teeth gnashing.

Would he be so blatant to--

Steven's breathing ceased when he saw the stranger lift the metallic object to his eyes.

Binoculars.

The stranger looked right at Steven through a pair of compact binoculars. Steven wanted to charge across the field and take him by the throat... but their locked stares caused Steven to hesitate.

People began to cross Steven's field of view, soft, somber voices filled the air, and suddenly strong hands yanked Steven into a tight hug.

"Beautiful ceremony, mon," Linton whispered in his ear.

When Linton released him, Steven saw the burial ceremony concluding. Mourners drifted back to their cars, Nichole hugged friends and neighbors, and Linton used his suit sleeve to wipe away tears.

Linton's brow fell when he noticed Steven's disorientation. "You don't look so good, mon."

"Come here." Steven hustled Linton aside, out of Nichole's earshot, then whispered, "I think the killer is here, right now. He's watching us."

"What?" Linton studied his best friend's face with alarm. "What are you talking about?"

Steven pointed. "That man over there, he--"

The old tombstone stood alone. The stranger, gone.

Linton followed Steven's gaze. "Where? I don't see anyone."

"He was there a second ago." Steven scanned the departing mourners. "He couldn't have gone far."

Linton's confused eyes picked over the crowd. "What did he look like?"

Before Steven could answer, Nichole approached, accompanied by a bald, bespectacled, middle-aged man, who Steven recognized as a frequent speaker at local functions. Steven couldn't recall his name, but he knew the owner of that perfect sympathetic smile, practiced as a priest or a reverend or a pastor, or something like that.

"Steven, this is Pastor Childs," Nichole said.

The pastor shook Steven's hand while his other hand patted Steven's upper arm. His voice strong and soothing at the same time. "My deepest condolences to you and to your wife. I'm aware you both are not religious, but I just wanted to--"

"Sorry. Pardon me." Steven spotted Detective Ahmad approaching. Abandoning the dazed pastor, he hurried over to intercept Ahmad.

The detective extended his hand to convey his condolences, but Steven wasted no time. "You need to get some men down here, right now. You have to search the cemetery."

"Steven, what's going on?" Nichole said, rushing to his side.

"Yes, Mr. Burns," Detective Ahmad said, "What's troubling you?"

Linton jumped in, "He thinks he saw the man who mur-- I mean, the man who hurt Luna."

"No." Steven shook his head. "It was him." He pointed. "He was right over there, sitting on that tombstone, watching with binoculars."

Nichole's hand went to her mouth.

Detective Ahmad frowned. "Mr. Burns, what makes you so certain the man you saw is the perpetrator?"

"I told you, he had fucking binoculars. He was watching the

burial like it was some kind of show. And the phone call. I'm telling you, it's him."

"What phone call?"

"Look, we're wasting time. Are you going to get people down here to search this place, or what?"

"Please calm down, Mr. Burns. And no, I will not."

Steven took a breath to dial back his aggravation. "Why? You don't believe me?"

"It's not that. It's just, I've seen this sort of thing before."

"What?" Steven traded baffled glances with Linton and his wife.

"Do you have any idea how many people come to cemeteries to watch the funerals of complete strangers? Some even take photographs. Especially when the ceremony involves someone in the news."

"That's horrible," Nichole said.

The detective nodded. "A distasteful hobby, I agree. But not illegal. Not in this state."

"You can't be sure," Steven said. His breathing returned to normal but he still itched to take action. "It still could've been him."

"True," Detective Ahmad said. "But what's more likely? You said this man used binoculars. I doubt the person we're looking for would be so conspicuous... or stupid." Detective Ahmad stroked his beard. "That said, this cemetery has no shortage of security cameras. I'll confiscate the files and examine them. Okay?"

As Steven nodded, he had trouble looking the detective in the eye. He liked Ahmad. He liked the man's measured and certain manner. During the past week Detective Ahmad had been unshakable and focused, and Steven had no reason to believe he wasn't giving the case his all. "Guess I'm going a little crazy," Steven said. "Sorry."

Steven extended his hand and Detective Ahmad shook it.

"It's alright," the detective said. "But what about this phone call you mentioned?"

Steven shook his head. "It was nothing. Some pushy reporter. Forget it." He wrapped an arm around Nichole and drew her close, then pinned Ahmad with anxious eyes. "Please be honest. What are your chances of catching this person?"

The detective paused to weigh his response. He glanced over at Pastor Childs, who still hovered nearby, looking deeply concerned. Then Ahmad turned back to Steven and Nichole and said, "In my faith it is permitted to swear an oath to God, and an unforgivable sin to break such an oath. To both of you I say this. I will do everything in my power to find the person responsible for your daughter's death. I will never stop looking until this individual is either brought to justice or dead. I swear this in Allah's name."

Steven and Nichole held each other tighter as they watched Detective Ahmad stride away.

16

The doorbell's singsong chime roused Steven from sleep.

Yawning at sunlight, Steven first thought he'd let Nichole answer it, then remembered he was in the guest bedroom. He and Nichole hadn't shared a bedroom or a bed in months, and every morning it took Steven a few seconds to orient himself. The guestroom sat on the ground floor, far closer to the front door than the upstairs master bedroom. Unless Nichole was already up, it fell to Steven by default to drag his ass out of bed and answer the door.

Steven scratched six days of beard as he rolled over to check the clock radio. His daily routine of shaving, like so many other micro deeds that made up a man's typical day, withered away months ago.

The clock read 8:54AM.

Who could that be at this hour?

In the weeks following the funeral, an early unexpected visitor or phone call would spark hope in Steven for news about Luna's case. But eight months of no answers and disappointment eventually extinguished that spark, leaving that particular corner of Steven's heart dark and numb.

Another deep yawn brought with it the recollection that he and Nichole had an appointment at noon with Detective Ahmad at the Sheriff's station. With a lapse of three months since their last face-to-face update, the thought of today's meeting should've inspired eagerness and anticipation. All Steven felt was a hollow knot in his gut that had nothing to do with morning hunger.

The doorbell chimed again.

Steven grabbed a T-shirt and jeans from a tangled pile on the floor. He found his ball cap on the bedpost.

Moments later, he stepped over and around more strewn clothing, soiled dishes, and a greasy pizza box, as he made his way across the living room. Seeing his home so disordered caused Steven a pang of sadness. Eight months ago, he never would have thought it possible, but now the detritus of his shattered family greeted him most mornings. He made a mental note to straighten up a bit, but as usual, he and Nichole would probably put it off until a real reason to clean presented itself, like a visit from Linton or their parents. In truth, even before Luna's passing, Steven rarely picked up, but Nichole fell just short of being labeled a neat freak. He used to laugh at her for cleaning up before the housekeeping service arrived. To save money Nichole cancelled the service months ago, and Steven couldn't remember the last time he laughed about anything.

Chimes resounded through the house again, just as Steven cracked open the front door.

Steven recognized the two sixyish women standing on his doorstep, but he couldn't recall either of their names. Almost certainly, the plump one with too much makeup lived in the huge house on the corner. The second woman, who wore narrow sunglasses and a floppy hat, brought no house to mind, but occasionally he'd see her jogging with a big chocolate lab. He also remembered her from the early volunteer searches, which made Steven regret forgetting her name. Why these two women awakened him, and were now smiling stiffly at him, was a complete mystery.

"Hi," Steven said, peeking out. "Can I help you?"

The plump one gave a little wave. "Hi, we've met before. I'm Sharon. I live at the corner. And this is Wendy."

"Hi." Wendy waved also. "I live right around the corner, on Elmwood."

"Yes, I remember," Steven fibbed. "I would invite you in but it's really early and--"

"Oh, no," Sharon said. "We don't need to come in. We just wanted to say that we know you and your wife have been through a lot, and have a lot to think about, so as a way of helping out, we'd like to hire a service to come in and tidy up your landscaping."

Heat rose on the back of Steven's neck, and his hand squeezed the door tighter. With effort, he pushed back his instinctive reaction. Yes, their concern for the condition of his lawn was shallow, and the absolute last thing he gave a shit about, but they were also being nice about it, not to mention generous.

Reacting to Steven's strained expression, Wendy said, "Please, Mr. Burns, we don't mean any disrespect. Like Sharon said, we know you're consumed with more important things right now. So we just thought--"

"I know what you thought," Steven said. "And I don't blame you. It's a mess. You're right. We haven't touched it since--" Steven paused to swallow the lump in his throat. Look, I've been meaning to deal with it, and I will. I'll figure something out. But I can't--"

Before Steven could finish the door was yanked from his

hand and swung wide open. Nichole, wrapped in a robe, now stood beside him, beaming at the two women. "Hello, Sharon. Hi, Wendy."

The two visitors appeared relieved by Nichole's sudden appearance. They waved pleasant hellos then Sharon offered Nichole a demure smile. "We were just asking your husband if--"

"Yes, I heard," Nichole said. "I think it's amazingly generous and thoughtful of you. Steven and I really appreciate the offer."

Nichole rubbed Steven's arm, which he took as his cue to smile and nod. He decided to let this play out her way for now.

"I'm sure it'll be fine," Nichole went on, "But let us talk about it, then I'll call you. Okay?"

Both women nodded in agreement.

"Of course," Sharon said. "Take all the time you need. Take care now."

When Steven shut the door and wheeled to confront his wife, she was ready for him, arms crossed. "I know what you're going to say," Nichole said, "we don't need their charity."

"That's right," Steven said. "We don't. I'll call the landscaper this afternoon, after we get back."

Nichole sighed. "Steven, we need to start saving more. What they're offering could really help. Why are you being so unreasonable?"

Steven stared at his wife as if he'd been slapped. He knew where this was going, and it wasn't good. He couldn't believe she'd, so casually, stoke an issue that, only a month ago, sparked their worst argument ever. Didn't she know how close they came to going over the edge?

"Talk to me," Nichole said. "Please."

But Steven couldn't, especially not today. "I need coffee," he murmured. Then he started for the kitchen.

17

The drive to the Crescenta Valley Sheriff's station was quiet. Steven and Nichole traded just a handful of words during the entire twenty minute trip. With each passing week their conversations had become more and more anemic, but the silence in the pickup truck felt unusually strained.

The way Nichole gazed out the passenger-side window without truly seeing a thing, told Steven her thoughts were troubled. This mood, while rare for Nichole, wasn't unprecedented, so Steven knew it would be fruitless to ask her what was wrong. She'd just shake her head and mumble 'nothing,' or not respond at all. Their noon meeting with Detective Ahmad seemed the likely cause of Nichole's brooding, but a hint of resolve in her distant eyes suggested something deeper.

At three minutes before noon, Steven and Nichole entered the low-slung station house. The female sergeant manning the reception desk greeted them with a formal smile and an apology. She explained that Detective Ahmad would be a few minutes late and that they could wait at his desk. Moments later, after being buzzed through a security door, Steven and Nichole trailed the desk sergeant through the heart of the station. Uniformed and plainclothes officers glanced up from computer screens and phone calls as the couple passed. Some offered a feeble nod or faint smile, others averted their eyes. Steven recognized many of these faces from those early, hectic days of organized searches and police escorts. He remembered their eagerness to help and the sympathy in their eyes. Now their glances almost looked shameful.

Detective Ahmad's desk abutted a window that looked out on the rear parking lot. After grabbing an extra chair from a nearby desk so that Steven and Nichole could both sit, the sergeant headed back to the reception area.

All previous face-to-face meetings with Detective Ahmad occurred in Steven and Nichole's living room, except the last, which transpired at the Harmony Diner on Foothill Boulevard, over lunch. While Detective Ahmad now knew the Burns' almost intimately, Steven and Nichole had seen little that reflected Ahmad's personal life, until now. Ahmad's desk looked meticulous, easily the neatest in the entire station. Case folders stacked just so, an outdated computer so clean it looked brand new, even a pair of miniature American and Pakistani flags, the only decoration, were void of even a speck of dust.

Steven wondered if Ahmad's desk always looked so neat, or if the detective straightened up a little in preparation for their visit.

"He has a beautiful family," Nichole said, nodding toward the computer monitor.

A bouncing screensaver displayed a photograph of Ahmad posed with an olive-skinned woman wearing a hijab head wrap and a small girl.

"Yes, he does," Steven murmured, a touch of hesitance in his voice.

Ahmad, his wife, and his daughter, all wore big smiles and

looked so damn happy, and the more Steven stared at that photo, the more his mood darkened. Ahmad talked about his family months ago, about how his daughter and Luna were so close in age. But to see it now, bouncing playfully in front of him, felt like a taunt. Like the universe was fucking with him.

When the screensaver finally transitioned to another photo, an old shot of Ahmad in uniform, Steven eased a bit and settled back in his chair.

Nichole turned and looked at him. Without uttering a word she reached out, took his hand, and offered the faintest smile. He and Nichole hadn't shared an intimate moment in months, so even this tiny gesture should've warmed Steven, but oddly, it had the opposite effect. Steven didn't understand why, but suddenly he felt very alone.

"Please accept my apology," detective Ahmad said, rushing toward them, a rolled-up prayer rug tucked under his arm. "An earlier meeting ran late, which made me late for my afternoon prayers. Again, I am so sorry." he sported a nice suit, as usual, and his beard appeared shorter since their last meeting.

After shaking their hands, detective Ahmad slipped his rug beneath his desk, grabbed Luna's file from a drawer, and launched right into the update. He discussed following up phone leads, questioning local sex offenders, a plan to reinterview certain witnesses, and summarized several other ongoing avenues of investigation. He also praised Steven's widespread posting of reward flyers, which had garnered an increase in calls to the tip line. But when Ahmad shut the thick case file fifteen minutes later, to Steven, only one disheartening fact stood above the rest. The police were no closer to finding Luna's killer now than three months ago.

"That's why you wanted us to drive in?" Steven asked, "To tell us the case is cold?"

Detective Ahmad pursed his lips. "No, I wouldn't say cold.

More like a lull. Very common in cases like this. Lots of ups and downs."

"It all seems down to us," Steven said.

"Yes. Of course." Detective Ahmad paused to look them both in the eye. "Please understand. I made a promise to you, and I intend to keep it. The investigation might hit a few snags, but I won't stop."

Steven joined Nichole in nodding their appreciation, but then his brow furrowed. "I'm still confused about why we're here. We appreciate the update, we do, but we could've done this over the phone."

"True, true," Detective Ahmad said nodding. "But it's been a while. I thought it might be good to reconnect in person." He knitted his hands and leaned back in his chair. "So, tell me, how are you two holding up?"

Steven and Nichole exchanged uncomfortable glances. Finally Nichole put on a smile and said, "Okay, I guess. It's a day-to-day thing."

Detective Ahmad turned to Steven. "How about you?"

"I don't know," Steven said, adjusting his ball cap. "Like she said, it's tough... but we keep going."

Detective Ahmad's brow fell. "Really? But what about your business?"

Blindsided by the question, Steven returned a guarded stare. "What do you mean? What about my business?"

"Well, I drive by your office almost every day. I can't help noticing it's still closed. Any plans to reopen soon?"

Steven paused to study the detective's face. His concern appeared genuine but Steven couldn't recall Ahmad ever asking about his business in the past. So why now? Finally Steven just shrugged and said, "Sure, we'll reopen someday. Of course. But I really can't focus on that right now. Not with all this going on. You know?"

"Of course. Completely understandable," Detective Ahmad said. "But you should keep in mind that 'all this' could go on for a very long time. I've seen others in your position become immobilized by their pain. They couldn't get past it, so it ate at them, and eventually destroyed them. I would just hate to see that happen to you two."

Steven dismissed the idea with a shake of his head. "It won't. Trust me. We'll be fine."

"I hear you, I do, but sometimes this sort of thing can creep up on you. Listen, do me a favor and yourselves a favor too." Detective Ahmad fished a business card from his desk and handed it to Steven. "Make an appointment to see her. She's very helpful in these matters."

Steven's puzzled eyes dropped to the business card. His jaw tightened and his breathing slowed when he read the raised type.

DEBORAH TIDDES, GRIEF COUNSELOR.

When Steven looked up again, his eyes burned into Detective Ahmad. He said, "We don't need a grief counselor."

"Sure, probably not," Ahmad replied with a disarming smile. "But just talk to her. It couldn't hurt, right?"

With a slow shake of his head Steven tossed the card onto Ahmad's desk. "No thank you."

"Steven, stop it." Nichole sighed and snatched up the card. To detective Ahmad she said, "Thank you. And thanks for your concern. We'll definitely think about it. Like you said, it couldn't hurt."

Steven's eyes narrowed as he watched his wife slip the grief counselor's card into her handbag. Suddenly memories flooded in of Nichole's endless complaints about her mother's therapy obsession. All Nichole's stories of being dragged into therapy sessions as a child, and how she hated every second. To see Nichole pocketing that card instead of ripping it to shreds made no sense, unless-- Steven winced as he experienced a jolt of clarity. Nichole's odd behavior in the truck, this pointless update meeting, Detective Ahmad's questions about his business, and all this talk about moving on, suddenly he understood it all.

Steven shot up out of his chair and glared down at Nichole. "I can't believe you dragged me down here for this bullshit." Then he snapped to Detective Ahmad. "What did she do, send you a fucking script?"

Nichole and Detective Ahmad traded busted glances.

Steven snorted at them. "Did you two rehearse this crap over the phone? You think I'm fucking stupid?"

Nichole reached for his hand. "I'm so sorry, we just--"

Steven shoved her hand away. "Don't you fucking touch me. I can't believe you would do this."

Detective Ahmad waved off concerned colleagues who began to approach, and stood up to face Steven. "Mr. Burns, please calm down. Your wife's just worried about you, and so am I. Everything I said was true. You need professional help."

Steven squeezed his eyes shut and took a calming breath. When he opened his eyes, several detectives had inched closer. Nichole was on her feet, her pained eyes pleading with him. Steven heard voices urging him to settle down, but they seemed faint compared to his thrumming heart.

Leveling a cold stare across the desk at Detective Ahmad, Steven spoke calmly, "You just find the animal who killed my daughter. That's all I need."

Then Steven brushed past Nichole and strode toward the exit.

18

S teven sat perched on the rear bumper of his truck, slumped forward, face buried in his hands. His head throbbed with sharp pain, as if an ice pick pierced his skull.

What's wrong with Nichole? She only cares about going back to work and making money. How could she think about anything else when he's still out there?

"The five stages of grief, have you heard of it?" Nichole's voice interrupted his thoughts.

Steven lifted his head. Nichole stood over him, arms crossed. Any guilt for deceiving him now replaced by cold eyes and a weary frown. Behind her, across the parking lot, he saw Detective Ahmad watching from the station house door.

Peering up at Nichole, Steven's brow furrowed. "Five what?"

"The five stages of grief. Dr. Tiddes told me that--"

"Hold on." Steven stood up quickly. "Are you telling me you already met with this person?"

Nichole sighed. "I did. Yes. But it was just a consultation."

"Wow." Steven shook his head. "And let me guess, your mother found her, right?"

"Yes, and she's also willing to pay for our sessions. Dr. Tiddes said it sounds like you're experiencing all five stages at once. She said it's not that unusual for--"

"Who the fuck are you?" Steven stared as if he didn't recognize her. "The Nichole I know hates all that psychobabble bullshit."

"I hate what's happening to you, no, to us, even more. I'm desperate to save our marriage. Steven, Luna is gone. We have to get on with our lives."

Steven scowled at her words. "Sure. That's so easy for you to say... isn't it?"

"What? What does that mean?"

"You never even wanted her, remember? You wanted to focus on building the business. Oh yeah, and working out. I had to practically beg you to start a family."

Nichole's mouth fell open. Her hands clenched into tight fists. "How dare you? I loved her."

"Exactly. You 'loved' her. Past tense. Now she's gone and look at you. You can't wait to return to your original plan. Time to forget all about Luna and get back to business. Let's make more money. Buy a bigger house. More cars. More time for yoga classes."

"Fuck you," Nichole hissed. "You're so screwed up you're not even thinking straight. All you want to do is lay around, and watch the news, and put up reward flyers, and play detective on the internet searching for lord knows what, while we slowly go broke." Nichole jabbed a finger into her chest. "Who am I? Who the fuck are you? You're driving me crazy. I can't take it anymore. I can't stand--" Nichole caught herself. Shut her eyes and took a deep breath.

In a calm, resigned voice, Steven finished her sentence. "You can't stand me."

For a moment Nichole just stared at him. Finally she frowned and said, "I never said that."

"You don't have to say it. I see it every time you look at me. And I get it. I convinced you to have a baby that you loved and cared for. Then I screwed up. Of course you can't stand me. Its my fault our little girl is dead."

"Steven, stop it."

"Why? Am I wrong?"

"Just stop it."

Steven took a step closer to her. "Look me in the eye and tell me you don't blame me."

Nichole met his gaze. Her breathing quickened and tears rolled down her cheeks. Her bottom lip quivered, but no words came.

"Come on," Steven pressed, "tell me I'm wrong. Tell me you don't blame me for Luna's death."

Nichole swallowed hard, shook her head, then reached out and drew Steven's hand into hers. "You're wrong," she whispered. "It's not your fault. I don't blame you at all."

Nichole's words were so soothing, her touch so gentle, and her eyes so radiant with love, that Steven almost believed her. But what she claimed was impossible. Luna's death was his fault, and Nichole was only human, so of course she blamed him. Of course she couldn't stand to be around him, he couldn't even stand himself.

Steven snatched his hands from Nichole's grasp and took a step back. "You're lying to yourself. I guess you really are desperate."

Nichole flinched as if struck. She gaped at her husband, the true depth of their disharmony registering for the first time. In that fleeting instance, Nichole seemed to frost over. She brushed away her tears and stood straighter. After a small sigh, she looked Steven in the eye and said, "If you won't meet with the therapist, I can't stay with you. I just can't. I'm sorry."

Steven replied with a somber nod. "I know."

19

A t 3:13 AM Steven's cell phone began to vibrate.

Steven snapped awake in the dark. His bleary eyes went to the nightstand. He saw the time glowing on the clock radio, but did not see his phone.

Where was it?

A deep buzzing came from somewhere within the bed.

"Shit."

As Steven patted the comforter and swept his hands beneath the sheets, he wondered who'd call so late. He first thought of Detective Ahmad, perhaps calling to report the arrest of a suspect. But Steven immediately dismissed the possibility. If nothing else, Ahmad was considerate. Even if he did have a suspect in custody, he'd wait until morning instead of disturbing their sleep. Steven also considered Nichole. It wouldn't be the first time she called him from upstairs. Maybe she changed her mind about moving out in the morning, and wanted to talk. But Steven doubted this as well. Nichole seemed dead set on getting the hell away from him ASAP, and he couldn't blame her. Far more likely, Nichole had snuck out after he fell asleep, and called now to let him know.

Another low buzz from the phone helped Steven to finally locate the device. When he read the caller ID, he froze.

BLOCKED CALL.

Instantly Steven flashed back to the last time he read those words on his iPhone. With all that had transpired in the last eight months, Steven almost forgot that strange phone call he received the night before Luna's funeral.

Steven squinted at the time on his phone, struck with the realization that the first call also came at 3:13 AM.

Could it be the same person?

Because of constant badgering from the media, he and Nichole had been forced to changed their phone numbers, cells and landline, several times in those first few months. They learned quickly not to share contact information with anyone, except police and close family members.

No, it couldn't be the same person.

Then who?

As if to answer, the phone trembled in his grasp, sending a ripple of dread through his entire body.

Steven sat up and switched on the bedside lamp. For some reason he didn't want to take this call in the dark. He swiped the screen and brought the phone to his ear.

"Hello?"

"Mr. Burns, I apologize for calling at such an unkind hour but I must ask you a question."

Steven's heart beat faster.

It was him.

Steven would never forget that scratchy, overly nice voice. "How'd you get this number?" Steven demanded.

"Did you mean what you said at the press conference? Please tell me."

Steven squeezed his phone tighter. "I told you I'd call the police if you called again."

"The police?" A slow, dry chuckle filled Steven's ear. "They're useless. You must see that now."

"Who is this, dammit?" Steven raised his voice through gritted teeth. "Is it you? Did you kill my daughter?"

The silence that followed the question gnawed at Steven's nerves. After what seemed like an eternity, the caller spoke again. "I will make you a deal, Mr. Burns. Answer my question, then I'll answer yours." The caller then repeated his question with deliberate slowness. "Did you mean what you said at the press conference?"

Steven said just one thing that morning, but that single provocative statement had made headlines and the evening news all over the country. Detective Ahmad and several of Ahmad's superiors expressed their displeasure about his outburst, and warned Steven not to repeat it. Even Nichole shook her head at his lack of restraint that day. But Steven didn't give a shit. He said what he felt in the moment, and now, as he searched himself he still felt that smoldering within.

"Damn right I meant it," Steven said. "Now who are you?"

"I knew it. I knew you meant it." The caller's tone sounded like a smile.

"Who are you? You said you would tell me."

"I apologize Mr. Burns but-- Well, I'm nobody really. I just needed to know to win a wager. Again, I apologize. Goodbye."

"No wait--"

The call went dead and the screen flashed, CONNECTION LOST.

"Fuck!"

Steven raised the phone, about to hurl it against the wall, but stopped himself. When Detective Ahmad warned them about the press invading their privacy, he also mentioned the possibility of prank callers. "There are some cruel people out there," Ahmad warned. "They take pleasure in other's pain."

Groaning at his own stupidity, Steven tossed the phone onto the nightstand, shut off the light, and tried to go back to sleep.

20

Instead of sitting around watching Nichole move out, with the help of one of her yoga buddies, Steven decided to spend the morning putting up new reward flyers.

About five weeks after the funeral, when the investigation began to lose momentum, Steven and Nichole got the idea to give the case a boost by offering a twenty-five thousand dollar reward. With literally hundreds of saved images of Luna to choose from, Steven photoshopped the reward flyer himself. Immediately after he and Nichole posted dozens of flyers around Flintridge and neighboring towns, the number of calls to the police tip line shot up. Now, once a month, Steven made the rounds, replacing old or torn down flyers with new ones. Sometimes he changed Luna's photo, and twice he raised the reward amount, the current amount being fifty thousand, but for nearly a year the flyer's promise had remained the same. Anyone providing information leading to the arrest and prosecution of the person or persons responsible for Luna Burns's murder will have a nice payday.

Although the reward offer kept the tip lines ringing, none of the calls provided a single useful lead.

But Steven remained ever hopeful.

As he wheeled his pickup out of the driveway with a stack of freshly printed flyers, a staple gun, and a roll of scotch tape on the passenger seat, he recalled an encouraging comment Detective Ahmad once shared with him.

"Always remember, just one good tip can break this case. Just one."

With the warm glow of morning cresting over rooftops and the looming Angeles Mountains, Steven cruised through Flintridge, following the route he usually took when posting flyers. First he stuck to residential streets, hopping out every other block to staple a flyer to a telephone pole or tape one to a lamppost. Early laborers like postal workers, garbagemen, and street sweepers, all waved good morning to the man they occasionally spotted defacing city property.

By 9:00 AM Steven reached the Foothill Boulevard commercial district, where his focus shifted to asking shop owners to display the flyer in their front window or inside their establishments. Some shop owners happily complied, and some refused. Steven never took rejection personally; he understood. Reminding customers of a murdered little girl didn't exactly contribute to a pleasant shopping experience.

After almost two hours of chatting with shop owners, most who had supported the flyer campaign from the start, Steven moved on to larger venues where crowds typically gathered. Supermarkets, post offices, movie theaters, a bowling alley, and Town Center Mall, where he tacked several flyers to public bulletin boards.

Several large churches and synagogues were on Steven's route as well. Every priest, pastor, or rabbi Steven spoke to always agreed to post the flyer, and most also promised to pray for the killer's capture. Steven and Nichole weren't religious, and they raised Luna likewise, but Steven never mentioned this fact during church stops. Just in case God did exist, he didn't want to forsake any source of help.

Faith Fellowship Community Church was the last house of worship on Steven's usual route. The nondenominational church, housed in a brick building void of any religious symbols, served one of the largest congregations in the city.

Normally, Steven just dropped off a flyer with Ellen, the church secretary, but this morning when he entered her office he was surprised to find the church's founder, Pastor Childs, chatting with Ellen while picking up mail.

A few weeks after their first meeting at the cemetery, Stephen visited Pastor Childs at the church to discuss posting Luna's flyer. Since then, despite Steven's monthly visits to the church office, he hadn't crossed paths with the popular pastor again, until now.

After greeting Steven with a gentle handshake and that soothing smile, Pastor Childs inquired about the investigation's progress. Acquaintances asked Steven this question frequently, especially when he distributed flyers. Usually it struck him as mere chitchat, no more significant than discussing the weather. But Pastor Childs sounded sincere, like he genuinely cared to hear case details. Disappointed by the lack of encouraging news, Pastor Childs promised to pray for swift justice, and of course to prominently post the reward flyer on the church's bulletin board, as always.

Steven expressed his appreciation and made to leave, but Pastor Childs reached out and laid a hand on Steven's shoulder. Eyes narrowed, the pastor asked, "What about you and Nichole? How are you two holding up?"

Steven froze, caught offguard by the question, but more so by the pastor's deeply concerned stare. Pastor Childs seemed to sense something troubled Steven, and he wanted to help.

"Mr. Burns?" Pastor Childs gave Steven's shoulder a gentle squeeze. "Are you okay?"

Steven forced himself to smile. "Yeah, I'm fine. Nichole and I are both fine. Thanks for asking."

The pastor cocked his head, as if trying to get a better look at Steven's soul. "Are you sure? You look... burdened. If you like, we could go up to my office and talk."

Steven shook his head. "Not necessary, really. But thanks again, Pastor." As Steven hurried out, he heard Pastor Childs call after him.

"Don't forget, Mr. Burns, my door is always open."

Moments later, as Steven drove away from Faith Fellowship, a lump formed in his throat and his eyes began to sting. Distributing flyers served to distract him from the painful truth unfolding at home that very moment, but Pastor Childs' question brought it all back. Nichole's departure not only marked the end of Steven's marriage, it felt like the last, tattered thread of a once happy family, slipping from his grasp. For an instant he considered racing back home to stop Nichole from leaving, but with that thought came a dark sinking feeling. Giving in to Nichole's desire to 'move on', essentially meant giving up his search for Luna's killer. No. Never. He had to focus all his time and energy on finding the bastard who murdered his little girl. And now with Nicole out of the house, he could do just that.

Instead of driving back home, Steven drove faster toward the location he always saved for last when posting flyers. Steven dreaded the place, but at the same time, he couldn't resist going there every chance he got.

21

Alonely, midday stillness permeated Memorial Park. Its sun-dappled green fields and winding footpaths were deserted, except for a pair of joggers and a lone woman walking a tiny dog. Bird song and white noise from passing vehicles on bordering avenues were the only sounds.

After tacking a flyer to the cluttered bulletin board outside the restroom building, Steven always strolled out to the middle of the great lawn, where a towering bur oak tree served as the park's natural centerpiece.

Two weather-beaten wood and wrought iron benches flanked the tree's massive trunk. One bench faced the park's north end, the other south. Steven always sat on the bench facing south, because it offered an unobstructed view of the location where his nightmare began.

Today the picnic area stood empty. Its wooden tables and charcoal grills occupied only by the phantoms in Steven's mind. Somedays, from his spot on the bench, he'd watch the picnic area for hours, mentally replaying that day over and over again. Giggling girls in fairy costumes. Hovering moms trading gossip to pass the time. Luna destroying that piñata with one perfect swing. Then chaos as girls scrambled for candy. Moms shouting for order. Two moms fighting. Steven rushing to break it up. Then Luna was gone.

Vanished.

The mere memory of that moment gut punched Steven with panic and helplessness as if it occurred that very instant. Sometimes he clenched the bench so tightly, his hands ached for several days after.

Because this was the last place Steven saw her alive, during these visits, memories of Luna laughing and playing were at their most vivid. Unfortunately, the same held true for the devastating pain of her loss.

Like the house he grew up in, or the Florentine cafe where he first met Nichole, the bench in Memorial Park was now a meaningful location in Steven's life. A place of wonderful memories, a place of soul-wrenching sorrow, and a place Steven was doomed to visit forever.

Steven glanced at the time on his iPhone.

12:30 PM.

If Meg arrived at the house at nine AM, like Nichole planned, three and a half hours should've been more than enough time for them to pack and leave. But to be safe, Steven decided to wait another half hour before heading home. He wasn't sure how he'd react if he ran into Nichole walking out carrying suitcases, so he thought it best to avoid the situation altogether.

"Pardon me."

Steven glanced over his shoulder, surprised to see a man standing over him. The man appeared to be in his fifties, with short cropped salt and pepper hair. He stood about Steven's height, but stockier. He wore squarish glasses with thick black frames, a beige windbreaker over a white dress shirt, black leather gloves, and gripped an old brown satchel briefcase.

The man's features were stern but not unfriendly. His gaze, confident and unabashed, as if accustomed to addressing complete strangers.

The man struck Steven as some sort of government worker, or perhaps a plainclothes cop, but Steven couldn't think of a reason why either would choose to ambush him in the park. Actually, despite being approached from behind, Steven didn't feel threatened at all, but something did seem off about the older man that he couldn't pin down.

"Mind if I sit?" The man offered a formal smile while gesturing to the spot on the bench beside Steven, currently occupied by leftover reward flyers.

That's when Steven noticed the gloves. It was seventy something degrees out, a beautiful spring day in La Cañada Flintridge, so why was this man wearing gloves?

It occurred to Steven that he might simply like wearing gloves, but the functionally dressed stranger didn't look like someone who cared much about fashion. No, the gloves were definitely odd. This combined with the fact that an empty bench was just a few footsteps away, made the hairs on the back of Steven's neck stir.

Noticing Steven's hesitance the man warmed up his smile. "Please?"

"Actually, I was just leaving," Steven said, picking up the flyers and rising to his feet.

"No, please don't leave." The man fixed a stare on Steven that made the request sound like a demand. "I've come a long way to see you, Mr. Burns."

Steven stiffened and his heart began to pound. Not just because the stranger knew his name. It was the man's voice. Steven would never forget that weird scratchy smooth voice. "It's you," Steven said, shocked and angry at the same time. "You're the asshole who's been calling me."

"Yes," the man said, looking regretful. "And I apologize for that, but I had to be certain."

Steven's eyes narrowed. "Certain about what? Who are you really? A reporter?"

The man shook his head. "Not a reporter. No."

"Then who? And why the hell are you stalking me? What do you want?"

The man gestured to the bench again. "Please, let's sit for a minute and I'll explain."

Steven pulled out his iPhone. "No. You explain right now or I'm calling the police. I mean it."

The man sighed. He glanced around to make sure they weren't being watched, then he said to Steven, "Those five minutes you asked for. I can make that happen."

"What?" Steven heard every word, but utter disbelief prevented him from understanding. "What the hell are you talking about?"

The man dropped his raspy voice to a whisper, and spoke with deliberate slowness, like a snake hissing words. "Mr. Burns, I know the name and address of your daughter's murderer... and I can deliver him to you."

22

S teven never stared at another person for so long. Anxious seconds felt like minutes, and all sounds from the desolate park drained away as he took in the stranger with new eyes. Steven weighed every possibility. Was this some kind of scam? Some sort of fucked up prank? Was this guy crazy? Or maybe he's-- Steven's hands squeezed into tight fists as an unthinkable possibility took hold.

Could this be him?

At first the man just stared back, cool, unthreatening, content to allow Steven time to absorb the situation. But the growing fire in Steven's eyes prompted him to raise a calming hand. He said to Steven, "To get it out of the way, no, I'm not the man who killed your daughter."

Steven's shoulders slackened. He didn't know if the stranger spoke the truth, but something about the man's composed manner left Steven inclined to keep listening, at least for now. He nodded. "Okay, then who the hell are you?"

The man gestured to the few remaining flyers in Steven's hand. "I'm someone who has seen those go up month after month, with no result. Someone who wants to help you."

"Help me how?"

"We'll get to that. Let's sit."

The man lowered himself onto the bench, rested his brief-case across his lap, then waved graciously to the vacant spot beside him. "Please."

Steven didn't budge. The last thing he wanted was to sit and chitchat with a stranger about Luna's murder. "Listen," Steven said, "If you really know something, let's go to the police. Even better, I'll call them right now." Steven raised his iPhone to dial, but froze when the man leveled a hard stare.

"Do not do that." The man's voice, forceful but respectful, like someone practiced at giving orders. "No police. Ever. Consider this your first and only warning."

Steven's brow clenched. "What do you mean, warning?"

The man adjusted his grip on his briefcase. "You don't believe me yet, but I do know who killed your daughter, and I'm here to help you. But if you try to involve the police or anyone else, including your wife, in our--" He paused to find the right word. "...Our business, I'll tell you nothing, and you'll never hear from me again. Do you understand?"

Steven felt confused and pushed, as if being backed into a corner. "No, I don't understand," he snapped. "What are you talking about? What business? And why no police? Listen, if this is about the reward, once the police arrest someone I'll--"

The man raised a gloved hand. "Mr. Burns, calm down. Please. I realize this must be confusing for you, but if you want my help you're going to have to sit and listen for a few minutes. During our conversation you will hear things that will make you extremely emotional, but at all times you must remain calm. Always calm. Can you do that? In order to find your daughter's killer, for a few minutes, can you sit and listen calmly? If not, our business is done." The man gestured again to the empty spot beside him. "For the last time, Mr. Burns, please sit down."

Time slowed as Steven stared at the man, torn. Part of him intrigued enough to want to hear the stranger out, the other part wanted to jump this asshole and drag him to the sheriff's station.

As if reading Steven's mind, the man frowned impatiently and said, "I'll simply tell the police I lied. They'll release me, and you'll never see me again. You'll never know what I know." He glanced at his watch. "What are we doing, Mr. Burns?"

As Steven's eyes shifted to that empty spot on the bench, a chill rippled down his spine. He wasn't sure why, but he had a gnawing feeling that sitting down with this man would lead to nothing good, and might even be dangerous. Still, he couldn't shake his peaked curiosity. What if this guy really did know the identity of Luna's killer? Was it possible? The longer Steven stood there fighting indecision, the more his body stiffened and the faster his heart raced. "Are you fucking kidding me?" Steven blurted out. "First the weird phone calls in the middle of the night. Now this bullshit about 'no police.' This isn't a fucking game to me, mister. My daughter is dead. If you really know something and want to help, great. Quit screwing around and start talking. Otherwise, I figure you're just full of shit."

The man nodded and rose to his feet. He paused to regard Steven with sympathetic eyes. With a sigh in his voice he said, "Have a good life, Mr. Burns." Then he walked away.

A panicked hollowness seized Steven as he watched the man striding away across the open field. Every departing step the man took, the emptier and more desperate Steven felt. Unable to restrain himself, Steven called out, "No, wait. Come back."

But the man kept walking, briefcase swinging at his side, no sign of having heard Steven's plea.

"Wait," Steven yelled louder. "Hey! Stop!"

The man just kept walking.

The realization that he was being intentionally ignored,

spiked Steven's panic. "Wait!" Steven broke into a sprint, quickly closed the gap, and grabbed the man's arm. "Please, I just--"

An angry crackling sound stopped Steven short.

The man whipped around and jabbed Steven's chest with a large black stun gun.

KZAPPP! Twelve million volts lanced through Steven's body. Grunting through gritted teeth, Steven jerked, seized up, then crumbled to the grass, convulsing in excruciating pain. Paralyzed, barely able to open his tearing eyes, Steven could just make out the man's bespectacled face peering down at him, watching his agony.

The man frowned disappointedly. "You'll regain muscle control in ten minutes or so. Sorry."

Then the man was gone... leaving nothing in Steven's blurred field of view but perfect blue sky.

23

"Damn! And you didn't call the police?"

"I already told you. He said if I involved the police or anyone else I'd never see him again."

"Good. Why would you want to see that psycho again?"

Steven stared at the rug, considering his reply. Finally he looked back up at Linton. "I guess I'm not so sure he really is a psycho. Maybe I made a mistake."

They were in Linton's living room, both seated on a dark green leather sofa that faced a seventy-inch plasma television. On screen, a muted basketball game played in 4K ultra high definition. Linton's two bedroom condo was located in Pasadena, a twenty minute drive from the Burns Remodeling home office. With its sleek decor, cutting edge gadgetry, and impeccable neatness, Linton's place always reminded Steven of a high-end electronics showroom. A photo of Linton hugging his mom in front of her Kingston home, and a blow-up of a Topps baseball card featuring Steven making a diving catch were the only visible evidence that Linton actually lived there.

"How about a drink?" Linton said. He rose from the sofa and

crossed to an impressive home bar that dominated one corner of the room.

"No. This is fine." Steven jiggled the half-full bottle of Arrowhead water he arrived with. He always kept a few bottles of water in his truck.

Linton flipped a switch behind the bar, illuminating well stocked shelves of liquor. "I got wine, vodka, gin, rum of course." He yanked open a compact fridge and took a quick visual inventory. "And about six types of beer."

Steven shook his head at the display. "I see you're prepared for every occasion, as always."

"If by 'occasion' you mean lovely ladies, absolutely." Linton held up a curvaceous bottle with an ornate gold label. "How about some Appleton? Best Jamaican rum you can buy off island. Ease ya down real nice, mon."

Steven shook his head. "Really. I'm fine."

"Suit yourself," Linton said with a shrug, then poured himself a short one over ice.

"So, you think I need 'easing down?'" Steven asked.

"You're being played, mon. That's what I think." The drink in Linton's hand tinkled as he returned to his seat on the sofa. "Did he ask you for any money?"

Steven shook his head. "I didn't give him a chance to."

"That's where he was headed, guaranteed. I'm telling you, he's just some crazy joker trying to scam you."

As Steven pondered these words, he unscrewed the top from his water bottle and took a sip. Linton's reasoning made perfect sense, in fact, Steven suspected the same thing himself, but like an itch he couldn't reach, two words kept nagging him.

Steven met Linton's concerned eyes and said, "What if?"

Linton's brow fell. "What if what?"

"What if he's not, like you say, a 'crazy joker?'"

"But he is."

"What if it's not a scam?"

"Trust me... it is."

"What if it's not? What if he really does know the identity of Luna's killer?"

Linton sighed. "Come on, mon. You said it yourself. If he knew something and truly wanted to help, he'd go straight to the police. None of this 'keep it secret' business."

"Okay, but what if for some reason he wanted to remain anonymous? A lot of people don't trust the police."

"Right... people like crooks and scammers." Linton rewarded his wit with a sip of rum.

"Okay," Steven said, "lets say he is some kind of criminal. Think about it. That could be the reason he knows something. Maybe he heard someone talking or--"

"Fine, fine." Linton conceded the point with a wave of his hand. "Then why not just tell you what he knows and walk away? Even better, he could just call in an anonymous tip, right?"

"True." Steven wrung his water bottle as he mentally juggled the problem. Suddenly his eyes lit up. "Okay, but what if he wants the reward money and also wants to remain anonymous? That's trickier because the reward is based on a conviction. If he's anonymous, how does he get paid?"

"Come on, they have to have a way to pay anonymous tippers."

"Sure, but maybe he doesn't want to risk it. He doesn't trust the system. Possible, right?"

Linton shook his head with a chuckle and took another sip of rum before replying. "Look, we can go back and forth all day, but we'll never know for sure."

"Exactly," Steven said. "That's the problem. I need to know for sure what he had to say, or I'll never stop thinking about it."

Steven could already see himself lying awake, night after night, pondering that ten-minute encounter at the park bench.

Constantly wondering what that strange gloved man really knew about Luna's murder. It was a life sentence of crippling doubt.

Steven groaned and raked his face with his hand. "Shit! I should've just let him talk. I'm so stupid."

"Listen," Linton said. "From what you described you already scared the guy off anyway, so going to the police now won't make a difference. What's the name of that Indian detective again?"

"He's Pakistani. His name is Ahmad."

"Right. Tell Detective Ahmad everything you told me. Let him track this guy down. If he really has information I'm sure the police will get it out of him."

Steven made a face. "No. They'll never find him."

Linton nodded. "It's a long shot for sure, but hey, you never know."

"Forget it," Steven said. "He's too careful, and the police will only have my description to go on. I'm sure he's already thought of that. I'm telling you, they'll never find this guy." Steven's eyes narrowed with realization. "The only way I'm going to get answers is to somehow get him to approach me again."

Linton cracked a impressed smile. "Smart. Use yourself as bait, then let the police grab him. A little crazy, but very smart."

"No, no, forget the police," Steven said. "I have to do this alone."

"Alone?" Linton's smile evaporated. "I change my mind. Steven, this is a very, very stupid idea."

24

L inton, now back behind the bar, refilled his glass as Steven tried to explain.

"He was absolutely clear about only one thing," Steven said, holding up an index finger. "No police involvement, period. And I could tell he meant it. True, I freaked out and scared him off, but I don't think I've done anything yet that could be considered a deal breaker. At least, that's my hope. But if I involve the police and he finds out, it's over. Done. Any chance of learning if he's real or not will be gone for good. Get it?"

"I get it, but I don't like it." Linton slapped the cork back into the bottle of Appleton and returned it to the shelf. "Also... aren't you forgetting something?"

"What?"

"The police is one thing, but you said he also warned you not to involve anyone at all, right?" Linton spread his arms like a show host. "I'm pretty sure I fit the 'anyone' category."

"True," Steven said, "but, unless he followed me, there's no way he could know I'm here. More importantly, this is between just us two. Calling Detective Ahmad means involving more people. Even an undercover operation would require a team of some sort. For all I know he could have a contact at the sheriff's station. Hell, he might even be a cop himself. He did have that stiff, formal thing about him that some cops have."

"But wait." Linton looked confused. "From how it sounds, this guy's been stalking you for a while. What makes you so sure he didn't follow you today?"

"Why would he? As far as he's concerned our business was done. Also, he assaulted me in broad daylight and left me squirming on the ground. Someone could have seen everything and called 911. Would you stick around?"

Leaning against the bar, Linton made an impressed sound as he swirled his drink. "You really thought this very, very bad idea through, huh?"

Steven almost laughed. He hadn't thought anything through. He was just doing what he knew best. Keeping his eye on the ball to avoid being struck out.

Steven stared across the room at his best friend and pinned him with driven eyes. "Linton, I must know for sure if this man is real. Getting him to contact me again, bad idea or not, is my best shot."

Linton sighed. He took a slow sip of rum, then crossed the room and plopped back onto the sofa, beside Steven. "Okay," he said. "How?"

Steven shrugged. "I have no idea. I guess I'll just go back to the park tomorrow... and wait."

"For how long? How do you even know he'll be watching?"

"I don't. If he doesn't show tomorrow, I'll try again the next day, and the day after that. I'll keep going back until he gets the message that I'm ready to listen."

Linton looked doubtful. "You really think that'll work?"

"All I know is, he put a lot of effort into contacting me. And if you're right, that this is about money, I'm betting he's still interested."

"Yes, but here's the thing." Linton's voice dropped ominously. "What, exactly, are you betting?"

Steven met Linton's portentous stare. "I'll be alright," he said. "Don't worry."

Linton laughed like Steven had just told the best joke in the world. "Why should I worry, mon? I'm gonna be right there with you. While you wait on the bench, I'll hide nearby. Keep an eye on..."

"No!" Steven snapped. "I'm doing this alone."

"The hell you are," Linton shot back. "And if you think I'm letting that happen..."

"It's not your choice, okay? It's mine. If he sees you, and he will, he'll never show. The only way this works is if I'm alone."

Linton took a settling breath, then leveled grave eyes on Steven. "What if it's him?"

A chill spidered down Steven's spine. He knew exactly who Linton meant, and Linton was right. "I thought about that," Steven said, "Of course I thought about it. But I don't think it is him."

"But it could be, right?" Linton leaned closer, pressing his point. "Maybe he doesn't like how hard you're pushing the police to catch him. Maybe he doesn't like you putting up all those flyers, or how you keep raising the reward. Maybe he's trying to kill you. Did you think about that?"

"If he wanted to kill me, why didn't he do it right there in the park when he had the chance?"

Linton threw up his hands. "Who knows why crazy people do what they do?"

Steven shook his head. "I don't think he wants to hurt me. I have no idea what he wants, that's why this has to happen."

Steven pointed his water bottle at Linton. "And you can't interfere. I want you to promise me."

Linton groaned. "Steven, brother... you sure about this?"

"No. But I need you to promise anyway."

"Fine. Okay. I promise. But at least take a little protection."

"Are you talking about a gun? Seriously?"

"Yes. Seriously. I know you don't have one, but I know this guy who..."

"Forget it."

"But--"

"Dude, you know how I feel about this. I'm not carrying a gun."

Over the years, and usually over a couple of beers, he and Linton have had several debates about gun ownership. Linton thought they were a necessary evil. Steven agreed guns were evil, it was that necessary crap he took issue with.

"Anyway," Steven continued, "I don't need 'protection.' Like I said... if he wanted to kill me I wouldn't be sitting here right now."

Linton tilted his head. "Good question. Why are you 'sitting here?' I mean, you don't want my help, you won't take my advice, you won't even drink with me. So why, exactly, are you here?"

Steven fidgeted with his water bottle. "I guess I just needed someone to talk it out with."

Linton laughed. "That makes sense. No way in hell Nicky would go for any of this craziness. So, how do you plan to explain these daily trips to the park?"

"I don't have to." Steven took a breath before continuing. "Nichole left me."

Linton sat up. "What?"

"She wanted me to stop... well, everything. Go see some shrink. Go back to work and move on. I can't do that so... that was it. She left. She went to stay with her sister."

Linton set his drink down on the coffee table. "Steven, you listen to me. Don't waste another second with this crazy park man nonsense. You gotta go get Nicky back."

"No. This gives me freedom to really focus on finding Luna's killer. Once that's done I'll contact her and..."

"But that could take years... or longer. Maybe never. What are you doing, mon? You already lost Luna... don't lose Nichole, too. Look, you gotta call her. Call her right now and fix this before..."

"I can't!" Steven pounded the sofa with his fist. "Why doesn't anyone understand that? Until the bastard who murdered my baby is in prison or dead, there's no moving on. Not for me. I can't do it."

Linton sighed, picked up his drink, and settled back on the sofa. Silent. Concerned.

Steven frowned at his friend. "Sorry."

Linton raised a hand. "It's cool. Look, I can't tell you what to do, but... I'm gonna be honest with you. I think Nichole might be right. Maybe you need to talk to someone. A professional."

"Maybe," Steven said, "but here's the thing." His voice dropped as if revealing a dark secret. "Until this is really over... I don't want to stop feeling what I'm feeling."

Linton just stared at him in numbed silence.

Steven set his water bottle down on the coffee table. "I need you to do me a favor."

Linton cracked a reluctant smile. "No worries, mon. I don't agree with any of this, but I will not say anything to Nichole. You have my word."

"I know. Not that. Another favor."

Linton spread his hands. "Anything, mon. You know that."

Steven acknowledged their camaraderie with a nod and a small smile, then said, "I changed my mind. I could really use that drink now."

25

A little past noon the following day, Steven sat down on the bench beneath the bur oak tree in the middle of Memorial Park, and waited.

He planned to arrive around 9:00 AM, but realized there was no reason to expect the stranger to appear earlier than the time of their last encounter.

Steven was confident he wouldn't have to wait long. His last minute plea and attempted pursuit, no doubt, conveyed his willingness to give in to the stranger's demands. And if the stranger was as motivated as Steven suspected, it seemed certain he'd return the next day and watch the bench, eager to get another shot at making his pitch.

So, with his right foot tapping incessantly, his palms sweating, and his stomach wavering... Steven waited.

His gaze pivoted back and forth between the three main entrances. Because he expected the stranger to change appearance, every adult male entering the park was suspect. Bikers, joggers, dog walkers, and especially men walking alone, all fell under Steven's scrutiny until his suspicion was satisfied. Intermittently, he'd scan the street outside the park, just in case the stranger watched from a parked vehicle.

Steven's hyperfocused state had the effect of compressing time. Only when the park's lights winked on did he realize the entire afternoon had slipped away. After more than five hours of waiting, the stranger had not shown.

As the somber light of dusk settled over Memorial Park, Steven picked himself up and started across the open field with a slight limp. His body was stiff from sitting all day. Any confidence in his plan to reconnect with the stranger, now shaken.

The next five days Steven spent waiting were equally long and disappointing.

Every day he'd show up around noon and occupy the bench until sundown. It occurred to him that doing nothing all day but watching and waiting was equivalent to staring at a clock.

By day three Steven began bringing along the signed copy of *Moneyball* that Nichole gave him for his birthday two years ago. He heard it was good and had always intended to read it, but never got around to it. Whether it was because he had little desire to relive the bullshit he faced in the majors, or just the fact that he wasn't a big reader, he wasn't sure. Probably both. A Subway footlong turkey sandwich and a bottle of Arrowhead were also part of Steven's daily supplies. No point starving while he waited for the stranger to decide it was safe to reapproach him.

That had to be why the stranger still hadn't shown, Steven kept telling himself; he was simply playing it safe.

But with each passing day, Steven's belief that he'd meet the stranger again withered a bit more. Linton was right. His hours spent on the bench could just be a waste of time. The truth was, he had no idea if the stranger was watching or not, or if he would ever return to the park. All Steven really had was a obsessive need to know the truth, and a feeble grip on hope.

During Steven's seventh day on the bench, at about three in the afternoon, a uniformed police officer approached him. The officer's youth and lack of cynicism suggested someone still new to the force. He explained that after driving by everyday and spotting Steven on the bench all week, he thought it best to come over and check that everything was okay. He accepted Steven's assurances with a smile, but dutifully requested Steven's ID. Normally Steven might question such a demand; after all, he was simply sitting in a public park, but to avoid the stranger spotting him with a cop, he immediately complied. Worried his name might be recognized and prolong the encounter, Steven held his breath until the young cop returned his driver's license, wished him a good day, and walked back to his cruiser.

Early, on the eighth day, Steven's cell phone rang.

The chiming ring startled him. Steven's phone hadn't made a sound in more than a week. Reaching into his pocket for the device, Steven hesitated, struck with a realization.

This could be him.

He took a breath then checked the caller ID.

It wasn't the stranger calling, but the name on the screen caused him to pause.

Nichole.

Steven watched the phone ring and vibrate in his hand, like a living thing frantic for attention. It felt wrong to ignore Nichole's call, but he didn't want to speak to her. Not now. He didn't want to risk Nichole asking to come back, because if she did... he wasn't sure what he'd say. But the answer had to be no. He had to see this thing through.

Finally, the phone quieted and the screen flashed: missed call. An instant later an alert signaled that Nichole had left a voicemail.

Steven hit play.

"Hey. Hope you're okay. I was wondering if we could meet and talk. Please call me when you get a chance. Goodbye."

For an instant Steven felt disorientated. Nichole's voice sounded so... normal. Not angry or curt, but like all was wonderful between them. It almost seemed like somehow his wife had called from the past.

As Steven slipped the phone back into his pocket, he decided he wouldn't meet her, and he wouldn't call either. If what they had was fixable, he'd do everything he could to fix it later. Right now he had to stay focused.

Not counting sharing his lunch everyday with a friendly black-tailed squirrel, Steven's next two afternoons in Memorial Park were uneventful. But on the tenth day, while driving home, what Steven noticed in his rearview mirror made his heart race. He wasn't certain at first, but after driving his truck a few more miles and making a couple of unplanned turns, he no longer had any doubt.

A charcoal grey Ford Explorer with dark tinted windows was following him.

26

S teven wasn't sure what to do, so he simply kept driving.

The grey SUV lingered two or three vehicles back. Even when traffic flow presented opportunities to maneuver closer, the SUV maintained an inconspicuous distance.

That was good, Steven thought. The SUV's continued attempts at stealth meant Steven's abrupt turns hadn't exposed the fact that he knew he was being followed.

Distance and obstructing traffic prevented Steven from getting a good look at the driver in his rear view mirror, but Steven didn't need to see the driver's face.

It had to be the stranger.

But why would the stranger follow him, instead of approaching him again in the park? And more troubling, how long has this been going on? Was today the first time the stranger tailed his pickup truck through the streets of Flintridge, or was this simply the first time Steven noticed? Steven decided it didn't matter. Most important now is that he avoided taking any action that would frighten the stranger away.

Steven made a left turn and headed south on Georgian Road, just as he did every night when driving home. In the mirror he watched the SUV mimic the turn and continue following. Being stalked quickened Steven's pulse, but he also felt a sense of relief. Those long afternoons on the bench had paid off. At some point the stranger spotted him, and was now preparing to make contact.

As Steven cruised closer and closer to home he considered the likeliest scenario. Before risking another meeting, it made sense that the stranger would take the precaution of shadowing him for a few days. When certain he wasn't walking into a trap, the stranger would show up at the bench again, ready to talk. Now all Steven had to do for the next day or so was continue his daily routine. Spend all afternoon waiting on the bench, at sundown drive straight home, repeat.

Steven's focus ticked up and down between the road ahead and his rearview mirror. He couldn't keep his eyes off that SUV. The man he'd been waiting for for weeks was now just a few car lengths away. Steven hoped that the stranger truly had been following him for several days. If so, maybe tomorrow would be the day they'd meet again. Maybe tomorrow he'd finally get answers.

But when Steven stopped at a red light at the intersection of Georgian and Woodleigh, just five minutes from his driveway, a voice he'd been trying to ignore since first spotting the SUV intensified.

The voice reverberating in Steven's head belonged to Linton, a memory that seemed to grow louder and louder the nearer he got to his front door. "What if it's him?" Linton's voice warned over and over. "What if he's trying to kill you?"

Nearby ramps for the busy 210 freeway made this particular intersection notorious for long traffic lights. While Steven waited, he eyed the SUV's reflection in his rear and sideview mirrors, hoping to spot anything that hinted at the driver's intent.

Linton was right, of course. The stranger's reasons for tailing him could be very different from Steven's fantasy. Instead of the park bench, maybe the stranger planned to show up on his doorstep armed with something more permanent than a stun gun.

But Steven didn't believe that.

During their first encounter the stranger meant him no harm, he truly wanted to talk. Of that much Steven was almost certain. Only after Steven freaked out and chased him, did things go badly. Still, there was something off about the man. Something beyond the creepy calls, and the gloves, and his rules about police, that, even now, filled Steven with a constant buzz of dread.

Steven glanced up to check the traffic light and found himself riveted. For an instant the world fell away as the burning red light dominated his vision, seeming to beam its implicit message directly to him.

STOP.

Steven blinked as if roused from sleep. And suddenly Linton's nagging voice was gone... replaced by his own.

What the hell am I doing?

What if it's him? What if he's...

You can't let... him just follow you home.

Then what?

Steven's eyes shot to the corner crosswalk signal. A glowing amber hand and numerals flashing down the seconds before traffic resumed.

27, 26, 25...

He had to think of something fast. He was too close to home to change course now. When the light turned green, if he did anything except continue along his normal route, it would look suspicious. The stranger would know he'd been spotted, then almost certainly vanish for good.

Steven couldn't let that happen.

22, 21, 20...

He considered pulling into a gas station to buy some time. Just across the intersection, a Shell station occupied the entire corner. But then he recalled filling the tank just the night before. If, by chance, the stranger had been trailing him for days, he'd know Steven had no reason to go near a gas pump.

18, 17, 16...

Think, Steven told himself, think.

When he glanced out the rear window to check the SUV's position, the answer struck him.

They were both boxed in.

The dark grey SUV, which still lingered two cars back, and his truck were both trapped by the cluster of idling vehicles waiting for the green light.

This was his chance. This might be his only chance.

14, 13, 12...

If he was going to do it, it had to be now.

Steven shifted into park, flung open his door, and jumped out. Holding both hands up chest-high, in a gesture of "I mean you no harm," Steven began walking back between the two lanes of rumbling vehicles, toward the SUV.

Drivers and passengers stared as the man with his hands up brushed past their windows. Hot exhaust fumes buffeted Steven's lower legs and stung his nostrils.

Just steps from the SUV, Steven spotted the driver through the windshield, but couldn't see his face. He was bent low over the passenger seat, fussing with some object out of Steven's line of sight.

A gun?

Steven's heart picked up at the thought, but the man's move-

ments seemed relaxed, even casual, not charged with the
urgency of someone grabbing for a weapon.

Steven rapped twice on the driver's side window. The tinted
glass was so dark that he could barely make out the man's startled reaction inside.

"I just want to talk," Steven said, voice raised above the din of
traffic. "Please."

With a motorized whine the window vanished into the door,
setting free a waft of cigarette smoke, stale fast food, and pine air
freshener.

Steven's upraised hands withered to his sides and his brow
tightened as he took in the individual seated behind the wheel.

It wasn't the stranger.

The driver was Asian, probably Chinese, forties, overweight
and balding. He shrank back from Steven, raising a defensive
hand. "Easy," he said, a tremor in his voice. "Just take it easy."

Steven stared, stunned, confounded by his error. He was so
certain the SUV had been following him. His desperation to
reconnect with the stranger must've gotten the best of his imagination. Steven found his voice. "Listen, I didn't mean to..."

"Just doing my job, okay?," the Asian man cut him off. "It's
nothing personal, Mr. Burns."

Steven blinked. "Wait, what?" Hearing the Asian driver utter
his name instantly reignited his suspicion. Steven's puzzled eyes
drilled into him. "Who are you? Why are you following me?"
Then an unexpected possibility seized Steven. "Hold on. Do you
work for him? Is that it?"

"Him?" The Asian man looked lost. "Him who?"

"I don't know his name," Steven snapped back. "The man
from the park. The man with the gloves."

The Asian man winced in bafflement. "I have no idea what
you're talking about." He held out a business-size white envelope. "This is for you."

Steven stared at the envelope like it appeared out of thin air.

Just two words typed on the front: STEVEN BURNS.

The Asian man waggled the envelope before Steven, like a fisherman twitching bait. "Take it, please. The light's about to change."

The instant Steven's fingers grasped the envelope the Asian man declared, "You've been served."

Before Steven could give voice to the confusion on his face, a cacophony of angry horns and grumbling motors erupted around him. The light had turned green. Traffic surged forward through the intersection, like a dam had given way. Drivers caught behind Steven's truck and the Asian man's SUV whipped into adjacent lanes, barking curses at the two men as they sped away.

The Asian man shouted over the chaos, "Like I said, Mr. Burns, just doing my job." Then he powered up his window and accelerated into the swarm of passing vehicles. Gone.

Standing in the middle of three lanes of hurdling steel, ignoring horns and shouts, Steven ripped open the envelope and removed a folded five page document.

Peeling open the pages, the first thing he noticed was a government seal, stamped in blue ink.

SUPERIOR COURT, LOS ANGELES COUNTY, CALIFORNIA

The next item that jumped out made Steven's legs go hollow.

A rectangular box on the left side of the page, labeled, in bold text: PETITION FOR DIVORCE. And within the box, two names. Petitioner: Nichole Burns. Respondent: Steven Burns.

27

S teven watched a couple walking, hand in hand. Both about his age. Warm smiles and a bounce in their step. Happy and in love.

Then Steven spotted a young man piggybacking a toddler. Dad adding extra giddy-up to his gait. Son giggling with each pronounced bounce.

A couple walking with a five-year-old girl strung between their outstretched hands next caught Steven's eye. The girl jerked up her tiny feet and dangled playfully from her parents' grip. Mom and Dad performed their duty, swinging her back and forth a few times before gently setting her down again, all without breaking stride.

After reading the divorce summons, Steven couldn't bring himself to drive home. He couldn't bear walking into that cold, lonely, five-thousand-square-foot shell of the wonderful life he once had. Not yet. Not when the shock of reading those pages still squeezed his heart. Not when all he wanted to do was bang his head against something hard.

So Steven went to the mall.

Flintridge Fashion Square offered one hundred and forty seven upscale shops and eateries on two sprawling levels. In one of several stylish yet durably decorated lounge areas, Steven sat slumped on an uncomfortable wire mesh chair, watching the world stroll by. The divorce papers were still clenched in his right hand, like a shackle he couldn't remove.

Steven thought he'd feel better being among people, even strangers, instead of alone in a house filled with ghosts. He was wrong. Everyone he laid eyes on seemed to remind him of the family he'd lost. A parade of happy couples and kids, each tamping down his sorrow a bit deeper as they passed.

Nichole did have a flair for the dramatic; Steven knew that. Just a year ago, after he'd repeatedly postponed the family ski vacation, he awoke one morning to an empty house and a note from Nichole. Be back next Sunday. Luna and I would love you to join us. XXX Your family. And it worked. Steven dumped everything into Linton's lap and hopped onto the next flight to Aspen. And two weeks ago, Nichole's ultimatum and suitcase packing exit was also one of her attention-grabbing powerplays, at least that's what Steven assumed. He was counting on patching things up with Nichole, as he'd always done, once Luna's killer was off the streets and out of his nightmares.

But the divorce summons was different.

It had nothing to do with drama or a demand for attention. There was too much at stake. Nichole wouldn't do that. She wouldn't stab that deep... not if she still cared. No, the summons was Nichole giving up on him, letting go of any hope that they were fixable.

Steven watched a young man, laden with shopping bags, kiss his pretty wife then plop down with a sigh into a nearby chair. The couple exchanged cute waves, then the wife set off toward the heart of the mall, most likely to inflict more damage on their credit cards. For an instant the young man's and Steven's eyes met. The young man flashed a polite smile, then surrendered his attention to the smartphone cradled in his hand.

Steven stared at his own hand. At the document coiled in his grasp. At that stamped government seal peeking out. He felt his head wag side to side even before consciously submitting to one undeniable realization.

I can't lose Nichole, too.

Along with that absolute, came another. He was running out of time. Waiting indefinitely on a park bench for some whack job to show up with information that's probably worthless, was no longer an option. Still, Steven desperately wanted to hear what the man had to say. Two days, that's what Steven decided to give himself. He'd wait in the park for two more days. If the stranger didn't show up by then, for the sake of his marriage and his sanity, he'd call Detective Ahmad and tell him about his strange encounter in Memorial Park two weeks ago.

"Excuse me."

Steven looked up.

An older woman, sixties, smiled down at him. A Lane Bryant shopping bag dangled from one hand, a venti Starbucks cup gripped in the other. "I've seen you on the news," she said. Her voice friendly and earnest. "I'm so sorry about your daughter. Every time I see a reward flyer with her adorable little face my heart breaks." She pressed the coffee cup against the small gold cross necklace that hung over her heart, and appeared about to cry. "You and your little angel will be in my prayers tonight."

Steven almost said thank you, but somehow that seemed wrong, so he just nodded with a tight smile. But as he watched the woman walk away and melt into the stream of shoppers, something she said echoed in his mind. A throwaway comment transforming slowly into inspiration.

Of course.

Steven got up, shoved the summons into his jacket pocket, and started for the mall exit.

He knew exactly what to do to get the stranger's attention, and it needed to get done tonight.

28

The following afternoon Steven was back on the bench beneath the big bur oak in the middle of Memorial Park.

He planned to pass the time completing the last chapters of *Moneyball*, but about fifteen minutes after sitting down, he glanced up from the book and froze.

He didn't see where the man came from. One moment the sprawling open field was deserted, and the next a figure was striding across the freshly mowed grass, heading directly toward him. Even from a distance Steven recognized that purposeful gait, that beige windbreaker and old brown briefcase, those squarish glasses, and most of all, those black leather gloves.

It was him. Finally.

Steven shut the book on his lap and watched him come. The pulse in his neck thrummed. His breathing quickened. The urge to jump up and rush forward to meet the stranger was overpowering, but Steven refused to repeat his mistake from last time. So he remained seated. Every tendon in his body ached with the effort to simply sit still and appear calm.

The stranger stopped two paces from the bench, just beyond

arm's reach, and offered a small nod in way of a greeting. No smile and nothing readable in his eyes, just the slightest dip of the head.

Steven returned the gesture, just as minimal and emotionless. He read somewhere that mirroring a person's actions increased rapport.

Before either man could break the silence, the black-tailed squirrel skittered down the bur oak's trunk and paused on its hind legs, right at Steven's feet. With its bushy tail curled high, the squirrel chirped a bright and friendly greeting to his human benefactor, in perfect contrast to the uneasy meeting he'd just interrupted.

"Shoo." Steven said, gently waving away the critter. "Go on, shoo."

But the squirrel just cocked his head, scooted a bit closer, and continued chirping.

"Get out of here!" The stranger shouted at the squirrel, while giving his briefcase three sharp slaps.

Steven flinched, almost as startled as the squirrel.

The terrified animal kicked up loose grass as it darted away.

Steven watched with a frown as his lunch companion skittered up the tree, toward the high branches.

"They're just rats with cute tails," the stranger said to Steven. "Not very wise to feed them; not to mention it's against park rules."

Struck by the implications of the stranger's comment, Steven whipped back to face him.

The stranger confirmed Steven's deduction with a slow nod. Then with that low, scratchy voice he said, "Yes, Mr. Burns, I have been watching you." He tipped his briefcase toward the bench. "I see you sitting there everyday. Waiting. I'll admit, your persistence is impressive, but I never planned to return. Not until I saw this." He withdrew a folded sheet of paper from his jacket pocket.

Steven knew what it was, even before the stranger unfolded the sheet and showed him the printed side. Last night, before leaving the mall, Steven stopped at a Papyrus Stationary store and purchased a red finepoint Sharpie. Then he spent the next two hours zipping around Flintridge, visiting every lamp pole, bus stop shelter, and bulletin board where he had posted a reward flyer. Along the bottom edge of each flyer, in block letters, he scrawled the same three-word message, a message he knew only one person would truly understand. Steven had no way of knowing if the message would reach its intended target, but if the stranger still stalked him, as he suspected, he gambled that the reward flyers were still being watched as well. And moments ago, when Steven spotted the stranger striding toward him, he knew his gamble had paid off.

The stranger held out the flyer with a gloved hand, confronting Steven with his own handiwork. The flyer was a black and white photocopy, so the three words scrawled on the bottom in bold red letters practically leapt from the page.

I'M CALM NOW

"Are you?" the stranger asked, giving the flyer a jiggle to underscore the question.

Mindful not to appear too anxious, in a measured voice Steven replied, "I am. I want to hear what you have to say."

"Good," the stranger said. "But I warn you, for the next few minutes, regardless of what you hear or see... you must remain that way. Calm, I mean. If not, I'm gone, and there won't be a third chance. Do you understand?"

The hairs on the back of Steven's neck stirred. *What could this man know about Luna's killer that warranted such a warning?* Pushing past dread, Steven replied, "Yes, I understand."

"Excellent." Somehow, without a change in expression the

stranger appeared genuinely pleased. He took his time refolding the flyer just so, then returned it to his jacket pocket. "Before we begin," he continued, "I have to ask you one more question."

Steven tensed. The stranger's words had the distinct tone of a trap springing shut.

"During our first meeting," the stranger said, "I made it very clear about my desire for absolute-" He rummaged for the right word. "Privacy." Then his voice dropped just shy of a whisper. "Did you tell anyone about me, Mr. Burns?"

Steven's heart seized. It took everything he had to conceal the fireworks of panic erupting inside him. "No," Steven answered, managing to conjure up a casual air. "I didn't tell anyone."

The stranger studied him in silence. He adjusted his glasses and cocked his head as if focusing on some particular spot deep within Steven's soul. Then, without a flinch in his stoic guise, he declared, "You're lying."

The stranger's dead certain tone ratcheted up Steven's distress. Did this man somehow know that he had told Linton everything? Deciding this was highly unlikely, Steven stuck to his story. "You're wrong," Steven said. "I swear, I did exactly what you--

The stranger raised an impatient hand, signaling Steven to save his breath. "I want to help you Mr. Burns," he said, "but I need to be able to trust you. I'm going to tell you a fact about me. Fair warning, it's a little unusual. Whether you choose to believe it or not is up to you." He paused to let his preamble sink in, then continued, "Ever since I was a boy, I could always tell when someone was lying to me. I don't know how it works. I'm not psychic or anything so fantastic. It's just a feeling I get." His eyes locked onto Steven's to underscore his next words. "And that feeling is never wrong. Never."

Steven just stared back, unsure how to digest what he'd just heard. Either the man looming before him possessed some weird knack for perceiving lies, or he was straight-up nuts. And if the stranger was nuts, what did that say about the information he claimed to have about Luna's murderer?

As if privy to Steven's thoughts, the corners of the stranger's mouth curled into the faintest smile. "No, Mr. Burns, I'm not crazy. Maybe just more observant than most." He took one deliberate step closer to Steven. "Now, I'll ask one last time. Did you tell anyone about me, or not?"

Despite being seated in the middle of a one-and-a-half-acre park, Steven felt cornered. If he told the truth, the stranger would, in all likelihood, leave. If Steven stuck to his lie, same result.

Maybe.

Could the stranger really detect deception? Steven realized it didn't matter. The boast was made with great conviction, planting the seed of doubt perfectly. Few people could deliver a convincing lie in the face of such a challenge. And perhaps that's the point. A clever mental maneuver by the stranger to keep Steven off balance and make him easier to read.

The stranger neither appeared impatient nor suspicious of Steven's hesitance. The man just stood there, waiting. His steady, watchful silence almost oppressive.

Steven swallowed into a dry throat and said, "Linton. I told my best friend, Linton. I didn't know if I'd ever see you again, so--"

"I'm not worried about him," the stranger said with a dismissive wave of the hand. "You didn't know much, so you couldn't have told him much."

Steven rose slightly in his seat, as if a load had just slipped from his shoulders.

"I'm more interested in your dealings with the police," the stranger continued. "Did you go to the police, Mr. Burns?"

Steven shook his head. "No. Just Linton. And I made him promise not to get involved. I swear."

Time slowed as the stranger scrutinized Steven head to toe, keen for the slightest hint of deception. If the stranger's lie-detecting claim was merely a mind fuck, his commitment to the ruse was unnerving.

Was it possible?

"Look," Steven said, giving a little under the pressure. "I told you the truth, and I'm calm. Now I just want to hear what you know about my daughter's killer. Please."

For several heartbeats, the stranger just continued to stare, as unreadable as a park statue. Then, after a quick adjustment to his glasses, he crossed to the bench, sat down beside Steven, and laid his briefcase across his lap.

29

The stranger smelled of aftershave lotion, cinnamon breath mint, and old leather, a scent combination Steven found agreeable. The stranger's seated posture was upright and rigid, too formal for a park bench, yet he appeared quite comfortable. The right lens of his eyeglasses was chipped in one corner, and what looked like a wedding band bulged beneath the glove on his left ring finger.

Steven could hardly believe that the man he'd obsessed about meeting again was now seated at his side. In the past two weeks, he'd visualized this moment so often that now it almost seemed unreal. If not for details like odors and chipped eyeglasses he'd swear he was dreaming.

Across the grassy field, a green garbage truck crept along the footpath. The grumbling vehicle paused every fifty yards or so, long enough for a sanitation worker to hop out and dump the contents of a trashcan into the rear compactor.

Immediately upon settling onto the bench, and without so much as a glance at Steven, the stranger devoted his full attention to the distant truck. For more than a minute he carefully observed the city employees going about their duty.

This behavior baffled Steven until it occurred to him that perhaps the stranger suspected the truck's presence wasn't merely a coincidence. Fearing he'd come off overly anxious, Steven stifled the urge to reassure the stranger of no police involvement. Instead, he waited in silence, making an effort to maintain his appearance of patience and calm.

The stranger lost interest in the garbagemen so abruptly that it appeared he'd secretly received an "all clear" signal. He began speaking before he had fully turned to face Steven. "I'm going to talk now. Do not interrupt me and, remember, remain calm."

Steven felt his heartbeat in his throat. "Okay."

Leather squeaked as the stranger interlocked his gloved hands atop his briefcase. "I'm very skilled with computers," he began, his tone measured and even. "Some might describe me as a hacker, but I dislike that term. Hackers are thieves and vandals. I use my skills strictly to help people with what I call justice problems." His head tipped toward Steven. "People like yourself, Mr. Burns."

Steven experienced a jolt of optimism. *That must be why he doesn't want to involve the police, because his information is obtained illegally. Maybe this guy was real after all.*

The stranger went on. "I locate individuals in need of my unique brand of assistance in several ways. By far, the most fruitful has been to infiltrate the hundreds of child pornography bulletin boards and forums hiding on the dark web. Unfortunately, that is how I came upon information concerning your daughter, Luna."

"Wait, are you--" Steven's voice cracked as he struggled to get the words out. "Are you saying that Luna was used for--?"

The stranger's impatient stare cut him off.

Steven swallowed the rest. Drew a deep breath to collect himself. "Sorry."

A nearly imperceptible frown, then the stranger continued.

"I rip and decrypt membership data from these cesspools, then trace IP addresses and break into each member's personal computer. Although consumers of child porn make me sick, I'm after far bigger targets. I scan these computers for evidence of individuals whose deranged sexual appetites aren't satiated by merely watching videos." He paused. His eyes hardened. His jaw set. His voice dropped to a slow, edged whisper. "I... hunt... monsters."

A chill rippled between Steven's shoulder blades. The feeling crept into his limbs as he watched the stranger slowly unbuckle the frayed leather straps of his briefcase.

"Now," the stranger said, "I'm going to show you what I found on the hard drive of one of those computers a few weeks ago." Loose buckles jangled as he flipped open the top flap.

From Steven's vantage point, the briefcase appeared empty. No papers, or books, or pens, just a satchel full of darkness. It almost looked like a magic trick when the stranger's gloved hand reached deep into the bag and came out holding an iPad.

Despite having no protective case, the black iPad was free of scratches and fingerprints. In fact, it looked brand new.

The stranger extended the device to Steven. "It's all set up for you."

Steven didn't touch it, instead his brow tightened. "What do you mean, 'set up for me?' What's on it?"

"I think it's best you find out for yourself." The stranger held the tablet closer to Steven. "Just take it and push the center button."

Steven dropped his gaze to the iPad's cold black screen and his gut went hollow. He had a feeling he knew what he'd see when the tablet powered on, and if he was right, there was no way in hell he'd ever touch that button. Hesitantly, Steven looked back up at the stranger. "Photos?" His voice strained with the effort to stifle his dread. "Is that what you found on those perverts' computers, disgusting photos of my little girl? If that's what you're trying to show me, I don't want--"

"Mr. Burns," the stranger interrupted, "remember when I said, for this to work I need to trust you? I assumed you realized that that has to work both ways." He paused to allow Steven to feel the weight of his words, then gestured to the iPad with a nod. "Take it. Trust me."

Steven wasn't naive enough to genuinely trust this man, but the threat in the stranger's voice seemed clear. If Steven didn't do what was asked, very quickly he'd find himself alone on that bench again, with no answers and little hope of finding any.

Steven took the iPad; the finely machined glass and metal casing, smooth and cold against his fingertips.

"Good," the stranger said. "Now... push the button."

Steven's trembling finger found the concave glass button at the bottom of the tablet. He took a deep breath, then pressed it.

Instantly, the iPad flashed to life.

The dark, grainy photograph that filled the nine-by-seven-inch screen made Steven gasp.

It was Luna, in her pink fairy costume, seated in the passenger seat of an old car. No child seat or seatbelt to protect her. Her diminutive body slumped on torn upholstery, clutching herself as if cold. Her face strained and tracked with tears.

Steven whipped to face the stranger. "Who's car is this? What's his name?"

"Calm, Mr. Burns," the stranger said. His tone was even but laced with a warning. "Remember, you must remain calm."

Steven caught himself. He took a slow breath, then said, "I'm calm. I really am. Please, just tell me you know who owns that car."

For an instant the stranger just stared at him, his expression betraying nothing. Finally he replied with a single word. "Swipe."

Confusion leaped onto Steven's face. "Swipe? What's that? Is that his name?"

A flicker of impatience pursed the stranger's lips, then he said, "There are two more photographs you need to see." He made a small sweeping motion with his hand. "Swipe the screen."

After a moment's hesitation, Steven's trembling fingers brushed across the iPad screen.

A new photograph slid into view.

Luna, still in her fairy costume, stretched out on a sofa, fast asleep. The glow from an unseen television the only light. Relics of a McDonald's Happy Meal strewn on the coffee table. Steven tried to discern other details in the room, but the image was too dark and grainy. Only his daughter could be seen clearly and that was probably intentional. Whoever took the photograph was careful with lighting and framing to avoid revealing information about the location. The deficit of detail between the foreground and background was so perfect that Steven suspected the image might have even been altered with an editing program like Photoshop.

Steven's knuckle cracked and he realized he was squeezing the iPad. To see Luna sleeping in some strange room, so vulnerable, sent a tense, dull ache through his entire frame.

"One more, Mr. Burns," the Stranger said.

Steven swallowed and reached to swipe the screen, but froze when the stranger raised a halting finger.

"The next one's a bit tougher," the stranger said. "Prepare yourself."

A wave of weakness passed over Steven like a gust of wind. If he was standing he might have fainted.

The stranger nodded for him to proceed.

Only when Steven's fingertips made contact with the screen again, did his trembling cease. He swiped to the next photo.

It was another image of Luna, this time in a dark bedroom. She sat perched on the edge of an unmade bed, wearing only a matching pink undershirt and panties, both adorned with tiny blue hearts. Beneath Luna's dangling bare feet, her fairy costume lay strewn on a stained carpet. For Steven, seeing his undressed daughter on a stranger's bed wasn't the most disturbing aspect of the photograph. It was the smile. Luna was smiling directly into the camera. It was a forced smile. A feeble smile straining to hold back tears. A smile brimming with absolute terror.

Steven winced and groaned as if a spear had ripped through his heart. His eyes were squeezed so tight that his temples stung. He barely noticed when the iPad was tugged from his grasp. He peeled open his eyes in time to see the stranger slip the device back into his briefcase.

As the stranger rebuckled the leather straps, he said to Steven, "I apologize for the unpleasantness, but in order for us to move on to the next step, you needed to see proof that the information in my possession is very real." He eased back on the bench and folded his gloved hands atop his briefcase. "Now you may ask your questions. Calmly."

"Who is he?" Steven blurted out with the eagerness of a starving man." Do you know his name? His address? How much do you know exactly?"

"I know everything, Mr. Burns." The stranger said this with the casual certainty of someone simply stating their name or favorite color. "I know the identity of the man who murdered your daughter, and I know exactly where to find him."

Rocked by the enormity of the stranger's words, Steven fell silent. His endless waiting, and doubt, and his war with Nichole, all about to be obliterated by a few pieces of information. And most importantly, there'd be justice for his baby girl. Finally.

"Tell me," Steven whispered in a slow, desperate hush. "Tell me... please."

For the first time the stranger's face registered an unmistakable expression. Puzzlement. He pushed his glasses higher on his nose and said, "I told you I used my skills to assist people with justice problems, but I didn't say I provided this service for free."

And there it was, just like Linton said. Just like Steven suspected. The stranger wanted money. The shock of seeing those photographs, and the excitement of realizing the stranger's claims were real had temporarily clouded his thinking, but Steven wasn't surprised. Of course the stranger was after a pay day. What else could this be about? Only a fool would believe someone would risk illegally mining sensitive data over the internet, simply to perform good deeds for perfect strangers. No, Steven wasn't surprised at all, and after seeing those three photos, he also wasn't opposed to paying for the information that would lead police straight to the man behind the camera. Undoubtedly, the very same man who murdered Luna. Steven's only concern now was whether or not he possessed the means to meet the stranger's price.

"Look," Steven said, his tone earnest. His eyes met the stranger's head on. "My business has been shut ever since this all started. I can definitely get my hands on a significant sum, but you have to understand, I'm not a rich man." Steven steeled himself with a deep breath. "Okay, how much? How much do you want for the information?"

"Nothing," the stranger replied with a small shake of the head.

Steven's brow fell. "But you said your help wasn't free."

"Because it's not. I'm not selling information, Mr. Burns. I'm selling something far more useful."

Steven's expression tightened further. He muttered, "Sorry, but I don't understand."

The stranger acknowledged Steven's bafflement with a nod, then said, "Do you remember what you said at the press conference?"

Steven shrugged. "I don't know. Maybe. What does the press conference have to do with what we're talking about?"

"You said, and these are your exact words, 'Five minutes. I'd give anything to spend five minutes alone with the monster who killed my little girl. That's all I want, just five minutes.'" The stranger paused to give Steven time to catch up. "When I asked you on the phone, you said you remembered. You also said you meant it. Do you still feel that way, Mr. Burns?"

Steven spotted something in the stranger's eyes, a faint gleam of ill delight, that made his forearms tingle. "What's this about, really?" Steven said. "Just say it. Please."

The stranger glanced around the park to ensure they were truly alone, then he returned his unblinking gaze to Steven. "I can get you exactly what you asked for," he whispered, his voice low and brittle like the rustle of dead leaves. "I can get you those five minutes alone with the man who killed your daughter."

"What?" That was all Steven could get out before he stopped breathing.

"Like I said, I sell something far more useful than information." He leaned in closer, the putrid scent of decay now faintly noticeable beneath his cinnamon laced breath. "Mr. Burns, I sell... revenge."

30

A ll the sights and sounds of the surrounding park were gone. Suddenly Steven's entire world had irised down to the stranger's impassive features. Those penetrating, bespectacled eyes, utterly vacant as he delivered a sales pitch for cold-blooded murder.

"I have a secure, very isolated location, so witnesses would not be a concern. Upon your arrival your prisoner would already be heavily restrained, unharmed in any way, and fully conscious and aware. There'd be a small selection of 'tools' at your disposal. Firearms, edged weapons, a few bludgeons, some acids, et cetera. And while five minutes sounds like plenty of time to set things right, once you're face-to-face with your daughter's killer you'll probably have a few things to say. Maybe you'll want to drag it out a little, you never know. Everyone's different. Point is, you can take as much time as you like, as long as it's reasonable. And after you're done, I handle the clean up completely. My disposal method guarantees that remains are never found. You simply return home and get your life back on track, knowing that justice for your daughter's death has been served." The stranger paused to adjust his glasses on his nose then continued. "As for how much, I'm sure you can see there's a lot involved. I'd be taking some extraordinary risks to ensure everything goes smoothly for you. I usually charge more, but I know you're telling the truth about your business closing. So let's just do the one hundred thousand you offered for a reward. I'm assuming that you can really get that, right?" He didn't wait for Steven's answer. "So it's one hundred thousand cash, tens and twenties of course, delivered to me on the day of the encounter. How does all of this sound to you, Mr. Burns?"

"It sounds-- It sounds fucking crazy," Steven said, dazed by disbelief. "You can't be serious. I mean, there's--" Steven stopped short, seized by a scary realization. "Wait a minute. Is this some sort of sting? Are you a cop?"

The stranger looked like he was about to yawn. "You're a smart man. Let's not waste time with ill-considered exclamations and questions."

Steven knew he was right. The stranger had just shown him rock-solid evidence connected to Luna's murder. Why would the police use that evidence to entrap him instead of going after the actual killer?

"Some initial shock on your part is to be expected," the stranger went on, "but right about now you should be arriving at the realization that what I'm offering you is very real."

Steven met the stranger's steady gaze. He saw nothing false or threatening there, just a cool, earnest confidence. The eyes of a man who could and would deliver exactly what he promised. This is really happening, Steven thought. I'm really having a conversation about committing murder.

With a slight shrug the stranger said, "All you have to do now is say four simple words... 'We have a deal', then I'll start making the arrangements." The stranger raised a gloved finger. "But be aware, once I start, there's no stopping. You have to see it through to the very end. This is a very important condition. Do you understand?"

Steven nodded numbly.

"Good." The stranger's stare continued to drill into Steven. "So, what do you say, Mr. Burns? Do we have a deal?"

Steven's gut reaction was to say 'Hell no' and get as far away from that psycho as possible, but one crucial detail held him there. Evidence. The stranger had evidence that lead right to Luna's murderer and there was no way Steven was leaving without it.

"I was angry," Steven said. "When I said what I said that day at the press conference I was out of my mind with grief. That was all talk. I'm not a violent person. What you're offering-- I couldn't-- I could never do that."

"You'd be surprised what you're capable of, Mr. Burns. Especially if I showed you the rest of the photos I found of your daughter. There were over a dozen. And several minutes of video. I plan to destroy them, of course, but if you need further motivation I can--"

"No! I don't want to see it." Steven's insides churned. He swallowed to hold down the contents of his stomach. "Look," he said. "I'll pay you the hundred thousand just for this guy's name and address."

With a slow shake of the head the stranger replied, "Impossible. I don't sell information. I told you that."

Heat flashed the back of Steven's neck. "I don't get it," he said, struggling to keep frustration out of his voice. "Wouldn't that be easier for you? For everybody? I mean, you'd still get your money. What difference would it make?"

"What difference it makes is not your concern." The stranger's eyes narrowed. "This will be done my way, or not at all. You have one week to decide. If we have a deal, tear a corner off the flyer at the intersection of Pine and North Street... then wait for me to get in touch. If not, do nothing and you'll never hear from me again. But remember, once I'm gone, any real chance of seeing justice for your little girl goes with me. Goodbye."

As the stranger stood to leave, Steven blurted out, "Just sell me the iPad. How about that?"

The stranger paused, glanced back at Steven, eyes tinged with impatience.

"I'm serious," Steven said. "I'm assuming all the photos are on there, right? That should be enough to help the police find him. That's my offer. I'll give you a hundred thousand just for that iPad."

With a sigh and a shake of the head, the stranger unbuckled his briefcase, withdrew the iPad and tossed it to an astonished Steven. Then, as the stranger strode away across the open field he called back, "One week, Mr. Burns. Don't forget. You have one week."

Steven's puzzled eyes dropped to the slim electronic device in his hands. Why would the stranger simply give him the iPad? It made no sense unless-- Ignoring a sudden sinking sensation, Steven hesitantly pushed the center button. The screen sputtered, then glowed bright white, then dimmed quickly until dead black. Steven had owned several iPads over the years, but he'd never seen one behave that way. He knew exactly what it meant, but he tried pressing and holding the other buttons anyway.

Nothing worked.

The iPad was completely dead.

31

After the strangest and scariest conversation he'd ever had, Steven knew the smart thing to do was go straight to the police. But that's not what he did. Steven also considered calling Detective Ahmad and sharing the unthinkable details with him, but Steven's iPhone never left his pocket. Instead Steven jumped into his pickup and drove straight to the mall, where he knew there was an Apple Store on the top floor.

Because Steven didn't have a genius bar appointment, a chipper female clerk informed him he'd have to join the standby list. As she rapidly thumb-typed his name into an iPhone, she assured him the wait wouldn't be too long.

To pass the time, Steven milled about the crowded store, poking powerbooks, iMacs, and Apple watches, but his focus was decidedly elsewhere.

What the hell was he going to do?

Steven's thoughts were a maelstrom of uncertainty, suspicion, and fear. Just the idea that he'd consider the stranger's offer made his head hurt, but as he saw it, he only had two choices. Either go to the police and hope they'll find the stranger and force him to reveal the killer's identity, or choose what seemed like the more certain path. Steven could pay the stranger his asking price, then take justice into his own two hands... literally.

Steven wasn't sure if, when the time came, he could really take another man's life, but he'd never forget the raw anger he felt immediately following Luna's murder. He remembered plotting ways to get his hands on the killer if the police actually did catch that bastard. During those first few hellish days, if somehow he'd found himself in the same room with his daughter's murderer, he would've done his damnedest to shoot, stab, or beat that fucker to death with his bare fists. This glimpse at his own primal rage is why he suspected the stranger was right. Steven might not have a violent nature, but if he ever came face to face with the man who violated and murdered his little girl, he'd probably be capable of anything.

Steven hoped he wouldn't have to put himself in that position, and that's why he now stood in the Apple store. After watching Detective Ahmad's investigation wither and ultimately stall over the course of a year, he had little faith the police would ever find Luna's killer. But, those awful photographs the stranger showed him could change everything. If those images could somehow be recovered from the iPad, there's a good chance the police could use them to track down their source. The possibility of a reinvigorated investigation would give Steven the confidence to go to the police and avoid the stranger's cold-blooded alternative.

After waiting a little more than forty-five minutes, a scruffy-bearded Apple specialist named Barry found Steven near the iPhone cases and politely lead him back to the genius bar.

Steven surrendered the dead iPad, then watched the specialist's brow sink deeper and deeper as he tried several methods to restart the device. He mashed buttons in numerous sequences, plugged it into a store computer, plugged it into the wall, then finally a portable charger, but nothing worked. Despite defeat, Barry flashed a professional smile and begged Steven's patience while he took the tablet into the back room for further testing.

Less than five minutes later, Barry returned, accompanied by a bald, bespectacled, also bearded, young man, who he introduced as an iPad technician named Jesse.

Jesse now had possession of the malfunctioning iPad. Steven noticed the odd way the iPad technician cradled the device with both hands. Steven also noticed a mix of bafflement and frustration on the man's face that easily surpassed Barry's earlier reaction.

Jesse said to Steven, "Barry tells me this iPad worked fine about an hour ago. Is that correct?"

"Well, now it's been more like an hour and a half," Steven said, glancing at his watch. "But, yes, it worked great, then all of a sudden... completely dead."

Jesse hummed with intrigue. "Let me ask you this. Between now and then, is it possible you set it down on something hot?"

"Something hot?"

"Sure, like an oven or some kind of heater maybe?"

"No," Steven said. "Nothing like that."

"What about direct sunlight, like a hot car seat or dashboard?"

Steven squinted at him. "It's not even that warm today. Why would you think that?"

The technician shrugged and wagged his head. "Because I'm stumped. I just don't know what else could explain the damage I'm seeing. Here, look." With just his fingertips, Jesse carefully began to pry the screen from its thin steel casing.

Steven suddenly understood why Jesse held the iPad so carefully. The device had been disassembled in the back room, and was now in two pieces.

Like opening the cover of a book, Jesse carefully folded back the iPad's screen.

The tangy stink of fried electronics hit Steven as he gaped at the device's blackened inner workings. Its micro solid-state circuitry was scorched and melted, as if blasted by a mini blow torch. "What the hell happened?" Steven said. "Did the battery explode?"

Jesse and Barry exchanged a look, then Jesse said to Steven, "Actually, that's what's so weird about it." He pointed to two thin rectangular black boxes that took up more space inside the iPad's casing than the circuit board. "These are the lithium batteries. Sure, it's possible for a faulty cell to combust, but when that happens, there's no mistake. It's like a small rocket engine igniting. As you can see, these batteries are untouched. Only the circuit board and drive are cooked. I've repaired iPads since they first came out and I've never seen anything like this."

Barry snorted in agreement. "I doubt anyone at Apple has seen this before."

Steven's shoulder's fell. The extreme damage to the iPad, and the stumped faces of the two Apple geniuses, told him all he needed to know, but he had to be certain. "What about information stored on the iPad?" Steven asked. "Photographs, for instance. Can they be recovered?"

Jesse winced. "Actually, a data dump was the first thing I tried when I saw all the damage. But no luck."

"Are you sure? Aren't there companies that specialize in data recovery?"

"Absolutely. They can save hard discs that have been smashed, water damaged, or even burned. But iPad drives are solid state. Just an array of high capacity memory chips. And unfortunately, the memory chips in this iPad are now charcoal." Jesse set both halves of the ruined device down onto the counter. He offered Steven a sympathetic frown. "I'm afraid anything you had saved on this iPad; music, movies, photos, it's all gone forever. Sorry."

Steven nodded glumly, thanked both men for their assistance, then turned and walked away.

"Mr. Burns, wait," Barry called after him. "Don't you want a replacement?"

Steven kept walking.

32

Five minutes later Steven was on the fourth level of the mall's garage, seated behind the wheel of his pickup truck. The idling engine grumbled, waiting for the driver to shift into gear and step on the gas, but Steven couldn't move. Not forward, nor in reverse. Faced with the biggest decision of his life, Steven found himself hopelessly stuck.

The decision was supposed to be simple now. The loss of the photographs almost certainly ruled out going to the police, which left one gut-wrenching alternative. But as Steven sat there gazing beyond the garage walls at the sun setting over Flintridge, he realized his uncertainty wasn't solely about ending a man's life, it was also about ending his own. Accepting the stranger's unique brand of help would be akin to making a deal with the Devil, and everyone knows those deals never end well. Despite the stranger's assurances, Steven knew something could go wrong, landing him in prison or in a grave, which was pretty much the same result. Even if he got away with it, he'd spend the rest of his life looking over his shoulder for flashing blue and red lights. Even a simple traffic stop would be a heart-pounding ordeal. Steven was also worried about Nichole. He'd have to tell her everything. It would be unfair to deny her the knowledge that justice for their daughter's murder had been served, a small comfort Steven himself eagerly anticipated. How Nichole would react to her husband committing cold-blooded murder, Steven wasn't sure, but he realized taking the law into his own hands might forever ruin any chance of saving their marriage.

Then, of course, there was the obvious risk of putting his trust in a man who lurks outside the law. A man who discusses stomach-churning matters with ease, and who possessed some seriously scary hacking skills. Steven had no idea how the stranger boobytrapped that iPad, but the reaction of those two Apple employees spoke volumes. What's to stop this stranger from luring Steven to some isolated nowhere, killing him, then simply walking off with his one hundred grand?

Absolutely nothing, that's what.

Steven groaned and wrung the steering wheel. The urge to speed to Linton's apartment so they could talk this madness out was almost impossible to resist. Just hearing himself talk some-times helped Steven sort out his thoughts, and his best friend and business partner was usually the sounding board of choice. But this time he couldn't count on Linton's ear. Linton was already convinced the stranger was a con man, or worse. If he found out Steven planned to hand over a hundred grand to that same man as part of some crazy revenge scheme, Linton would go into DEFCON 1. In the name of protecting Steven, he'd do everything and anything to kill the deal, even if it meant going to the police himself.

Steven also considered calling Nichole. Luna was her daughter, too, after all. Maybe it was right to let her in on the decision. But Steven didn't entertain this notion for long. Nichole was tough for sure, but more than that she was practical to a fault. If Steven confided in his wife after the dirt was done, there was a chance she'd accept his grim decision. But Steven could never imagine Nichole agreeing beforehand. She'd see a thousand ways for things to go wrong, and as usual she'd probably be right.

Steven didn't want to be talked out of it, he just wanted to talk it out... until he could settle on a decision for himself.

The last sliver of sun clung to the horizon, setting the streets and rooftops of Flintridge ablaze in a fiery glow.

If Steven believed in such things he might have taken the hellish light show as a sign. A prophetic vision warning him to stay far away from the wicked man in black leather gloves. Instead, the burning heavens inspired another revelation.

Steven fastened his seatbelt, shifted into reverse, and backed his pickup out of the parking space, fast.

Suddenly, he knew exactly who to seek advice from about making deals with the Devil.

"You have arrived at your destination," the GPS announced. "2245 Apple Tree Road."

Steven pulled to a stop in front of a postcard-perfect craftsman-style home. He knew the place well, but only from afar. Since moving to Flintridge he must've driven by countless times, and each time he'd slow down to admire the well-maintained classic house. Once he even considered knocking on the door cold, with a plan to convince the owner to give him the nickel tour. Not just to satisfy his curiosity about the interior, but to possibly pitch some restoration or remodeling work. Old houses, no matter how beautiful the exterior, always needed work. Despite his long standing interest, Steven never took the time to research who owned the property, but now that he knew the owner's name, he wished he had. Steven was absolutely certain the man who held the deed to one of the most beautiful homes in Flintridge would've welcomed him inside with open arms.

Steven made his way up a brick walkway to a square-columned portico and rang the doorbell.

It was dark out now. LED street lights, like the ones installed all over town a year ago, bathed the quiet suburban street in a ghostly white glow. In the near distance, the silhouette of the Santa Monica mountains loomed against a backdrop of endless stars.

The porch light winked on and the front door swung open. A fiftyish woman wearing a kitchen apron and with a streak of silver in her hair greeted Steven with a polite but uncertain smile. "Good evening. May I help you?"

They'd never met before, but Steven assumed she was the wife of the man he came to see. "Hi," Steven replied, returning the smile. "Sorry to disturb you. My name is Steven Burns. If your husband's home I was hoping I could speak to him."

A warm smile leaped onto her face. "Oh, Mr. Burns. Of course. Hello." She wiped both palms on her apron, then reached out and cupped Steven's hand. Her voice dropped to a pious whisper. "I'm so sorry for your loss and for what I'm sure has been a day-to-day struggle." She leaned in a little closer. "I've prayed so often for your little angel. God bless her soul."

It took some effort for Steven to keep smiling. "Thank you," he said. "I appreciate that. I really do." And he meant it. Whether he was a believer or not, he could appreciate someone making an effort to do him a kindness. Withdrawing his hand as politely as he could, Steven said, "So, is your husband home?

"Oh, yes. He is, but...," Her brow tightened. "He didn't mention any company tonight. Is he expecting you?"

"No. This is kind of a last-minute thing. I would've called first, but I didn't have his personal number." Steven gestured to her apron. "Listen, If I'm interrupting dinner or something I could come back--."

"Oh, no. Not at all. I'm just baking. I'm always baking." With a chuckle she pulled the door wide open. "Come in. Please. The Pastor will be so surprised to see you."

Mrs. Childs was right.

After trailing her through the old house's handcrafted interior, Steven found himself in a bookshelf-lined study, seated before Pastor Childs.

Reclined in a high-back leather chair, the Pastor stared across his perfectly ordered antique desk at Steven with raised eyebrows. "The groundskeeper gave you my address? Really?"

"Not your actual address," Steven replied. "He just described your house. He did try to tell me to return to the church tomorrow morning, but I was pretty pushy. Look, I don't want to get anyone in trouble."

"Oh no, not at all," the pastor said with a chuckle. "I don't mind visitors. My door's always open to members of my congregation in need of, what I call, urgent counseling. Rarely a week goes by where someone isn't seated right where you are now, unloading their troubles. I've even let a few stay in my guest house." He gestured to the window behind his chair that looked out on a sprawling moonlit backyard, complete with a pool, grilling area, and a two-story bungalow that looked to Steven like an oversized dollhouse.

Steven reseated his ball cap then said, "Is this "urgent counseling" reserved only for church members?"

Pastor Childs shook his head. "Absolutely not. All are welcome. And I will admit I'm terribly curious. Nonreligious people don't usually seek out their local pastor."

"The reason I'm here is simple," Steven said. "I have a really tough decision to make. I figure you help people make tough decisions all the time. So, maybe you can help me. Religion's got nothing to do with it. No offense."

Pastor Childs returned a small smile. "None taken. I just hope I can help." He straightened up in his chair. Interlocked his hands. "So, what's this decision you need to make? Does it have anything to do with your daughter's death?"

"Murder."

"Excuse me?"

"My daughter didn't just die," Steven said, "she was stran-gled." It was a small point, Steven knew that, but every time someone made that same mistake his jaw cinched. Smoothing over the truth somehow lessened the severity of the crime, and felt like an affront to Luna's memory. He took a deep breath to take the edge off, then calmly continued. "I just think it's impor-tant to call it what it is. Murder."

Pastor Childs nodded. "Of course. I understand completely."

"And yes," Steven said, "the reason I'm here is connected to Luna's murder, but I can't get more specific than that."

Pastor Childs' eyes narrowed. "Why? Is there a question of legality? Just so you're aware, everything discussed between us falls under clergy-penitent privilege. Just like attorney-client privilege, but for the church. So you can tell me anything, anything at all, and it stays between us." Pastor Childs raised a finger. "And, in case you're wondering... who falls under that protection is solely at the church's discretion. So, no, you don't have to actually be a church member."

Steven fidgeted with his cap. He was definitely tempted. Talking out every detail and possibility would help him see straight. But he couldn't accept the pastor's offer. Confiding in the pastor would be equivalent to opening up to Linton or Nichole. Their focus would turn immediately to talking him out of doing something crazy... even if *something crazy* is exactly what's needed to get justice for Luna.

"Sorry," Steven said, "but I really can't go into detail."

The pastor sighed and rubbed his bald spot. "Mr. Burns, if I don't know the details of your problem, how can I possibly help you make a decision?"

"Really, I just need you to answer one question for me."

Deep creases appeared on the pastor's brow. He reclined in his chair and crossed his arms. "Okay. I'm listening."

"I have two choices," Steven said. "Both have the potential to solve a huge problem or ruin my life forever. So, short of flipping a coin, how do I choose?"

"Hold on," Pastor Childs held up a hand as if stopping traffic. "When you say 'ruin your life'... do you mean your life's in danger? Because if you do, I wouldn't be comfortable giving--"

"No," Steven said, cutting him off. "It's nothing like that. My life isn't in danger. I swear. I mean, I promise. Sorry."

For several heartbeats the pastor just stared. Finally he said, "So, you're saying these two choices are somewhat equal, correct?"

Steven gave a half-hearted nod. "Yes. Somewhat."

"Well, in cases like this, where your brain has reached a stalemate, all that's left is to let your soul decide."

Steven almost rolled his eyes. He knew seeking guidance from a church leader meant risking an earful of spiritual mumbo jumbo, but in his dealings with Pastor Childs, the pastor always struck him as down-to-earth. In a way the pastor seemed less devout than a few of his bible-toting neighbors who paraded off to church every Sunday morning.

Seeing Steven deflate, the pastor said, "I can imagine how that sounds to you... but in this particular instance, when I say soul, I don't mean in a religious sense."

If the pastor had sprouted antennas Steven's expression would have been the same. "Then how?" Steven asked "How else could you mean it?"

"You ever go to bed with a problem on your mind, then you wake up the next morning and, *bingo*, you have the answer?"

"Of course. I'm sure that's happened to everyone."

"Exactly." The pastor dropped his voice. "Now think about it. Has that answer ever been wrong?"

Steven couldn't remember details from any of his morning

"bingo" moments, but he did remember being pleased whenever they occurred. "No, I guess not," Steven said.

The pastor thew up his hands. "Well, there you go. Go home, get a good night's sleep, and when you wake up tomorrow morning the choice you really want to make, the choice your soul wants you to make, will be clear to you."

Steven looked at him sideways. "So basically, Pastor, your advice to me is... sleep on it?"

"Just give it a try," the pastor said with a smile and a shrug. "God works in mysterious ways... and so does the mind."

34

W hen Steven peeled open his eyes the following morning, he didn't know where he was. Not at first. But squinting against shafts of sunlight streaming into the room, he noticed baseball posters, shelves crowded with T-Ball trophies, rubber-banded stacks of baseball cards, and dangling from one bedpost, a small glitter pink Boston Red Sox baseball cap.

It all came rushing back.

Steven hadn't stepped foot into Luna's bedroom since the day of her murder. But last night, somehow, he found the strength.

He remembered pushing open the bedroom door, switching on the light, and for a few seconds forgetting to breathe. He remembered giving in to the impulse to touch everything in the room. He remembered smiling at all the framed photographs of Luna playing baseball, and curling up with his favorite photo atop her tiny bed. And lastly, Steven remembered Luna's sweet laughter echoing in his head as he drifted off to sleep.

If he dreamed about his little girl, his mind kept it a secret.

Steven sat up on the edge of the bed, yawned, rubbed his

eyes, then took in Luna's bedroom again. Slowly. Carefully. Every object his gaze fell upon stirred a memory, but in the harsh light of day, despite the childhood clutter, the room felt... empty.

Steven could feel the emptiness pressing in on him. Seeping through his pores. Crushing his heart.

And the emptiness spoke to Steven. Not with words, but with a plunging hollowness that turned his stomach.

The emptiness told him this lifeless bedroom was all wrong. A wrong that poisoned everything. A wrong so big that nothing could ever be right again.

And with that realization something strange happened to Steven. He began to laugh. He laughed because the pastor's cliche'd advice was right on the money. After a good night's sleep, suddenly the answer to Steven's problem was ridiculously clear.

Working with the police wasn't an option because even the slightest chance of Luna's killer escaping what he had coming was unacceptable.

Screw the law, screw the universe, screw every-fucking-thing. If his baby girl could be raped and murdered by some maniac motherfucker, then all bets were off.

He murdered my daughter... now I'm going to murder him.

Plain and simple.

35

"Liquidate whatever you have to, but I need to draw one hundred thousand in cash. Can you do it?"

"Hmmm. Let me take a look."

Jerry Raymond, CPA, took a quick sip of Diet Coke, slipped on the wireframe readers tethered to his neck, then swiveled to face his desktop computer and began poking keys. Jerry was overweight, five years past retirement, incapable of getting through a day without staining his necktie, and a hardcore Diet Coke addict.

Steven was seated across from him, attention divided between watching Jerry's usual struggle with modern technology, and the breathtaking thirty-second-story high view of Los Angeles beyond picture-window walls. Along with a perpetually cluttered desk and dated plush furniture, Jerry's spacious corner office featured a full-sized refrigerator that his secretary, Barbara, kept stocked with cans of Diet Coke.

Grimacing at his monitor, Jerry said, "Well, you've been living off second mortgages for almost a year. You've pulled the equity out of almost everything you own, including your primary residence."

Steven gnawed his bottom lip. "I know, but there's gotta be something. What about Long Beach or Orange County?"

"Possibly. Hold on." After another sip of soda, he moved the mouse and tapped more keys. His bushy grey eyebrows rose. "Yup, a second on the property in Long Beach could get you there... barely."

"Great," Steven said. "How soon could you get me the money?"

Jerry let out a deep sigh and swiveled to face him. "Actually, I can't get you that money at all. You're two days too late. Sorry, kid."

Raymond and Associates, CPAs, specialized in servicing professional athletes, and Jerry had personally overseen Steven's finances since Steven first signed with the Boston Red Sox. Jerry wasn't just his accountant, Steven saw him as a friend, and when it came to business matters, a trusted mentor. Throughout their thirteen-year relationship Jerry had only called Steven 'Kid' when the accountant had bad news to deliver. Like two years ago when Jerry unexpectedly called Steven into his office, then dropped a bomb. "The IRS has tagged you for a random audit. Tough break, kid." So, now, to hear his accountant dust off that term, just when he needed a large sum of cash, caused Steven's heart to beat faster. Straightening up in his chair, Steven said, "What are you talking about? What happened two days ago?"

Jerry sifted through a large pile of open mail that occupied one corner of his desk. He held up a business envelope bearing a California Superior Court seal. "Two days ago this arrived," he said. "It's a subpoena from Nichole's attorney demanding your financials for the last six years."

Steven averted his gaze from the envelope as if it stung to stare at it too long. He had compartmentalized his marital troubles into some deep dark corner of his mind, and in order to remain focused on avenging Luna, he was determined to leave it there for now.

Jerry wagged his head. "Jesus, I had no idea you were going through this mess too, on top of everything else. You got a good divorce lawyer? If not, I have a few names that--"

"Forget it," Steven said. "I can't think about that right now. Give them whatever they need, just leave out the one hundred grand."

Jerry winced. "See, that's the problem. I can't knowingly help you hide marital assets. If we got found out, I could lose my license, and the fines they'd hit you with are brutal. Take my advice, as long as you have a good lawyer it's better for you to just come clean."

"Actually, I'm not trying to hide anything," Steven said with a shrug. "Handle it however you see fit, but I still need the cash. And I need it soon."

Jerry's eyebrows drew together. "Steven, what the hell do you need one hundred thousand dollars in cash for?"

Earlier that morning, after deciding he'd pay the stranger, Steven instantly faced a new problem. How to get Jerry to give him the needed cash without raising suspicion? Now, with Jerry eyeballing him, eager for an explanation, this was the moment Steven dreaded. While it was true that Steven could do whatever he pleased with his own money, he knew the fatherly accountant wouldn't simply hand over such a large amount, no questions asked. So, as Steven drove the thirteen miles between his driveway and Jerry's office in Century City, he crafted a story he hoped was good enough to satisfy his wise old friend. Working to maintain a casual and confident appearance, Steven said to Jerry, "I need it for a business deal. Something I'm very excited about. And before you start drilling me with questions, I signed an NDA, so it's not something I can really talk about right now."

Jerry blinked. "What? Not even with your accountant?"

"Nope. My attorney even said this was the toughest NDA he'd ever seen."

"Is that so?" Jerry took a slow sip of his soda. Stared at the can, mind working. He squinted at Steven. "Okay, but why only cash?"

"In order to explain that," Steven said, "I'd have to break the NDA."

"I see." Jerry took another thoughtful sip of Diet Coke, then said, "So your attorney has reviewed this deal, correct? And he's okay with it?"

"He reviewed the NDA," Steven said, "but it doesn't contain details. Like I said, these guys are really protective."

Jerry shook his head and sighed. "Okay, let me get this straight. You're about to enter a business deal that requires you to hand over one hundred thousand in cash, and you're restricted from seeking advice from your lawyer, from your accountant, from anyone. Is that about it?"

"I know it sounds a little crazy," Steven said, "But this is a ground floor opportunity that I can't pass up. I have a good feeling about this deal. I really do." Steven concluded with a big, assured smile.

The gesture was not returned by Jerry.

Instead, the old accountant eased back in his chair, cocked his head, and for a long tense moment just studied Steven. Finally, in low voice, he said, "Are you in some sort of serious trouble?"

Steven's heart hammered like it wanted to get out. It was like Jerry could see right through him.

"Because if you are," Jerry continued, "I have a client who's a detective. Good guy. I'm sure he could help you."

Steven forced himself to laugh. He laughed like Jerry had

just told him the best joke ever. "Wow! All the caffeine in those Diet Cokes are making you paranoid. Jerry, it's nothing like that. I'm fine. It's just a kick-ass business opportunity. That's it. I promise."

Jerry nodded and said, "Okay... then you're being conned my friend."

All amusement vanished from Steven's face. "What?"

It was Jerry's turn to laugh. "Jesus Christ, Steven, do you even hear yourself? A cash-only deal? An NDA that prevents you from discussing this so called "ground floor opportunity" with anyone? And let me guess, I bet they're promising you some ridiculous ROI, like fifty percent or sixty percent a year, am I right? That's what's called a tip-off to a rip-off." Jerry drained his Coke then tossed it into a soda can filled trash bin, where it landed with a loud *clank*. "Wake up, Steven, clearly you're being conned." Jerry lifted his desktop phone. "I'm gonna call that detective and--"

"Goddammit, Jerry," Steven shouted. "You're not listening to me. I'm not in any trouble and I'm not being conned. It's my money and I fucking want it."

Slowly, Jerry returned the handset to its cradle, his eyes brimming with concern. "Now I'm really worried. What the hell is going on?"

Already regretting the outburst, Steven sighed. "Listen, I'm sorry. You're just going to have to take my word for it. Everything is fine. I just need you to get me this money as soon as possible. Can you do that? Please."

For a moment Jerry just stared, caught between professional responsibility and loyalty to a friend. Finally his shoulders sagged. With a small nod he said, "Okay. Sure. I can have it for you in three days. I just need you to sign a waiver stating you were notified about the asset demand. That's it."

"Thank you," Steven said. "And don't worry. I know what I'm doing."

Jerry slumped back into his seat and shook his head. "I sure as hell hope so, kid."

36

J erry did better than he promised.

Two days later, in the early evening, Jerry delivered the cash to Steven's house personally. Ten neat packets of used one hundred dollar bills. Each packet tightly bound with a $10,000 mustard-yellow currency strap. Jerry made no last minute attempt to talk sense to his client. After Steven signed both a receipt and a waiver, the accountant promptly transferred the packets of cash from his briefcase to Steven's coffee table. Very professional, and a bit cold. When Steven and Jerry shook goodbye at the front door, there was a frozen instant of eye contact. A flash of deep concern in Jerry's gaze, quickly pushed aside by a forced smile and a friendly slap on Steven's shoulder.

Then Jerry was gone.

Steven stashed the cash in the kitchen cabinet where his pots and pans were stored. Not a particularly clever hiding spot, but Steven felt little need to hide the money at all. He did it because it felt weird to leave one hundred thousand dollars atop a coffee table, or dumped in a sock drawer. The kitchen cabinet was a compromise to satisfy that buzz of paranoia that always came with the possession of an enormous sum of cash.

Not wanting to waste any time, that same evening Steven jumped into his pickup truck and drove to the intersection of Pine and North. The reward flyer that he'd taped to the northeast corner lamp post more than a week ago was noticeably weathered but still there. In the amber wash of street light, the faded photograph of Luna's smiling face took on a spectral quality. A haunting reminder that with each passing day his little girl became more and more just a memory. Life moved on without her... but not for him. Not yet.

Steven ripped away all four corners of the flyer to make certain the stranger got the message.

He was ready.

Steven didn't truly begin to worry until a full week had come and gone with still no reply from the stranger. Then, like a dam bursting, relentless anxiety and second guessing rushed in to fill the void.

Was it possible tearing all four corners of the reward flyer had confused the stranger? The agreed upon signal was a single torn corner, not four. Maybe the stranger thought Steven sent a different message, like "fuck off."

Maybe the stranger was watching the house when, the morning after Steven left the signal, Linton unexpectedly showed up at Steven's front door. Steven pretended to be sick and immediately sent his best friend away, but Linton's ill-timed appearance might've been enough to poison the deal.

What if the stranger's offer was merely a ruse to get him to bring home a shitload of cash? Was the stranger, possibly along with an accomplice or two, now waiting for the perfect opportunity to break in and steal his one hundred grand? For this reason Steven moved the cash from the kitchen cabinet to a more challenging hiding spot behind the washing machine in the basement.

Steven's biggest concern was also the simplest. Maybe the strange gloved man had simply changed his mind, and Steven would never see or hear from him again.

Eight days after ripping the corners from the reward flyer, at 9:38 PM on a cloudless Wednesday evening, all of Steven's worries were obliterated by the chime of his cell phone.

Steven was on his sofa, trying to distract himself with some mindless program. When he checked the caller ID his heart began to pound.

Unknown Caller.

Steven killed the TV and lifted the phone to his ear. His hand trembled. He could feel each heartbeat in his fingertips. "Hello?"

The deep scratchy voice on the other end, unmistakable. "Mr. Burns... you have the money?"

"Yes," he exhaled, remembering to breathe. "I have it. Yes."

"Good. Then we're all set for tonight at two AM."

"Wait. What do you mean? We're doing it tonight?"

Steven's question was answered with silence.

"Hello? You still there? Hello?"

"Calm, Mr. Burns. Always remain calm. Never forget that."

"Right. I won't." Steven took a deep breath before continuing. "Sorry, I just thought I'd have more time to prepare."

"You have what I want... and I have what you want. You do still want it, correct?"

It was real now. It was about to happen, and Steven still wasn't sure he'd be able to do what was necessary. But he had to... for Luna.

"Mr. Burns?"

"Yes. Yes, I still want it."

A lingering silence, then... "I know you do."

There was a hint of amusement in the stranger's voice that made Steven's skin crawl.

"I'm going to give you a set of instructions," the stranger said. "You might want to get a pen."

37

Steven glanced at the glowing digits of his dashboard clock.

1:46 AM.

He was just six blocks away, which meant he'd get there ahead of schedule. Not a problem; at least he didn't think so. There was nothing in the stranger's instructions that forbade arriving a few minutes early.

Steven's pickup truck cruised along a dark desolate avenue toward the northern end of Flintridge. No other vehicles on the road, no pedestrians about, and except for the low rumble of his engine, strangely peaceful. Staring out at the endless stretch of darkened storefronts and barren sidewalks, he felt like the only person awake in the entire town. But Steven knew that wasn't true. He knew for certain that at least one other soul stalked about at that moonlit hour.

There was no need to write down the stranger's instructions because they were pretty simple. Meet at two AM at the municipal parking structure on 4th and Fairview Ave. Park on the sixth level, leave your cell phone in the car, then take the stairs up to the seventh. Come alone and, of course, bring the money. The stranger concluded his instructions with his usual warning. Any attempt to involve the police or anyone else and Steven would never see or hear from him again.

Steven knew the municipal garage because it was only two blocks from Sunset Canyon Elementary School. Luna attended first grade at Sunset Canyon until toxic mold was discovered in the cellar and the century-old building was shuttered by the health department. While the city council debated whether or not to save the ailing building, Luna and her fellow students were transferred to other schools.

1:49 AM.

Minutes later Steven cruised past the now-abandoned school. A shadowy field of neglected trees and shrubbery fronted the single-story brick building. Every window and door barricaded by sheets of weathered plywood, each plastered with a health department warning sign. Darkness and distance made it impossible to read the signs now, but Steven remembered their frightening message from when they were first posted.

DANGER. MICROBIAL HAZARD. DO NOT ENTER SCHOOL BUILDING BY ORDER OF THE HEALTH DEPARTMENT.

1:51 AM.

Steven pulled to a stop directly across the street from his destination. The municipal garage building stood seven levels high without one distinguishing characteristic. It was the kind of concrete edifice you drive by everyday and never notice. The entrance booth's windows were permanently blacked-out, the attendant job long supplanted by an automatic ticket dispenser. A sign over the entry gate declared 24-hour parking, the hourly rates, and a disclaimer in bold letters: PARK AT YOUR OWN RISK.

The warning resonated mentally as Steven, hoping to spot an arriving vehicle, glanced up and down the avenue. The endless stretch of vacant blacktop lined with blinking traffic lights looked more like an airport runway than a city street. Steven found it odd how a place so filled with people could at the same time be so empty.

The dashboard clock flashed 1:52 AM.

Steven considered waiting outside until exactly two AM, but worried the stranger could be watching and somehow find his hesitance suspicious.

Steven wheeled his pickup across the avenue, pulled into the entry lane, then paused at the ticketing machine. He powered down his window and was about to press the button when something he spotted caused him to pause.

High on a nearby pillar, a security camera pointed directly at his vehicle.

Glancing around Steven noticed three other cameras focused on various sections of the garage's entrance. And for an unmanned 24-hour parking garage, that made perfect sense. In fact, he was certain there'd be multiple cameras on all seven levels, each keeping a record of every vehicle that comes and goes. So why, Steven wondered, would someone as cautious as the stranger choose an after-hours parking garage to meet? It didn't add up, unless-- He recalled the amazing hacking ability demonstrated by the stranger. Maybe he had a method of accessing the garage's surveillance system and could delete video files with just the push of a button. Or maybe he didn't give a shit about the cameras because he knew, even with grainy video footage, he'd be impossible to track down. Whatever the answer, it didn't really matter to Steven. If the stranger didn't mind the cameras, why should he?

Steven reached out the driver's side window and pressed the button.

The machine whined and spit out a timestamped ticket.

The instant Steven grabbed it, the orange barrier arm swung upward, allowing entry.

Steven drove through the gate then turned right, following a large painted arrow into the level one parking area.

Tight spaced rows of parked vehicles bathed in sickly fluorescence. The grumble of Steven's engine reverberated as he wound through the low-ceilinged space. Considering the hour and the neighborhood, Steven was surprised by the number of parked cars. Level one did have a fair amount of available spaces, but most were occupied. As far as he knew there weren't any clubs or 24-hour diners in this part of town, so where were all these drivers? Even better, why would they park in the garage when at this time of night there was ample free parking on the street? A closer look at the parked vehicles sliding past his window revealed many coated with an accumulation of dust. Perhaps, because of the low monthly rates, vehicles were being stored here long term.

Steven wheeled his truck up a steep curving ramp to the second level. There were fewer parked cars on level two, but still a surprising amount for two o'clock in the morning. By level three the number of parked vehicles had dropped sharply, with each subsequent level significantly less crowded than the last. When Steven finally reached level six, he stared out at a vast grid of white lines and concrete pillars. Except for three lonely parked cars... level six was empty.

Steven pulled into a space just steps from a scuffed and dented orange door with a large number 6 painted on its surface.

When he killed the engine, an uneasy quiet settled in. The ambient buzz of aging florescent fixtures the only sound.

Steven checked his mirrors and glanced out the truck's windows. As far as he could see, he was alone. He picked up his cell phone from the passenger seat and stuck it into the glove compartment. Next, he reached under the passenger seat and came up with a white plastic shopping bag. A glance inside revealed the ten packets of banded cash were still there. Of course they were, but he couldn't resist checking anyway. He wrapped the bag into a tight rectangular bundle, drew a deep breath, then exited the vehicle.

The solid thud of the shutting door seemed to echo through the entire garage.

Another cautious glance around as his heart picked up a little. If it was the stranger's intention to rob him, this was the perfect moment. But all he saw was a desolate garage, as still and gloomy as an old photograph.

Steven moved to the orange stairway door and pulled the jiggling handle. The door swung open with a mournful creak and a waft of escaping air that reeked of urine and filth. The steel stairway's dingy lighting was barely enough to see the litter. Stepping over beer cans, food containers, and cigarette butts, Steven topped the stairs and pushed open a green door marked 7.

Cool night air and a million stars greeted Steven as he emerged onto the rooftop parking level. The moon, hidden behind a patch of clouds, loomed over the craggy peaks of the Santa Monica mountains like a wispy apparition. The lights of the surrounding town stretched away in all directions.

The pale yellow wash of outdoor sodium vapor lights illuminated rows and rows of empty parking spaces. Out of hundreds... just a single space was occupied.

The lone vehicle sat in a corner of the lot furthest from the stairway door. It was also the darkest corner, by far. Every light fixture on the rooftop worked... except for the two nearest that vehicle.

Cloaked in darkness with its lights off made the vehicle difficult to visually fix. From where he stood, all Steven could make out was a full size sedan, probably old. Perhaps an older Chrysler or Taurus. The lone car appeared so lifeless, so part of the scenery, that Steven wondered if the blown light fixtures were just a coincidence. Maybe that car was being stored here longterm, like the others on the lower levels.

Steven checked his watch.

1:54 AM.

Six minutes early. Maybe the man he came to meet had yet to arrive.

The headlights flashed. Two quick bursts of light, then that corner of the lot fell back into darkness.

It was him.

This is it.

Steven took a deep breath, readjusted his grip on the bag containing the money, then started walking. Because there were no parked cars to circumvent he cut a diagonal path across the center of the lot, directly toward the far dark corner. Drawing closer he could see that he guessed right about the car. The black Chrysler 300 looked about ten years old. No dents or other distinguishing marks that he could make out in the dark. Steven did notice that the license plate frame beneath the front grill did not contain a license plate or even a dealer plate. The space was just bare, and Steven had a feeling that was intentional.

Just when Steven was close enough to make eye contact through the windshield, the driver's side door swung open and the stranger climbed out. The color of his windbreaker was now black instead of beige, other than that his outfit remained unchanged. Thick square framed glasses, windbreaker over a white dress shirt, and of course those black leather gloves. He stepped forward and paused adjacent to the nose of the car.

Steven stopped six feet in front of him.

There was a silent pause to allow the moment to settle in. An exchange of stares underscored by the roar of a jet passing overhead.

Finally, with no expression at all, the stranger gave a small nod. "Good evening, Mr. Burns."

Steven returned the gesture. Stiff. Uncomfortable. "Hey."

The stranger's eyes dropped to the plastic bag clenched in Steven's hand. "That for me?"

Steven tossed him the bag.

The stranger uncoiled the plastic and peeked inside. "Good."

Steven watched, puzzled, as the stranger rewrapped the plastic bag back into the shape of a brick, opened the driver's door, and tossed it into the passenger seat. As the stranger returned to the front of the car, Steven asked. "Aren't you going to count it?"

"Later. Now I need to search you. Did you leave your phone in your truck as instructed?"

"Yes."

"Are you sure?" The stranger studied him a moment. "I find any electronic device on you at all I'm leaving. Understood?"

Steven nodded and raised his hands in the pat me down position.

The stranger brushed his hands across Steven's body. He apologized before brushing his hands over Steven's crotch and buttocks.

"I've done everything you've asked," Steven said. "Now what?"

"Now you get what you paid for."

Steven watched as the stranger walked to the rear of the Chrysler 300 and lifted open the trunk.

Peering around the raised door, he beckoned Steven over with a wave. "Come."

Steven didn't budge. Instead, his entire body went rigid. What the hell was in that trunk? Was it Luna's killer? He thought they were supposed to drive to some secret place where the man would be restrained. Had he misunderstood?

"Mr. Burns." The stranger was staring. Scrutinizing him. "Is there a problem?"

Steven shook his head. "No. I just thought we were driving somewhere."

"We are. But first things first." Again, he waved for Steven to join him at the open trunk. Very casual. "Please."

Steven started moving. Slowly, he walked the length of the sedan and stopped beside the stranger. What Steven saw inside that trunk caused his face to collapse into confusion.

There were no spare tires, or tools, or jugs of antifreeze, or anything else typically stored in a car. The spacious trunk contained just three items. A folded blue moving blanket, a small LED flashlight, and two sixteen ounce bottles of Arrowhead water.

He wasn't sure why but the longer Steven stared at those items, the shallower his breathing became. He turned to the stranger. "What is this? What are you showing me?"

The stranger gestured to the waiting trunk with the casualness of a welcoming chauffeur. "You'll have to get in. Please."

"What?"

The stranger leveled an impatient stare. "I told you, the location I'm holding him is confidential. The drive takes just forty-two minutes. You'll have light. Water. You'll be fine."

"Are you crazy?" Steven took a step back. "No fucking way I'm getting in there. Forget it."

"Calm, Mr. Burns. Always calm. You must never forget that."

Hearing the threat in the stranger's voice, Steven took a breath. "Okay, look. There's gotta be another way. Blindfold me. I'll lay on the floor in the back seat. Let's do both. Anything. But I'm not getting in your trunk. No fucking way."

The stranger just stared a moment, as if waiting to make

certain Steven's speech was done. He ended the silence with a sigh. "Mr. Burns, please listen carefully so there will be no misunderstanding. I think I've made my reason for requiring you to ride in the trunk very clear. Considering how we met and what we're about to do, I can understand your hesitance. But I also warned you that a great deal of mutual trust was required for us to work together. Now you need to trust me. If you don't ride in the trunk, you don't ride, and our business tonight is done. You will get no refund and you and I will never meet again." The stranger laid a gloved hand on the raised trunk door, ready to shut it. "I'll only ask you this once. Are you coming, or not?"

Steven's eyes fell to the waiting trunk space. A gaping steel maw waiting to swallow him whole. He could physically feel the conflict within himself. His desire to avenge his murdered daughter at any cost tugging him toward the car, his innate survival instinct anchoring him to where he stood.

What was really holding him back?

The iPad photographs proved the validity of the stranger's information, and if the stranger simply wanted to rob and murder him, what better place than this deserted parking lot? Why would the stranger bother with this trunk business unless it was what he said it was, a precaution to protect some secret location. Still, it didn't feel right. Maybe it was fear of being locked in a confined space. Maybe it was the complete surrendering of control. Steven wasn't sure what set off his alarm bells, but he couldn't shake the feeling that getting into that trunk would be equivalent to climbing into his own grave.

Slam! The stranger shut the trunk and rounded the car. "Goodbye Mr. Burns."

Steven's breathing ceased as he watched the stranger yank open the driver's side door and climb in. The roar of the starting engine and the crimson flare of tail lights hit Steven like a slap in the face.

"Wait," Steven called out. But it was too late, the Chrysler already pulling away.

"NO, WAIT!" Steven bolted forward. Ran beside the accelerating vehicle, pounding on the trunk with his open hand. "WAIT! WAIT!"

The engine revved and the car surged away, cutting fast across the parking lot.

Steven filled his lungs to shout again, but stopped himself. Instead, he stood watching calmly as the Chrysler 300 sped toward the down ramp.

Suddenly, the brake lights glowed bright red and the departing vehicle came to a stop.

Staring across the dark expanse of parking lot, Steven heard a *clack* and saw the Chrysler's trunk door spring open.

He's giving me one last chance.

A rush of adrenaline and the crush of fear hit Steven simultaneously.

A deep settling breath, then he started walking. Heavy, deliberate steps carried him closer and closer to the waiting car. Nearer and nearer to that dark open trunk.

"Stay calm," he whispered to himself. "Stay calm."

38

T he small LED flashlight was unnecessary. Light bleeding from the tail light assembly filled the trunk space with a crimson glow.

Steven was flat on his back, legs folded to one side, arms outstretched to brace himself, and rigid with fear. His only movement was the rise and fall of his chest with each shallow breath, except when jostled by the speeding car.

The trunk smelled of grease, gasoline, and damp carpet.

Intermingled with engine grumble and the shush of tires, Steven heard muffled voices from the passenger cabin. He couldn't discern a single word but the nonstop cadence, occasionally interrupted by music, suggested the car's radio was tuned to a talk show.

As minutes ticked away and the Chrysler 300 traveled farther and farther, Steven struggled to remain composed against the onslaught of panic that began the second the trunk door slammed shut.

Steven regretted climbing into the car's rear almost instantly, but once he felt the sedan surge forward he knew it was too late to back out. It took every ounce of will to just lie there, motionless and quiet, but he remembered the stranger's warning.

"Calm. Always remain calm."

If Steven had given in to the urge to kick and pound and holler to be let out... there was no telling how the man in the driver's seat would've reacted. The last time he violated the stranger's "stay calm" edict, Steven found himself writhing on the ground after receiving a fifty thousand volt time-out from a stun gun. And the stranger committed this assault in broad daylight, without the slightest hesitation. Now, in the dead of night, with so much money at stake, Steven feared that if he gave into panic, instead of a stun gun... the stranger would quiet him with a more permanent weapon.

Steven had no choice but to remain quiet and go for the ride.

It didn't take long for the dark, cramped space to impact Steven's sense of time. How long had they been traveling so far? Ten minutes? Half an hour? Longer? He tried to work it out by recalling the number of radio commercial breaks he'd over-heard, but decided he hadn't paid close enough attention to the muffled broadcast to trust his memory. Then he remembered the stranger's assurance that the drive would only take forty-two minutes. The Chrysler hadn't slowed once since they pulled off, which meant his time in the trunk had to be less than that, unless...

What if he lied?

The stranger didn't say 'about' forty-two minutes, he said forty-two minutes exactly. How could he be so sure? Not even the GPS in Steven's truck nailed arrival times so precisely.

The stranger had to be lying. And if he lied about that, he probably lied about everything else... like where he was really taking the man imprisoned in his trunk at two in the morning.

Steven's breathing quickened. The squat compartment suddenly felt darker, narrower, like the steel walls were closing in. Steven clenched his jaw to hold back the cry for help gathering in his throat. He drew a deep breath and shook his head to dislodge the demons. "Calm," he whispered through gnashed teeth. "Stay calm."

Why, Steven wondered, would the stranger bother with this entire production if he simply planned to murder him for the money? Back at the garage the stranger had ample opportunity to surprise Steven with a bullet to the brain or a tire iron across the skull, far less risky then driving through downtown with a terrified man in your trunk. No, the careful and methodical individual who approached Steven in Memorial Park so many weeks ago, would never take such a huge chance... unless forced to fulfill his end of the deal.

It's going to be okay. Just stay calm.

This flimsy rationalization eased Steven's pounding heart, but he knew the lull wouldn't last. The longer he remained trapped in the trunk, hurtling toward the unknown, the more irrepressible the panic churning inside him became.

To distract himself he turned his thoughts to memories of Luna.

He remembered the first time he held his daughter. She was just a few minutes old. Her hands clenched into teeny fists, one over the other, as if clutching a baseball bat. The grin that sprang onto Steven's face at that moment lasted for days. Steven rummaged for other memories. Luna taking her first wobbly steps, teaching Luna to ride her bicycle, that silly dance she did with her stuffed giraffe, how she'd crawl into bed between him and Nichole after a scary nightmare, and the way Luna gasped when she entered a baseball stadium for the first time.

And Steven remembered the last time he saw her... a winged fairy princess sporting a glittery pink Red Sox cap. The memory brought a small smile to his face... along with warm tears.

The drag of deceleration snapped Steven back to the red

gloom of the trunk. He felt the car slow to a near stop then dip sharply and creep down a steep grade. The flashlight and water bottles rolled forward across the carpeted trunk floor. Steven wedged both feet against the rear of the trunk to prevent himself from sliding.

The descent was brief. Breaks squealed as the Chrysler leveled off and eased to a stop.

Steven next expected the car to shut off, instead he heard the driver's side door open. Beneath the idling engine's low grumble he could just make out the solid crunch, crunch, crunch of footfalls. Steven tensed until he realized the steps were growing fainter. The stranger was moving away from the car.

Steven shuddered at the thought of the Chrysler being abandoned in some desolate spot with him still locked in the trunk... until he heard the unmistakable squeal and clatter of a roll-up steel gate. Roll-up gates were commonly used to secure retail storefronts, but also used as industrial garage doors for warehouses and factories.

Could that be where the stranger had taken him? To one of those abandoned buildings along Highway 14?

Twenty minutes west of Flintridge, Highway 14, also called the Antelope Valley Highway, winds north through the high desert. Steven had only driven the desolate route twice, both times for remodeling quotes in Palmdale, but remembered spotting several derelict structures along the way. Most were just collapsed shacks, but some were quite large, like weatherbeaten aircraft hangars and crumbling manufacturing plants. The drive time from Flintridge seemed right. If the stranger were truly holding Luna's killer prisoner, what better place than some forgotten ruin miles from nowhere? It occurred to Steven that such an isolated spot would also be the perfect place to bring a man you intended to murder and dump.

As this thought sank its icy teeth into Steven's spine... he heard the footsteps returning.

Crunch, crunch, crunch.

The driver's door slammed, the car advanced briefly then braked again.

This time the engine died.

The sound of the door opening then thudding shut was louder now. More resonant. Steven could feel it in his bones.

Crunch, crunch, crunch... footsteps again. This time definitely headed toward the rear of the car.

Steven tensed as the steps drew closer and closer. But instead of stopping at the trunk, the footsteps kept going. Moving away again.

But to where?

Steven was startled by the clatter and bang of what had to be the roll-up gate slamming shut. He should've expected that sound. He was right. They had pulled into a garage. And taking into account their steep descent moments earlier... the garage was underground.

Crunch, crunch, crunch... The footfalls paused just outside the trunk.

Steven stopped breathing, ready for the trunk to open. Instead, just silence.

No... there was a faint sound. A soft shuffling followed by a muffled click.

What the hell was that?

As he strained to hear more... the latch clicked, the trunk door sprang up, and Steven found himself staring down the barrel of a gun.

39

"Are you calm?" The stranger's voice was even and cool. His bespectacled eyes unblinking. He held a 9mm trained on Steven with a terrifying casualness, as if squeezing the trigger would be the simplest thing in the world.

"Wh- What?" Steven said, still crammed in the trunk, his eyes riveted to the pointed gun. He failed to hear the question over his hammering heart.

The stranger's lips flattened. He nodded at the weapon in his hand. "Just a precaution. Being locked up can make a man unpredictable." His eyes narrowed. "So I ask again... are you calm?"

After a settling sigh, Steven said, "Yes. I'm calm. I just want to get the hell out of here."

The stranger stared at him, coal black pupils darting as he scanned Steven's face.

Steven remembered the stranger's odd boast about being a human lie detector. Was that even possible? Is that what he was doing now, trying to sniff out a lie? Steven wasn't concerned. The trunk was finally open, he was still breathing, and with each passing second he grew more confident the stranger intended to deliver Luna's killer as promised. Although his stomach was now doing flip flops... Steven was as calm as could be expected for a man lying in a trunk with a gun pointed at his face.

"Good," the stranger muttered, then tucked the 9mm into his belt.

Steven couldn't see much beyond his host's looming form; just peeling paint, cobwebs, and faint shadows cast by a dingy unseen light source. He could almost taste the dry musty air.

The stranger pulled what looked like a black ski mask from his jacket pocket and tossed it to Steven.

The object Steven held was sack shaped, made from dense opaque material, with no eye or mouth holes. It wasn't a mask, it was a hood. Exactly the type of hood thrown over a condemned man's head right before he's executed.

"Put it on," the stranger ordered.

Steven's heart thudded, but he could see the stranger watching him. Waiting for any sign that Steven might lose it.

Steven drew a deep breath, sat up on the trunk floor, and pulled the hood down over his head. Instantly his entire world became darkness, the huff of his own breathing, and the unexpected scent of laundry detergent.

The pleasant freshly-washed fragrance was a good sign. If the stranger intended to murder him, why bother cleaning the hood?

Steven felt a gloved hand grip his right upper arm. "Come."

With the stranger's firm help Steven climbed blindly out of the trunk. Finally on his feet again, he groaned as he flexed stiff limbs. He discovered that if he stared straight down, he could see his own feet through the hood's opening.

"Okay, just walk slow and let me guide you," the stranger said.

Steven felt a tug on his arm and walked forward, keeping pace with the stranger's lead.

"Turn."

Steven let the stranger pivot him right, then continued forward. Peering down, he could see an unpainted concrete floor, cracked and buckled with age. After advancing about ten yards the stranger tugged back on Steven's arm.

"Hold it."

Steven froze. He heard keys jingle. A lock clicked followed by the squealing creak of an old door swinging open. A waft of cool air brushed Steven's skin accompanied by the unmistakable dank smell of a basement.

"There's a flight of stairs directly ahead of you," the stranger said. "Eight steps down. No rail. So, take your time." With that the stranger nudged him on.

Steven stepped down, slow and careful. A loud creak startled the silence as his foot found the first step. A peek downward confirmed the staircase was constructed of old wood. That probably meant the building was ancient. Of course, that was assuming they were in a building at all.

"Good, keep going."

Steven descended the remaining steps with similar caution. Once they reached the bottom the stranger steered Steven to the left before leading him forward again.

The space they moved through now was darker. Glancing down, Steven could barely see his own feet, much less the floor. Wherever the stranger had taken him, it seemed pretty remote. So why the hood? Just one explanation made sense. Something about the building's interior, like old signage, threatened to reveal their location.

"Wait."

The stranger tugged Steven to a stop.

The piercing squeal of another door being opened caused

Steven to wince. The stranger guided him forward two steps, then paused. Steven winced again when he heard the door shut behind him. Steven assumed they entered a room, until they began walking again. The slight reverb of their footfalls told Steven they were now moving down a hallway. He wanted to reach out and touch the wall to confirm this, but fought the urge.

"Almost there," the stranger said. "Just a few more--"

A booming, agonized moan filled the darkness, until finally trailing off.

Steven froze. "What the hell was that?"

He felt the stranger lean in close. He heard the stranger's measured breathing just before that scratchy, emotionless voice whispered in his ear. "That, Mr. Burns, is the reason we're here tonight." The stranger squeezed Steven's arm. "Keep walking."

Ignoring the sinking in his gut, Steven continued forward.

The moaning rose again. Muffled. Desperate. Helpless. And with each step, that awful sound grew louder and louder. Steven was relieved when he felt a halting tug on his arm.

"Stop here," the stranger said. He waited for a lull in the moaning before continuing. "I'm going to remove the hood now. Hold still."

Steven braced for the hood to be snatched off, but the stranger lifted it away slowly, seeming to show genuine concern for Steven's comfort.

It only took Steven a few blinks to adjust to the dark surroundings. He and the stranger stood facing a closed door. Behind them, a dark corridor lined with corroded pipes stretched away. Several puck-sized battery-powered LEDs spaced out along the dust-caked floor provided just enough light.

Another moan drew Steven's eyes back to the door before him. Its metal surface dented and scratched with age. Nothing special about it, except those awful sounds coming from the other side.

Steven began to breathe faster.

The man who killed my baby is in there.

As the moaning waned again, the stranger's black leather-gloved hand reached out and grabbed the rust-pitted door knob. He turned to Steven and said, "Last chance to change your mind. Once I open this door there's no turning back. What you came here to do... must be done."

Steven could feel his heart thrumming in his fingertips.

The stranger's gaze drilled into Steven, unrelenting. "Well, do I open the door or not?"

After a pause, Steven swallowed, reached out, and pulled the stranger's hand from the knob. "No," Steven said, his voice just above a whisper. "Let me." As another keening moan filled the corridor, Steven gripped the knob, gave it a twist, and pushed the door open.

40

F or an instant Steven thought he was staring at a man strapped to an electric chair. This was merely a trick of shadows and nerves... but the reality was no less startling.

The room he and the stranger now stood in was lit by a single LED camping lantern hung from the valve of a corroded ceiling pipe. The lantern's stark bluish glow revealed a classroom-sized space once used for storage. Several tall racks of empty shelves stood huddled in a dark corner, pushed aside for the medieval-looking contraption that dominated the center of the room.

The wide, high-backed chair was constructed solely of square steel tubing. No fabric or padding, just unfinished metal joined by crude weldwork, and each leg was bolted to the concrete floor.

The chair's occupant was restrained by heavy leather straps around his wrists, ankles, and torso. A narrower strap, pulled taught across his forehead, made any head movement impossible. A ball gag, reinforced by strips of heavy-duty duct tape, did little to quiet his grunting and groaning, especially now that company had arrived.

From the moment Steven entered the room, the prisoner's eyes fixed on him. Pained, terrified, desperate eyes, bulging with every pleading moan.

And Steven returned the stare, paused by the enormity of the moment.

This is... him.

For the last few days, while waiting for the stranger to call, Steven wondered endlessly about how he'd react when he came face to face with Luna's killer. Would he fly into a rage? Would he crumble in tears? Would fear paralyze him? Never once did Steven consider the disembodied numbness that seized him now.

This is the man who killed Luna.

The man in the chair looked Caucasian, in his forties or fifties. The silver tape covering his lower face made guessing his age difficult. His sweat-soaked button-down shirt and torn black slacks suggested he'd been waylaid while headed home from some office job. The wet stain over his crotch and the small puddle beneath the chair explained the taint of urine in the musty air.

This is the man who killed my baby.

Only when Steven felt a hand squeeze his upper arm did he remember his host stood beside him.

"Look here," the stranger said. He pivoted Steven to face a drop cloth-covered table about two paces from the steel chair.

Four distinct objects bulged beneath the dusty covering. Three were indistinguishable, but one, despite the drop cloth's thickness, was unmistakable. Seeing that all-too-familiar outline sent a cold ripple through Steven.

This is it. This is really happening.

The stranger reached to remove the drop cloth but Steven said, "Wait."

He turned back to face the man in the chair, who continued to grunt and groan and plead with his eyes. Steven asked the stranger, "How do you know he's the one? How do you know for sure?"

The stranger stared at Steven and sighed. He crossed to a dark corner crammed with what appeared to be stacked equipment and supplies. Despite the gloom, Steven spotted portable welding gear, power tools, and boxes of various sizes. After rummaging, the stranger returned carrying an object that made Steven's heart pound.

Another iPad.

Steven winced at the memory of the stranger's prior use of the popular tablet computer. Those awful photographs of Luna sliding across its screen. His frightened baby girl in the palm of his hand, yet unbearably out of reach.

The black and silver iPad the stranger pulled from the shadows was an exact match for the one he handed Steven in the park two weeks ago, with one exception. It was damaged. A single angry crack sliced down the middle of its otherwise perfect black screen.

The stranger extended the iPad to Steven. "You want irrefutable proof? Take it. But, prepare yourself. It's video. He recorded everything he did to her. Everything."

Steven just stared at the tablet. Its shattered screen only added to the device's menace; a portent of the sickening images festering within its circuitry.

"Go on," the stranger said. "Take it."

Steven shook his head. He couldn't bring himself to even touch the damn thing.

Encouraged by Steven's hesitance, the man in the chair groaned loudly and jerked at his restraints.

Steven turned and watched the man struggle desperately to speak, but the gag reduced his words to feeble grunts and moans.

"Do you want to see more evidence or not?" the stranger asked, his voice raised above the prisoner's muffled utterances.

Riveted by the man in the chair's determination to communicate, Steven hesitated before pivoting back to the stranger. "I want you to remove the gag."

The stranger's reply was immediate. "No. That is not an option."

"What do you mean? Why? I want to talk to him."

The stranger's adjusted his glasses, as if to get a better look at Steven's face. "Mr. Burns... I didn't bring you here to converse with this animal."

Steven could feel the stranger's stare challenging his resolve. "I know exactly why I'm here," he shot back. "I just want to ask him one question first."

The stranger was shaking his head before Steven even finished the sentence. "If I remove that gag all he'll do is scream we got the wrong man. You won't get a single word in. Even worse, you might actually begin to believe him. The gag stays on."

Steven bristled at the implication he'd allow Luna's killer to manipulate him. "I just paid you a lot of money. I should be able to ask one goddamned question."

The man in the chair affirmed Steven's demand with eager grunts and groans. But the outcry made Steven cringe. Luna's killer presuming to side with him was just too much to stomach. Steven wheeled around and shouted, "YOU SHUT UP!"

The prisoner recoiled in silence, pinned by Steven's glare.

Steven took a deep breath then stepped closer to him. "Why did you do it? Why my baby girl?"

The prisoner moaned in denial and strained to shake his head. Leather straps creaked.

"Why?" Steven yelled. He lunged, grabbed the man by the collar, and shook him violently. "Why, why, why?"

The prisoner clenched his eyes as if bracing against a hurricane.

"Why? Tell me!"

The stranger grabbed Steven's arm, squeezed gently, and whispered, "Save your anger for what comes next."

Reminded of the night's true purpose, Steven caught himself. He released the man in the chair and allowed the stranger to lead him back to the covered table. Once again Steven found himself staring at a familiar bulge beneath the drop cloth. That elongated shape could only belong to one object, an unsettling hint to the nature of what else lay hidden beneath the cloth. Steven's insides went hollow.

"Ready?" Not waiting for an answer, the stranger snatched away the drop cloth with a subtle, but unmistakable, flourish.

At that instant Steven suspected the stranger's motive wasn't strictly money or helping victims.

Could he be enjoying this?

Through swirling dust motes Steven stared at four objects laid out on the table before him. They were aligned and spaced just so, like merchandise in a department store display case. They varied in shape and size but shared one vile characteristic. Each was an excellent tool for brutally ending a human life.

Over his shoulder, Steven heard the man in the chair whimper in reaction to the dire sight.

The stranger's gloved hand gestured to the object furthest left on the table, a large fixed blade hunting knife. The handle was made of stained and laminated natural wood, oddly elegant for an object so deadly.

"That's a Fallkniven VI," the stranger said. "Handmade.

Perfectly balanced. Razor sharp." Next he gestured to the second object, a small black hand gun. "That's a Beretta nine millimeter. Low recoil. Easy to handle, even for a novice." The stranger glanced over the top of his glasses at Steven. "Any firearm experience?"

During a weekend getaway to Vegas with Linton, Steven allowed himself to be talked into visiting a firing range. To attract tourists, the range offered customers the opportunity to shoot firearms straight out of action movies like Uzis and AK-47s. Linton entertained himself with several choices but Steven tried just one, a Thompson submachine gun, better known to gangster movie fans as a Tommy gun. While truly a thrill to fire the classic weapon, he couldn't wait to get the heavy, hot, and noisy thing out of his hands.

Realizing his Vegas experience in no way prepared him for this moment, Steven answered the stranger with a shake of the head.

"Exactly what I assumed," the stranger said.

Steven stiffened at the remark, although he wasn't sure why.

The stranger pointed to the next object on the table, a length of piano wire strung between two wooden handles. Unlike the other weapons, this one appeared handmade.

"That's a garrote," the stranger said. "I made it myself. Most people don't know what it's called but how it's used I assume is obvious."

Steven responded with a stiff nod. He knew the simple tool was perfect for strangling a man, and thanks to some forgotten TV show he also knew its odd name.

Instead of pointing, the stranger paused and watched Steven's hesitant eyes settle upon the final weapon on the table.

Steven was right. The long object, now uncovered, turned out to be exactly what he expected. Something so familiar, so much a part of his past, that he could already feel it gripped in his hands.

The stranger cracked a slight smile as he watched Steven's hands squeeze into fists. "Usually I'd include a lead pipe or a crow bar," he said, "but for you this would be more satisfying, don't you think?"

Steven stared in silence at an object he once used everyday during his stint in the major leagues. Same make, same color, same length and weight. A black Louisville Slugger pro stock baseball bat.

41

W *as this really happening?*
During his darkest period of mourning, Steven imagined, more than once, using a baseball bat to bludgeon Luna's killer to death. He envisioned himself shattering every bone in the killer's body before finally smashing the bastard's skull. But these thoughts were just flashes in his mind's eye. Whatever satisfaction they provided, fleeting. Presented now with the opportunity to live out this brutal revenge fantasy made his head swim.

As if not to disrupt Steven's musings, the stranger whispered, "I imagine the bat would be more, dare I say, poetic."

Again Steven sensed a jocular note in his host's tone. It was clear now. This display was as much for the stranger's fulfillment as it was for Steven's.

He enjoys this. He enjoys watching people die.

The stranger picked up the bat and waggled it, his leather gloves squeaking against the wood shaft. He relished the bat's lethal heft in plain view of the moaning prisoner. Finally, he extended the handle to Steven. "Go on, give it a feel."

Steven shook his head. "I want the gun."

The stranger's brow fell.

"I'm here to get justice for my daughter," Steven said. "Not put on a show."

After a blank stare the stranger returned the baseball bat to its spot on the table. He gestured to the small handgun. "Go ahead, pick it up. It's loaded but the safety's on."

Steven stepped closer and lifted the Beretta 9mm. The weapon felt cold in his grip, and despite its size, dense. The thick metallic scent of gun oil struck him immediately.

"The safety's that small lever on the left," the stranger said.

Steven reached for the tiny switch, but froze when the stranger pulled his own gun from his waist and racked the slide. Steven didn't resume breathing until the stranger raised a reassuring hand.

"Calm," the stranger said. "My weapon's just a precaution. Keep yours pointed away from me and I'll do the same. Understand?"

Only now did it occur to Steven that his host would be just as uneasy about their late night rendezvous. The stranger had no way of knowing how Steven would react once handed a lethal weapon. Unchecked emotions, violence, and a shitload of cash was the perfect recipe for unpredictable behavior, so the stranger was taking no chances.

"Got it," Steven said with a stiff nod, then returned his attention to the weapon gripped in his hand. He flipped the safety lever. *Click.*

Behind them the prisoner flinched at the sound, then jerked and moaned with renewed desperation.

Ignoring the outburst, the stranger locked eyes with Steven. A lingering, searching stare.

Perhaps a final measuring of my resolve, Steven thought. He

returned the stranger's gaze, refusing to let his hands tremble; refusing to hyperventilate, or even blink. His jaw was clenched so tight he feared his teeth might shatter.

After endless seconds, the stranger nodded and said, "You're calm. Very good." Then he backpedaled three steps, leaving Steven alone at the table.

The prisoner, aware these were his last seconds, bucked and writhed against the straps, rattling the steel chair. His moaning was ceaseless now.

Steven's insides went hollow. Even from the man who murdered his baby girl, that pitiful wailing was almost unbearable.

The stranger's next words to Steven were quiet and measured, a striking contrast to the prisoner's death throes. "Time to do what you came to do. Don't overthink it. Just turn around, aim for the center of his chest, and squeeze the trigger."

Steven nodded like his head weighed a ton. He drew a deep breath, turned, raised the Beretta, aimed and--

The prisoner's eyes stopped Steven cold. Wide, terrified, streaming tears.

Steven could actually hear his heart thrumming. His trigger finger twitched in time with his racing pulse.

"Go on," the stranger said. "Do it. Squeeze the trigger."

Steven's trembling hand tensed again and again as he struggled to find the will... but he couldn't stop staring at those eyes.

"What are you waiting for?" The stranger said. "This animal raped your little girl."

Steven flinched as if punched. Tears flooded his eyes.

The stranger took a step closer and said... "Then after he was done with Luna, he wrapped a belt around her neck and--

Steven let out a loud, mournful groan. He clenched his eyes shut, raised the gun, and squeezed the trigger. He fired again and again. The sharp report of each shot deafening. Finally the Beretta clicked empty. Steven dropped his arm and let the weapon slip from his hand. He heard it clatter to the floor. Then he just stood there, eyes still closed, waiting for his heart to slow and his breathing to return to normal.

When Steven opened his eyes the prisoner was still staring at him, only now with a shocked expression.

Steven had intentionally fired into the far wall, so he wasn't surprised to find the restrained man unharmed. The hate Steven had harbored for so long, hate that cost him his marriage, his business, and pretty much ruined his life... just wasn't enough to turn him into a cold-blooded killer.

"Mr. Burns, you might want to step back."

Steven turned and saw the stranger striding towards the prisoner with the raised Louisville Slugger.

"No." Steven shouted. "Wait!"

The stranger planted himself and swung with everything he had.

The baseball bat caved in the prisoner's face with a thick, wet crunch.

Steven felt warm blood speckle his left cheek. He watched in numb shock as the stranger swung two more times, pounding the prisoner's skull into a sagging, pulpy mass.

Steven cringed against a rush of nausea.

The stranger tossed the bat back onto the table. It landed with a loud bang and a splattering of blood and brain matter.

Steven watched the stranger use a shop rag to wipe his bloodstained leather gloves. He didn't see where the rag came from. Mental flashes of the prisoner's head imploding made it difficult to focus.

The stranger flipped the rag to Steven. "There's some on your cheek."

Steven reached up, touched his cheek, then stared at the glistening blood on his fingertips. His gut spasmed. He clamped a hand over his mouth and dry heaved.

The stranger sighed. "If you're going to be sick it's better you do it here than in the-"

Steven doubled over and vomited.

42

The drive back was a different experience.

Although the stranger insisted Steven ride in the trunk again, knowing he was headed home instead of to an unmarked grave, was an obvious relief. Still, the depth of emotion Steven experienced during the return trip had little to do with concern for his own safety.

Despite the cramped trunk space, Steven felt relaxed and free of tension. The engine noise and drone of tires failed to disturb his inner quiet. His breath smelled of vomit, yet he breathed easier. And for the duration of the trip, tears rolled from his eyes. Not tears of sorrow or joy... but tears of peace.

The man who murdered his baby girl had finally met justice.

Steven didn't agree with the stranger's use of brutality, but he felt no sympathy, either. No longer would he have to live with the knowledge that the man who murdered Luna was out there, somewhere, living his life. No longer would he lose a second of sleep wondering when Luna's killer would be caught, if ever.

Finally... it was over.

Another difference about the return trip was that it seemed to take half the time. Steven knew that weird feeling of "getting home quicker" was a common phenomenon, but the disparity in this instance felt so real. He decided to blame his heightened emotions, the sensory-depriving effects of traveling in a dark box, and a touch of shock. Whatever the cause, when the stranger popped the trunk allowing him to climb out, Steven was relieved to see that they were back where they started.

The rooftop parking level, with its endless rows of empty spaces, seemed less creepy now that dawn rimmed the distant mountains. The dark deserted streets below were slowly awakening as early morning delivery trucks rumbled along their routes. Steven smelled baking bread from some nearby eatery, preparing for the breakfast rush.

When the stranger slammed the trunk shut the sound seemed to reverberate forever.

"Feeling better?" the stranger asked.

Steven wasn't sure if the stranger meant his stomach or his hunger for justice. Not that it mattered. The answer to both questions were the same. "I do," Steven said with a nod.

"Good," the stranger said. Then he cocked his head in an almost playful manner. "What happened tonight is our secret. No talking. You understand that, right?"

"Of course," Steven replied immediately.

"Not to your wife, or that black friend of yours, or your future therapist. No talking to anybody. Ever."

"Trust me," Steven said. "I get it." Steven had expected his partner-in-crime to warn him about keeping quiet, and knew it was important to ease the man's doubt. And although he sensed no immediate danger, Steven thought there was a slight chance his life depended on his next words. "I understand completely," Steven went on. "I'll never breathe a word about this to anyone. You have nothing to worry about."

The stranger's brow tightened. "I think you're a little confused. By this time tomorrow the body and any evidence will be destroyed. And yes, that does include all photos and videos of your daughter. This is the last time you and I will meet. You won't be able to contact me, and even the FBI won't be able to find me. So if you ever run your mouth and end up in a cell, I won't be dragged down with you, because... I won't exist." He shrugged. "So, you're right. I have absolutely nothing to worry about. You on the other hand can ruin your life with one slip of the tongue. When I say no talking... that's not for my protection, it's for yours."

Steven blinked. Was it possible this man truly cared? Was the stranger exactly who he said he was from the very beginning? A good man with a dirty... but very necessary job.

The stranger reached out and squeezed Steven's arm. "You did right by your daughter. Now, forget tonight. Forget me. It's time to go back to your life and move on. Okay?"

Steven swallowed a lump of emotion and nodded.

The stranger extended his gloved hand and Steven shook it. Grips interlocked, the two men exchanged a fleeting stare. A lifelong bond sealed in a heartbeat. Finally the stranger said, "Goodbye, Mr. Burns," then he released Steven's hand and moved to the driver's side door.

As Steven watched him open the door, he realized this was his last chance to get an answer to one remaining question. If Steven didn't ask now, he'd wonder forever.

"Wait," Steven said.

About to climb behind the wheel, the stranger paused and looked back.

"I understand why he had to die," Steven said. "But you could have done it quick. Why... like that?"

The stranger pointed to his own eyes and said, "It was your eyes."

"My eyes?"

"I told you, I can read everything in a man's eyes."

Steven shook his head. "I don't understand."

"When you turned down the baseball bat... I saw in your eyes you were lying. You wanted to bash his brains in more than anything. So I did it for you." The stranger offered a slight smile. "Have a good life, Mr. Burns." With that, he shut the door and drove away.

Steven watched in numbed silence as the Chrysler 300 cut across the empty parking lot, then started down a steep ramp. As darkness devoured the descending vehicle, a sudden chill made Steven shiver.

43

T ime heals all wounds.
     Not really.
     Not the deepest wounds.
Not wounds of the soul.

But time does make it easier to cope... and move on.

These were Steven's thoughts as he stood with a jubilant gathering of friends, watching Nichole unwrap gifts beneath a polka-dotted banner that read, BABY SHOWER.

The party was held at the offices of Burns Home Remodeling because of the ample parking out back, and the generous floor space inside. Balloons, streamers, and wall hangings transformed the work area into what looked like an oversized pink and blue pastel-colored nursery.

Nichole was seated in an office chair festooned with satin ribbons and bows. On either side of this seat of honor, dozens of wrapped presents and gift bags waited their turn. Nichole wore a form fitting white lace dress with a pink and blue ribbon corsage pinned to her chest. An embroidered patch at the center of the corsage declared, MOM TO BE. A matching DAD TO BE corsage adorned the lapel of Steven's sports-coat. He tried to get out of wearing it, but Nichole reminded him the shower was a co-ed event, a fact that neatly nullified any counter argument.

A chorus of oohs went up as Nichole unboxed a Marc Jacobs paisley-printed diaper bag. After announcing her mom sent it, she stood up and showed off the gift with a playful twirl. As she turned carefree circles, Steven and Nichole traded smiles across the room. If Nichole was at all self-conscious about how her eight-months pregnant figure looked in that clingy dress, it didn't show. To Steven she looked perfect. In fact, he couldn't remember another day, or moment, when his wife looked more beautiful.

A hand slapped Steven's shoulder. He turned to find Linton and his wife, Sharon, wearing apologetic frowns. Sharon cradled a beautifully wrapped present under one arm.

"Sorry we're late," Linton said. "Sharon insisted on taking her car and you know how she drives, so-"

"Hey," Sharon nudged Linton playfully. "Tell the truth. The traffic was messy. Not I." She spoke with a thick Jamaican accent that was almost musical.

Linton screwed up his face in a look of utter confusion. "What traffic? I don't know what you're talking about."

"Ha ha," Sharon said rolling her eyes. "Silly man. You t'ink you're soooo funny."

Linton laughed and gave his wife a gentle kiss.

Two years ago Linton flew to Jamaica to visit his mother and returned a month later married to a woman gorgeous enough to be a supermodel. Sharon was slender, yet buxom, with an unreal shade of chocolate skin, and a perfect smile. Linton said they met at a fruit market and it was love at first sight. Knowing his best friend, Steven was certain it was more like lust at first sight, and feared Linton had acted impulsively. But after two years, Steven was happy to see that Mr. and Mrs. Clarke still appeared to be very much in love.

Sharon said to Steven, "We really are sorry."

"It's fine," Steven said. "You haven't missed much. Nichole's just opening presents."

Remembering the gift in her arms, Sharon said, "Be right back," then made her way toward the gift table.

"It's a tummy time play mat," Linton said to Steven. "In case you're wondering."

Steven chuckled. "Thanks."

Linton nodded across the room towards Nichole. "She looks like she's having a good time."

Steven smiled as he watched his wife hold up a teensy jumpsuit with a colorful unisex pattern. Because he and Nichole had decided against knowing the baby's sex ahead of time, all gifts had to be suitable for either a girl or a boy. Steven next watched Nichole unwrap and hold up a silver picture frame. Instead of the typical factory-supplied family photo, the frame's center was occupied by a blank black card. A lifeless void in a room filled with warmth and joy. Steven's smile withered, his insides suddenly as empty as that frame.

"Are you okay?" Linton asked.

Steven looked at him. "Do you realize how close I came to also losing Nichole?"

"But you didn't," Linton said. "As bad as things got, you never gave up. You put in the hard work and got your life back on track. That's what's important."

Steven nodded. "You're right."

The hard work included couple's therapy, which turned out to be not so terrible. Steven even began to look forward to the sessions. After a few months Steven and Nichole were house hunting together. They agreed their old place held too many memories for a true fresh start. Once they were settled into their new home, they shifted their focus to reviving the business. With Linton back on board, but now as a twenty-five-percent partner, in less than one year Burns Home Remodeling was booking more contracts than ever. During those first few months back together, Steven and Nichole barely touched each other. When lovemaking eventually resumed with some regularity, they took steps to avoid pregnancy. They both agreed they weren't ready yet to have another child, if ever. Then one evening, over dinner, Nichole told Steven that if it was okay with him, she'd like to have another baby. Steven reached across the table, took her hand, and told her nothing would make him happier.

Less than a month later, for the second time in their lives, Nichole and Steven were expecting a child.

Now here Steven was, holding a baby shower in the offices of his thriving business, just weeks away from being a dad again. It all seemed too good to be true.

As he watched Nichole put down the empty picture frame and reach for another present, Steven couldn't help thinking the universe had somehow reset itself. He and Nichole had been given a second chance at the life they once had. A chance to fill a void that never should have been.

Linton said to Steven, "Not many people have the strength to come back from what you went through. Hell, I'd be a total mess. I'm really happy for you, man."

"Thanks," Steven said, rubbing the back of his neck. He wondered if Linton would feel the same way if he knew just how far he had to go to find that strength.

True to his word, Steven never told anyone, not even his wife, about the night he stood eye to eye with Luna's killer, or about the mysterious individual who arranged the encounter. In the immediate weeks following, Steven was gripped by crippling paranoia. Terrified the police were coming for him at any minute, or that the stranger would call demanding blackmail. In the darkest moments, the need to purge his soul to anyone who'd listen was overwhelming. Still, somehow, he kept his secret. As time passed, dedication to repairing his life pushed aside his fear. For three years, two months, and six days, Steven kept his mouth shut and planned to do so forever. What was done that night, had to be done, and the sooner forgotten, the better. Time to focus on the future. And his future was seated just a few yards away, wearing a white lace maternity dress, and holding two gifts. One wrapped and held in her hands... the other due to arrive in about two weeks.

"I can't find a card," Nichole said, turning the shoebox-shaped gift in her hand. Every wrapped present adhered to the party's pink and blue theme, except this one. Both wrapping paper and bow were a matching shade of solid green. Not pastel green, but a dull, earthy green. An odd choice for a baby shower present. Nichole held up the gift so everyone could see. "Okay, who's favorite color is green?"

There were chuckles and curious looks, but no one claimed the oddball gift.

"Don't be shy," Nichole said, scanning the faces of her friends. "Come on. Who's this from?"

More head shakes and shrugs and now everyone looked around for the culprit.

Linton said to Steven, "Did you notice anyone leaving early?"

Steven shook his head. "No. Not really."

Linton's brow furrowed. "Maybe Nichole shouldn't open it."

Steven stared at his friend. "Why would you say that?"

"I don't know." Linton shrugged. "It's just... weird."

When Steven turned back to Nichole, she was already ripping away ugly green wrapping paper to reveal a white box. She opened it and removed a stuffed toy pickle with a cute grinning face.

Everyone laughed, including Linton, who called out to Nichole, "Who'd give you such a silly thing?"

Nichole used the pickle to point across the room at Steven. "My silly husband. Who else?"

Gasps and chuckles of surprise as everyone turned to Steven, who cracked a guilty smile. He said, "Hey, if you guys knew how many pickles that lady consumed in the last eight months you'd understand. Pickles and ice cream. Pickles and Oreos. Straight pickle juice. Yuck."

The laughter that filled the room was cut short by a sharp gasp from Nichole. Wincing, she dropped the toy and grasped her belly with both hands.

The crowd of concerned faces parted as Steven rushed to Nichole's side and placed his hands over hers. "What's wrong?"

No one in the room breathed, except Nichole who slowly inhaled and exhaled. Finally, she smiled weakly at Steven. "I'm okay... but maybe we should cut the party short."

44

As Steven drove through downtown Flintridge, he divided his attention between the road and keeping an eye on his wife. Nichole was in the passenger seat, flipping through a beautifully illustrated children's book. The book was a gift from Nichole's aunt, Penny, who lived in New York. The rest of the baby shower loot was piled in the rear of the pickup truck, secured under a tarp.

It was a late Saturday afternoon and shopping traffic made traversing downtown a challenge, but once Steven turned onto residential streets, driving became easy. The truck Steven owned now, a Silverado 1500, had a bigger engine, a roomier interior, and like their new home, fewer memories.

Steven braked at a red light, then watched quietly as Nichole continued to admire the book's whimsical watercolors. Whenever Nichole came across artwork or a particular design that struck her as exceptional, her eyes would actually twinkle.

Maybe she really was okay.

Although Nichole showed no signs of discomfort now, Steven couldn't help worrying. Two weeks ago, seven weeks before her due date, Nichole experienced painful contractions and had to be rushed to the hospital. Their obstetrician was able to stop premature labor with drugs, but cautioned Nichole against strenuous activities for the remaining term of her pregnancy. The doctor also warned that if she felt any unusual pangs to call him immediately. After that close call, Steven wanted to postpone the party, but Nichole flat out refused. She was really looking forward to having a baby shower, and had already postponed twice due to work conflicts. Maybe Steven could've insisted they reschedule, but he knew better than to get in the way of a determined pregnant woman.

Sensing Steven's stare, Nichole looked up. "What's wrong?"

"Nothing," Steven said with a shrug. "Just checking out that book. Looks nice."

Nichole rolled her eyes. "Would you stop worrying. I'm okay now. Really."

Steven reached out and took Nichole's hand. "I know you think you are. But do you remember what the doctor said?"

"Yes. Of course I remember. But what I felt wasn't unusual. It was just a kick."

"You're sure?"

"Yup, strong one, too." Nichole stroked her belly. "Hey, maybe we got ourselves a soccer player."

Steven's eyes narrowed. "Excuse me?"

"Ooooo, or maybe a football player. Wouldn't that be great?"

"That's not funny." Steven pointed to Nichole's belly. "Only baseball players allowed in there. Family rule."

Nichole chuckled and pointed straight ahead. "You got the light."

Steven cruised along the quiet, home-lined streets for another five minutes before slowing to a crawl behind a mini traffic jam. A long line of cars crept toward the intersection where a flashing police cruiser blocked the next street. Two uniformed officers stood in the roadway directing traffic to turn either left or right.

"Must be an accident," Steven said as he craned to peer around the traffic. But as the pickup trucked inched nearer and nearer to the corner, both Steven and Nichole spotted the true cause of the delay.

In the next block, a small fleet of police vehicles, all with emergency lights flashing, were parked outside a single house. Not just Sheriff's Department cruisers, but also vans, panel trucks, and a few unmarked sedans. Officers in green windbreakers with 'Sheriff' printed large on the back, flowed in and out of the besieged home. Some carrying evidence bags and boxes, others wielding cameras. Several local news vans were positioned around the perimeter, their roof-mounted satellite antennas raised skyward.

"Wow, I've never seen so many cops," Nichole said to Steven. "Looks like a scene from a movie. What do you think happened?"

Steven opened his mouth to respond but paused, struck by a realization. "I know that house. I know who lives there."

"Really? Who?"

"Remember Pastor Childs? We met him years ago, at the funeral."

"Of course. That's his house?"

Steven nodded. "He lives there with his wife."

Nichole stared at him. "How do you know that?"

Steven continued inching the pickup truck forward with traffic as he answered. "After you left, I needed someone to talk to. Sure, there was Linton, but I wanted someone who didn't know me... or you."

Nichole's eyebrows rose. "So you went to a church? Really?"

"No. I kind of ran into him one day. He could see I was a

mess. Offered to listen... and it really helped. He's smart. Nice, too."

Nichole nodded. "Well that explains the gift."

"What gift?"

"I forgot to mention it. UPS delivered it yesterday. A baby photo album with a beautiful silver cover. I was surprised it came from Pastor Childs since we barely know him. Now I get it."

"I hope he's okay," Steven said, frowning at all those flashing lights and uniforms outside the Pastor's house. "This doesn't look good."

Nichole shook her head. "No... it doesn't."

When they finally reached the intersection a uniformed cop directed Steven to turn right, but instead Steven braked and powered down his window. "Excuse me, officer. I know the people who live there. What happened?"

The bored cop continued to robotically wave them forward as he answered. "All I can tell you is that it's a police action. Now, please keep moving. You're holding up traffic."

As Steven powered up his window and turned left, Nichole said, "Look at all those news vans. Whatever this is, it'll be on the news."

45

Steven and Nichole's current residence, a four bedroom, two bath, ranch style home, was about four hundred square feet smaller than their previous house. The front lawn and backyard were a little smaller as well. The trade-off was a better neighborhood, where property values were rising steadily, and the school district was one of the highest rated in California.

After pulling into the driveway, Steven and Nichole decided they'd unload the shower gifts later, so they could hurry inside and switch on the news.

Moments later they were on the sofa, gaping in disbelief at the fifty-inch flatscreen that hung over the fireplace.

Nichole was right, the commotion unfolding at Pastor Childs' house was on the news. In fact, all three local stations had cut into scheduled programming to broadcast special reports. After flipping from channel to channel, Steven had settled on KCAL, the only news show airing live helicopter shots of the house and the surrounding area.

Seen from two hundred feet up, the scale of the police raid was even more surprising. There were as many emergency vehicles behind the house as there were in front. Portable work lights blasted the backyard, where several work crews could be seen digging. The entire property, inside and out, twinkled with constant camera flashes.

Steven was reminded of watching news reports of some terror attack aftermath, but what was going on just a few miles from his front door, in some ways, was far more chilling. The bold graphic at the bottom of the TV screen, beside the KCAL logo, summed it up with clinical bluntness. And after reading that graphic over and over, Steven still couldn't believe it.

TIANA KELLY FOUND ALIVE. HELD CAPTIVE BY LOCAL PASTOR.

How was this possible? He knew this man. He sat in his home. Met his wife. Even listened to his advice. How could Pastor Childs be responsible for such a monstrous crime?

For weeks the mysterious disappearance of an eight-year-old girl named Tiana Kelly dominated the local news. She was last seen drawing on the sidewalk with chalk outside her Altadena home on a sunny Saturday afternoon. There were no witnesses or clues to what everyone assumed was an abduction. One moment she was playing happily; Tiana's mother recalled hearing her daughter singing a song from *Moana*, and the next moment she was gone.

Steven and Nichole had avoided watching all newscasts since the story broke. Reports of volunteer search parties, police press conferences, and devastated parents and friends stirred too many painful memories.

The helicopter shot of the Pastor's home dissolved to a full-screen photograph of Tiana Kelly as a reporter's voiceover delivered the latest update. The image of Tiana was an elementary school portrait. Her hair in twisted ponytails with pink barrettes, her brown eyes sparkling, and her smile bursting with life.

Steven didn't want to think about what that poor child experienced during her captivity, so he focused on the positive. She survived, she was relatively healthy, and she still had her whole life ahead of her.

Suddenly the television shut off.

Steven turned and saw Nichole, remote in hand, staring at him with a shocked expression. "Oh my God," she said. "Do you think it's him?"

Steven blinked, baffled by the question, but more so by the level of emotion in his wife's voice. "I guess so," he replied. "I mean, it looks like they found the girl at the Pastor's house, so--"

"No, no, not that," Nicole cut him off, tears welling in her eyes. "Do you think he's the one who took Luna?"

Steven was struck by a rush of realization. The secret he'd protected for three years prevented such suspicions from ever entering his mind. But Nichole's reality was different. For her, as for the rest of the world, Luna's murder remained unsolved and the perpetrator was still out there. Steven now understood the torment in Nichole's eyes, and regretted the only comfort he could offer was an earnest assurance.

Steven said to Nichole, "Absolutely not. You saw the news report. The Pastor held the girl prisoner in his shed for months. In Luna's case, she was found less than a week after she was taken."

"I know, I know," Nichole said. "But maybe his plan was to hold Luna longer, but then something happened."

"Something like what?"

"I don't know. Maybe Luna fought back too much." Nichole brushed tears from her eyes. "You know how tough she was."

Steven sighed. "You're trying to make it all fit, but--"

"I'm not. I know it seems that way, but really think about it. Pastor Childs lives so close. Also Tiana and Luna are around the same age. They even look alike."

"What do you mean?"

"You didn't notice? Their skin color, they both have light brown eyes, even their hairstyles are similar. They could almost be sisters."

Picturing both girls, Steven decided Nichole was being a bit dramatic. Still, there was enough resemblance to make him wonder why he hadn't noticed earlier. "You're right," he said to her. "They do look a similar. But that's just a coincidence."

"You don't know that." Nichole was beginning to sound frustrated. "The men who do this usually have a type, right? And why'd he send a baby shower gift? For that matter, how'd he even know there was a shower? I never sent him an invitation. Did you?"

Again, Nichole had a point, but Steven could think of several ways the Pastor could have found out about their party.

"Well, did you?" Nichole pushed.

"No," Steven said. "But he interacts with a lot of people. Anyone could've mentioned it to him."

"Or maybe he's been watching us all this time. You know, keeping tabs on us in case something develops with Luna's investigation. If he's guilty, that's what he'd do, right?"

Steven sighed. He took her hand and squeezed gently. "Listen to me. Please don't do this to yourself. I'm telling you... Pastor Childs is not the man who took Luna."

Nichole cocked her head and stared at him with narrowed eyes. "I don't get it. How can you be so sure?"

Steven's jaw clenched. He wanted to tell his wife the truth so bad it hurt. It would be so easy to ease Nichole's unending uncertainty and share the peace of mind he'd enjoyed these last few years... but the truth might do more harm than good. Steven couldn't be sure how Nichole would react if she knew he had participated in a brutal act of revenge. Would she be horrified and repulsed, or overcome with relief? Would she run straight to the police, or straight into his arms? And there was also the matter of complicity. If the police ever came knocking and learned Nichole had knowledge of what Steven had done, she'd be arrested along with him. If that happened, what would become of their child? As much as Steven wanted to tell her the truth and trust that everything would be okay, the stakes were just too high.

"I can't explain how I know it's not him," Steven said. "Call it a feeling. Point is, you're getting yourself all worked up. Dr. Chou would not be happy. How about we drop this for now and wait for all the facts, okay?"

Before Nichole could answer Steven's cell phone rang. He glanced at the caller ID but didn't recognize the number. The instant he answered a woman began talking rapidly. "Hello, am I speaking to Mr. Steven Burns?"

The voice was unfamiliar and her direct tone off-putting. Steven hesitantly replied, "Yes, who's calling?

"My name's Gladys White. I'm a reporter with KTLA news. I'm contacting you in regards to the recent arrest of Pastor Edmund Childs. I assume you're aware of what happened today."

Steven bristled. Clearly this reporter had made the same incorrect assumptions as Nichole, and now in an act of gross insensitivity was calling to pester them with questions.

"Of course I'm aware," Steven snapped. "It's all over the news."

Nichole whispered to Steven, "Who's that?"

"Some reporter," he whispered back, then into the phone said, "Sorry, but what's going on with Pastor Childs has nothing to do with us. Goodbye."

"Mr. Burns, wait. Please. The police are holding a press conference as we speak. You're not watching it?"

"No. Our TV is off."

"They just released new information that might connect--"

"I don't care about any new information. I told you, that story has nothing to do with us. And if you know anything about what we've been through, you should know how inconsiderate it is for you to call here. You're upsetting my wife. Please don't call back. Thank you."

As Steven hung up and turned off his phone, Nichole aimed the remote at the TV.

"Wait," Steven said. "What are you doing?"

Nichole's eyes flashed with purpose. "If there really is new information, I want to hear it."

"I thought we agreed to drop this for now."

"Steven, it's far more stressful for me to just sit here wondering. Trust me." With that, Nichole hit the power button and the fifty-inch flatscreen returned to life.

The onsite press conference was still in progress. Chief Frank Roberts, flanked by other uniformed brass, stood before a bank of microphones fielding questions from reporters. Behind the chief, the pastor's house still buzzed with investigation activity. Steven remembered Chief Roberts from that awful morning, three years ago, when he and Nichole stood at a police podium sharing their grief with the world. Chief Roberts was part of the gaggle of fresh-pressed uniforms who took turns before the cameras, congratulating themselves for finding Luna's body. Steven remembered how hollow he thought their words were. He remembered feeling helpless and furious at the same time.

The bold headline at the bottom of the TV screen had changed since their television was last on. Steven and Nichole noticed the new graphic a few heart beats apart.

When Nichole read it, she gasped.

When Steven read it, he muttered, "Oh my God."

PASTOR CHILDS A SERIAL KILLER, EVIDENCE OF MORE VICTIMS FOUND.

46

Nichole clung to Steven's hand as they sat there watching a police press briefing that, to Steven, seemed disturbingly surreal.

"Has Mrs. Childs been arrested as well? The question came from a reporter gripping a mini digital recorder in her outstretched hand.

Chief Roberts shook his head. "No. We currently believe Mrs. Childs had zero knowledge of her husband's illegal activities. As I explained earlier, these girls were kept prisoner in a bungalow behind the house. Mrs. Childs claims she was strictly forbidden from ever entering that bungalow, and we believe her story. That could change of course, but I've questioned her personally and I don't think it will."

Every reporters' hand shot up, vying for Chief Roberts' attention.

The Chief pointed to a man near the front who immediately fired off a question. "You stated that personal items belonging to three other victims were found. Do you think evidence of more victims will be discovered?"

"God, I hope not. The items recovered were found in a very

specific location, leading us to believe that's all there is. That said, as this case proves, anything is possible." The Chief next pointed to a female reporter.

She thanked him with a formal smile then asked, "So, to be clear, you're saying no human remains were found on the property at all? No bone fragments, hair, nothing?"

"That is correct," Chief Roberts said. "It appears his M-O was to secretly keep his victims prisoner, then after a week or two he'd end their life and dispose of the body somewhere off property. We believe he kept these personal items as souvenirs."

The same reporter blurted out a follow up. "Can you tell us what these items were?"

The Chief paused to consider his response, then said, "I'm pretty sure that would be okay." He glanced at his colleagues beside him, who all nodded in agreement. Turning back to the reporter he said, "The items recovered were three sets of shoes. The type that would've belonged to girls about five to eight years old."

Murmurs rippled through the crowd as eager hands shot up. The Chief pointed to another reporter.

"Chief, can you confirm that these shoes have already been matched to past victims?"

The Chief again glanced at his colleagues, offering them a chance to object, before nodding to the reporter. "Yes. We are confident we know the identities of his other victims."

The reporters erupted with excitement, shouting questions simultaneously. The Chief raised a hand. "One at a time. Please." He pointed to a reporter at the rear of the crowd. "You."

"Thank you, Chief. When will you release the names of these other victims?"

"Not until their families have been officially notified."

Hands shot up again and Chief Roberts scanned the crowd, but before he could select another reporter, a voice shouted above the din, "Jessica Green, Monica West, Luna Burns... are these the girls on your list?"

Dead silence as all eyes turned to the tall, grey-haired man who called out the names. He was easily the oldest reporter in the crowd, and also the best dressed. He stared back at Chief Roberts with the unblinking confidence of a seasoned journalist. He continued, "All three went missing in the last eleven years, within five miles of the Pastor's home. All were close in age and appearance to Tiana Kelly. And in each case no suspect was ever arrested. All the pieces seem to fit. So is it safe to assume these three girls are the victims you're referring to?"

For a moment Chief Roberts just stared out over the heads of the reporters, lost in thought. Finally, he cleared his throat and spoke slowly. "As I said, names of the victims will not be released until all families have been officially notified. That process is underway as we speak. Now, out of respect for the families, I ask that everyone be patient."

Hands flew up along with a flurry of shouted questions, but the Police Chief waved them off. "Sorry. That's all for now. There'll be another update in about three hours. Thank you." With that Chief Roberts and the police brass strode away.

As Steven switched off the television, Nichole gaped at him and said, "Oh my God. Did you see the Chief's reaction to that last question?"

Not only did Steven see it, a chill had crept along his spine. Chief Roberts looked deeply conflicted, as if fighting the urge to confirm every word of the reporter's deduction. But Steven knew that was impossible. Maybe the other girls had fallen victim to Pastor Childs' evil perversion, but not Luna. The man who murdered Luna paid with his life, and was now probably buried somewhere in the vast brush-covered hills of the Antelope Valley.

Probably.

For the first time since the night Steven watched Luna's murderer succumb to justice, the comfort of that secret knowledge was accompanied by a twinge of doubt. And with that doubt, a three-year-old question resurfaced. A question Steven never bothered to ponder again, until that very instant.

How did he know the man strapped in the chair that night was truly Luna's killer?

The answer came immediately. Photos. The stranger had shown him awful photos of that very same man with Luna, in some disgusting bedroom. What better evidence could there be? Yes, photos could be faked, but to achieve that level of realism wouldn't be easy. Also, the stranger had video. Photoshopping an image is one thing, but to convincingly fake a video required far more expertise and planning.

Then Steven was struck by a troubling realization.

I never saw any video.

When Steven asked for proof that the man in the chair was truly Luna's killer, the stranger offered to show him a video on an iPad. But Steven couldn't bring himself to watch it. Was it possible the stranger had gambled on Steven's queasiness, and offering the video was just a bluff?

That twinge of doubt began to metastasize into a ever tightening knot in Steven's gut. Why wasn't he allowed to speak to Luna's murderer, or even know the man's name? The reasons the stranger gave seemed logical at the time, but could just as easily have been total bullshit.

Was it all a lie? An elaborate con game to swindle a grieving father out of a small fortune? No. It couldn't have been. Steven was certain because of one tiny detail he knew to be absolutely true.

A man was brutally murdered that night.

Steven not only witnessed this murder, he heard it, smelled it, and wiped it from his face. That was no act. And if the murder was real it all had to be real, because the alternative didn't add up. Why kill some random person as part of a scam to get Steven's money, when it would be easier to simply kill Steven?

"Yes, I did see the Chief's reaction," Steven finally said to Nichole. "But try not to get your hopes up, okay?" He gently laid a hand on her swollen belly. Through the lacey material of her dress he could feel the soft shape of their unborn child. "Remember, whatever happens, it's important you stay calm."

"Steven... he did it." Nichole stared at him with dead certain eyes. Her voice, assured and even, the tone of someone stating absolute fact. "It was Pastor Childs. He killed our little girl."

In the light of what he now knew about the Pastor and his young victims, to hear those words spoken with such conviction froze Steven's heart. Despite those awful photos of Luna, despite watching a man die that night... something deep down told Steven his wife was right. Suddenly, beneath the weight of common sense, a gut feeling, and Nichole's unwavering stare, Steven's carefully considered rationalizations crumbled.

And at that very instant... Steven thought he felt the world shift.

He withdrew his hand from Nichole's belly and gripped the sofa to steady himself.

"Are you okay?" Nichole asked.

Steven just stared at her. His mouth moved but nothing came out. His mind was now flooding with so many questions about the stranger that it was nearly impossible to focus.

Who was he really? Who was the man in the chair? Was the murder real? Where was the stranger now?

Nichole's brow tightened. "Steven, what's wrong?"

Before Steven could reply the doorbell chimed. Nichole glanced across the room at the front door, then quickly back to her husband. Eyes brimming with emotion, she said, "Oh God, it's them. They said they were contacting families. I know it's them."

"Stay here," Steven muttered. Then he rose and started across the living room. The walk from the sofa to the front door was only twenty-two feet, but tonight it seemed further. The hardwood floor felt odd beneath his feet. Spongy and slightly lopsided. The surrounding walls seemed to drift sideways, as if not anchored to the floor. When he finally grabbed the doorknob, he held on a moment to steady himself, then pulled the door open.

Steven found himself staring at a face he hadn't seen in over three years.

Detective Ahmad was dressed impeccably, as always, and wearing a tight smile. It was a proud and contented smile. The smile of a man who had just completed a grim, but worthy task.

Detective Ahmad said, "Good evening, Mr. Burns. I have some news regarding your daughter, Luna."

The world shifted again.

Steven's hand slipped from the doorknob as the floor rose up and slapped the side of his face. He heard his wife's voice shouting his name as everything went black.

47

S teven roused to a light flashing in his eyes and a gloved hand lightly slapping his cheek.

"Mr. Burns, wake up."

Steven squinted and recoiled from the bright light.

The light winked out.

Someone was kneeling over him.

He blinked and focused on the face of a young woman he didn't recognize. She wore some kind of uniform and light blue rubber gloves.

She flashed a nice smile. "Hi there, Mr. Burns. Do you know where you are?"

Steven blinked again and his surroundings came into focus. He was flat on his back on the sofa in his living room. A black man, also wearing a uniform and blue gloves, stood over the young woman. A stethoscope around his neck.

Paramedics.

Behind the paramedics, Nichole stood with her hand over her mouth, watching with anxious eyes. And there was another man standing beside Nichole. His arm wrapped around her shoulders, comforting her.

It was Detective Ahmad.

Suddenly it all rushed back. The police press conference, Pastor Childs a serial killer, Luna one of his victims. The stranger lied about everything, they killed an innocent man.

The female paramedic waved her hand in front of his face. "Mr. Burns, do you know where you are?"

"Yeah," he said rubbing his temples. "My living room. What happened?"

"Looks like you had a panic attack."

Steven groaned. "Great." He swung up into a sitting position.

The paramedic grabbed his shoulders. "Whoa. Take it slow. Might be better to remain lying down for a moment."

"I'm fine."

Nichole sat down beside her husband and hugged him. "You had me so worried. It's a miracle I didn't give birth right here in the living room."

Steven grimaced. "Sorry."

"How do you feel, Mr. Burns?" The female paramedic asked. "Any dizziness? Blurred vision? Headache?"

"No. I'm fine. More embarrassed than anything."

"Nothing to be embarrassed about," the male paramedic said. "A panic attack can happen to anyone under a great amount of stress. From what I hear from the detective, I'm surprised you didn't have one sooner."

Steven's eyes shifted to Detective Ahmad. "Then it's true? Luna's one of his victims?"

The Detective frowned. "Let's focus on making sure you're okay first. After they finish, we'll talk."

The female paramedic said to Steven, "No worries, we're almost done. Just need to check your vitals." She pulled a blood pressure cuff from her bag. "Could you roll up your sleeve for me, please?"

Steven ignored her, still riveted to Detective Ahmad. "It's

been three years. We deserve to know right now. Did Pastor Childs kill our daughter or not?"

Tense silence ensued. Finally Detective Ahmad turned to the paramedics. "Could you both wait outside a moment?"

The female paramedic shook her head. "No need. He's fine." Then to Steven she said, "But if it happens again go to the hospital. Get yourself checked out. Okay?"

Before Steven could respond, Nichole jumped in, "He will. Thank you."

The instant the door shut behind the paramedics, Steven and Nichole turned back to Detective Ahmad. They didn't utter a word, they just stared, and waited.

After a deep breath, Detective Ahmad said, "What hasn't been reported yet is that the Pastor is being very cooperative. Besides all the physical evidence, we already have his confession. And yes, he did identify Luna as one of his victims."

To Steven the words sounded distant. His body felt numb and detached. He heard a whimper and saw Nichole brush tears from her cheeks. Steven pulled her into an embrace and held her tight. He felt Nichole's body shudder against his.

After a respectful pause, Detective Ahmad continued, "Mr. Burns, I know this isn't the best time but we'd like you to come in to answer a few questions."

Steven and Nichole both leveled puzzled looks on the detective. Steven said, "I don't think that's a good idea. Nichole's supposed to avoid stress, and this day has already been too much. Could we do it tomorrow?"

"You misunderstand," Detective Ahmad said, "Your wife can wait here. We only need to speak to you."

Steven's brow tightened. "Why just me?

"Do you recall visiting the Pastor at his home about three years ago?"

Steven felt his heart thud in his chest. Was it possible the police somehow connected his meeting with Pastor Childs to his dealings with the stranger?

"Mr. Burns?"

"Of course I remember," Steven said finally. "I was going through tough times. Nichole and I were split. My business was going under. I needed someone to talk to. Why would this have anything to do with the case?"

Detective Ahmad shrugged. "I'm not sure. It's the D.A. who wants to speak to you. Things are moving fast. He's probably just tying up loose ends. You can ride into the station with me. Once you're done I'll have a squad car bring you back. Sound good?"

Steven felt something he hadn't felt in years, an uncomfortable tightening around the base of his neck. He believed Detective Ahmad, and knew it was highly unlikely the D.A.'s request had anything to do with the stranger. Still, the invisible hands clasping his throat seemed to grow tighter and tighter.

Steven rose suddenly and brushed past the detective as he crossed to the front door. Pulling open the door, Steven said to Ahmad, "I'll come in tomorrow. Right now I really need to be with my wife."

"I really don't mind waiting," Nichole said to Steven. "You can go. It's okay."

"No," Steven said, "It's not okay. Not now." He turned back to Detective Ahmad. "We appreciate everything you've done, but I'd like you to leave now. Please."

"Steven!" Nichole exclaimed with a gasp.

Detective Ahmad raised a calming hand. "No. It's okay." He gave Steven a formal smile. "Mr. Burns, I completely understand, and honestly I don't blame you. I'll call tomorrow morning to arrange a time. Goodnight."

As Steven locked the door behind the detective, Nichole stared at her husband with puzzled eyes. "What's wrong with you? He's been so nice to us."

Steven rejoined Nichole on the sofa. He gently took her hand, paused to take a deep breath, then said, "I have something to tell you. Something I never wanted to tell you... but now I have no choice."

Nichole straightened up and gripped his hand tighter. "You're scaring me."

48

W hen Steven was done talking, without a moment's hesitation, Nichole scooted closer on the sofa, threw her arms around him and hugged him tight. The embrace was long and quiet, and with each passing second Steven felt lighter and more clear-headed. When they parted they both brushed tears from their eyes.

Nichole said, "Oh my God. It must have been so hard living with that secret for so long."

"So many times I wanted to tell you," Steven said, "but I wasn't sure how you'd take it. I was afraid you'd see me as some sort of monster."

"Never," Nichole said shaking her head. "If that man approached me I would've done the same thing. You did it for us. For Luna."

"Also, I wanted to keep your hands clean. Keep you out of it in case something went wrong." Steven pinned her with grim eyes. "Tomorrow when I go into the station, I'm going to tell them everything."

Nichole gasped. "What? No."

"Think," Steven said. "It's the smart thing to do. Instead of waiting for the police to figure it out, it'll look better if I come forward first. Conspiracy to commit murder is bad, but I didn't actually kill anyone. He did. With a good lawyer, there's a good chance--"

"Stop it." Nichole snapped. "You're not turning yourself in. I won't let you. Absolutely not."

Steven sighed. "Come on, you heard Detective Ahmad. They're already asking questions. For all I know they already know something."

"Or, they know absolutely nothing and it's exactly what Detective Ahmad said. They're just tying up loose ends. Also, from what you've told me, I don't see how they could ever connect your meeting with Pastor Childs to anything."

"That's not the point," Steven said. "Don't you get it? I can't just do nothing. Because of me an innocent man is dead."

For a moment Nichole just stared at him, understanding yet impatient. Finally she reached out, took his hand and laid it upon her swollen belly. As she held his hand there with a loving firmness, she said, "The only innocent person involved is right in here. If you turn yourself in that man will still be dead, and his murderer will still be out there. All that will change is that your wife will be without a husband, and your child without a father. Doing nothing... will save your family."

Steven felt movement beneath his hand. A brief, slow shifting within Nichole's belly. It was as if their unborn child was siding with its mother by reminding its father what was truly at stake.

Steven sighed and settled back onto the couch. He said to Nichole, "You're right. I don't know what I was thinking." Then, struck with a realization, his expression darkened.

"What is it? Nichole asked.

As quickly as it came, the shadow passed. Steven shook his head dismissively. "Nothing important."

Nichole's eyes narrowed. "No more secrets. Tell me."

Steven frowned. "Pretty soon Luna's name will be all over the news. Then he'll know that I know the truth. That he's just a con man and worse, a murderer. And I can identify him."

"You're worried he might come back?"

"I thought about it but... why would he? He got what he wanted. He knows I can't talk without getting myself in trouble. Also, he seemed pretty damn confident the police would never be able to find him." Steven shook his head. "No, if he's as smart as I think he is... he's long gone."

Nichole smiled.

Steven smiled back... despite the sudden sensation of a spider crawling up his spine.

49

A t 7:55 the next morning, Steven and Nichole were awakened by Steven's ringing cell phone. A bleary-eyed glance at the screen instantly cleared the morning fog from Steven's head.

It was Detective Ahmad.

Steven felt a pang of nerves as he answered the call, but was surprised to discover scheduling a meeting with the District Attorney was not the detective's priority. Instead he invited Steven and Nichole to attend a noon press briefing, wherein the names of Pastor Childs' victims would be released to the media. Steven's initial reply was negative. What would he and Nichole gain by submitting themselves to a media circus? But Detective Ahmad explained that making an official statement in a controlled setting would forestall nonstop phone calls and stalking by reporters.

Steven thought this made sense. He told Detective Ahmad he felt confident Nichole would agree and, in all likelihood, they would attend the briefing.

Detective Ahmad thanked Steven, made some comment

about seeing them later at the station, then, to Steven's bewilderment, simply said goodbye. Had Steven missed something? The detective was about to hang up without any mention at all of the District Attorney. In the fractions of a second between Detective Ahmad's goodbye and the line going dead, Steven considered letting him go. Why remind him? Just wait for them to ask again. But Steven was now curious to personally gauge the District Attorney's interest. Was he truly tying up loose ends... or was there something more? Now that he knew the D.A. had questions, waiting to be summoned seemed far more stressful than just getting it over with.

"Wait," Steven said into the phone. "What about the District Attorney? You said he wanted to talk to me."

"Oh, right," Detective Ahmad said. "I told him what you said about your personal troubles and needing someone to talk to, et cetera. He said fine and to drop it. So, forget it." Detective Ahmad apologized for his forgetfulness, reminded Steven to arrive at the briefing early, again said goodbye, then hung up. Just like that, he was gone.

Steven stared at his phone, relieved but also feeling a bit foolish for blowing this D.A. business out of proportion. Suddenly he felt a hand on his arm.

"Well," Nichole asked. "What did he say?"

Steven rolled over in bed to face his wife. He smiled at her, said good morning, and gave her a gentle kiss.

Once again, the press briefing was staged in the staff parking lot of the Crescenta Valley Sheriff's Station. The nearby mountains, aglow with noonday sun, made for a dramatic backdrop. Unlike the press briefing Steven and Nichole had suffered through three years ago, this time there were twice as many reporters in attendance. Steven wasn't surprised. The capture of a serial killer was major news, especially when the suspect was once a trusted clergyman.

District Attorney Angel Nieves was slender, well dressed, and an energetic speaker. As he addressed the media from the podium, Steven and Nichole stood behind him along with the parents of the other two victims, and a large group of police and city officials.

Minutes before the briefing began Detective Ahmad gathered all the parents together, including Steven and Nichole, and made quick introductions. There was only enough time to trade tragic smiles and supportive hugs before it was time to face the cameras. Nichole suggested they trade numbers later, and all agreed that was a good idea.

The first part of District Attorney Nieves' speech was an acknowledgment of the work done by the investigators who broke the case. When particular mention was made of Detective Ahmad's persistence, Steven noticed the Pakistani American hold his chin a little higher.

Finally, the District Attorney got to the part of the briefing the press had been waiting for. Respectful silence fell over the crowd as he read the names of the three young girls who'd fallen victim to Pastor Childs' depravity. He also gave the date each girl went missing, and the date and place their bodies were found. When Luna's name was read, Steven and Nichole took hold of each other's hand and squeezed.

The instant D.A. Nieves looked up from his notes, reporters began shouting questions at Steven and Nichole and the other parents. But Nieves raised his hands and quieted the crowd by announcing he wasn't done. After a pause he said, "We have a great deal of evidence, but there will be no trial. Last night Pastor Eric Childs, aka Pastor Childs signed a detailed letter confessing to all the murders. With the exception of sentencing, this case is closed."

Like Steven and Nichole, the other parents were already notified about the Pastor's confession, but to the press this was a bombshell. A roar went up as the crowd bombarded D.A. Nieves with questions. With professional poise he quickly regained control and began answering reporters one by one.

Up until that instant, the idea of doing another press conference made Steven's insides flutter. But now, seeing the excitement and smiles inspired by the capture of Luna's killer, he was glad he and Nichole had decided to come. This is how justice is supposed to feel, he thought. Not dirty and hidden, but shouted and celebrated.

As if she'd heard his thoughts, Nichole turned and smiled at him. Steven smiled back and they embraced. Suddenly he felt lighter. Heady with thoughts of family and a boundless future.

The moment was interrupted by Steven's cell phone vibrating in his back pocket.

As Steven dug for his phone, Nichole returned her attention to the briefing.

Steven stared at the phone's screen... and stopped breathing.

A text message. Just two words. All caps.

STAY CALM.

Steven stared at the text as the stranger's sandpaper voice resurrected in his mind.

Suddenly, Steven felt watched. He whipped to the crowd of reporters. Scanned the faces.

So many.

His phone vibrated in his hand again. Another text.

I'M CLOSER THAN YOU THINK.

Steven's heart thudded. His eyes shot back to the sea of faces. He searched the front rows... and froze.

Every person in the crowd was riveted to the District Attorney... except one man. He stood about thirty feet from the podium. He wore a simple black windbreaker, black leather gloves, and a pair of black, thick framed glasses. And those glasses were trained squarely on Steven.

It's really him.

The stranger gave Steven a nearly imperceptible nod, then dropped his gaze to the phone in his hand and typed a message.

Despite his jangled nerves, Steven couldn't help thinking the stranger's leather gloves must be touchscreen sensitive. An instant later Steven's cell phone pulsated and a new message filled the screen.

WE NEED TO TALK. 6 PM TONIGHT. THE BENCH.

"Are you okay? Nichole asked.

Steven looked up and saw his wife staring at him.

"I'm fine," Steven said, making an effort to appear casual as he slipped his phone into his back pocket. "Just checking my email."

A smattering of applause drew Nichole back to the podium, where the District Attorney was turning over the mic to Detective Ahmad.

Steven peered back out at the front of the crowd, but the stranger was gone. Steven immediately spotted him wending slowly through the crush of reporters, towards the parking lot's exit.

The stranger wasn't fleeing or in a rush of any sort, he was simply leaving.

Surrounded by so many uniforms, the urge to point the stranger out and yell for his arrest did spring to Steven's mind. But so did Nichole's words from last night. There was far more at stake than his guilt and freedom.

He wants to make sure I'm going to remain calm. That's all this is.

Steven watched the stranger peel from the rear of the crowd, stroll out the exit gate, and disappear from sight.

A moment later Steven's back pocket buzzed again. He pulled out his phone and glanced at the screen.

Somehow... all the stranger's text messages were gone.

50

A t a little before 5 PM that same evening, Steven lied to his pregnant wife.

He told Nichole the unexpected press briefing had caused him to cancel an earlier quote appointment in Glendora. The soonest the client could reschedule was 6 PM. Because the job was a ground-up, six-thousand-square-foot remodel, he didn't want to schedule for another day and risk losing a huge contract. Steven made this fabrication airtight by adding he tried to get Linton to go in his place, but their partner had previous plans that could not be changed.

Twenty minutes later Steven was behind the wheel of his Silverado pickup, driving along Foothill Boulevard toward Memorial Park. Sunset painted the bustling shop-lined thoroughfare with golden light. As Steven cruised past the currently closed offices of Burns Home Remodeling, he saw the automated dusk-to-dawn security lights wink on in the parking lot.

To Steven, the idea that he was on his way to meet the stranger again almost felt surreal. Three years ago, when the stranger said they'd never meet again, not only did Steven believe him, he was relieved. Steven wasn't ashamed to admit that the man who seemed to never take off his black leather gloves scared the shit out of him.

The stranger was clearly smart. Anyone who could program an iPad to self-destruct, make text messages vanish from someone else's phone, or create impossibly realistic fake images had to be some sort of hacking genius. The stranger had lied about everything, which meant those disgusting photographs of Luna were lies as well. Photoshop tricks. But where did the stranger get images of Luna to start with? Steven's best guess was the stranger hacked into his home computer and down-loaded everything he needed. In a world dominated by technology, a man who could so expertly manipulate that technology was not someone you wanted as an enemy. And more so if that same man was also a cold-blooded killer.

The indelible memory of that baseball bat caving in that man's skull was disturbing enough, but what haunted Steven more was what happened immediately after. Most people, after stepping on a roach, lift their foot to check the result. Some out of morbid curiosity, others only to make sure the creature is dead. But after the stranger took his final swing, he simply tossed the blood-soaked bat onto the table and wiped his hands. Never once did he bother to glance back at his victim. And there was nothing in the stranger's eyes, not even disgust at the mess he'd just made. It was as if he were some sort of robot, and human life meant nothing to him.

Steven abruptly pulled to the curb and slammed on the breaks.

The pickup came to a skidding halt.

"What the fuck are you doing?" Those whispered words slipped from Steven's gaping mouth as if uttered by someone trapped inside him. He was the sole witness to a murder committed by a very dangerous man. Yes, going to the police would hurt them both, but now Steven knew he'd been robbed of both money and justice. Undoubtedly, the stranger feared their delicate balance had been upended. For all he knew, Steven might now be more interested in revenge than common sense... which would make Steven a loose end that needed to be dealt with. The stranger's text said he just wanted to talk, and for now that was probably true. Why else reveal himself and ask for a meeting? But the problem was... what happens if that meeting doesn't go well? What if the stranger tries his human lie detector trick? Only yesterday Steven was prepared to march into the Sheriff's station and confess everything. Would the stranger be able to see that in his eyes?

One thing Steven knew for certain... for now, voluntarily going anywhere near that man was far too risky. He wanted nothing more than to tell the stranger to keep the money; just stay away from him and his family. But before that conversation could happen, Steven needed some insurance. He needed more leverage than simply being able to point the stranger out in a lineup. He needed a name, an address, and most of all, hard evidence.

It instantly occurred to Steven that the planned 6 PM meeting presented a rare opportunity to get everything he needed.

He glanced at the dashboard clock.

5:35 PM

That gave him only 25 minutes to prepare. That should be enough time, but he'd have to move fast.

Steven threw the truck into drive, cut a sharp U-turn through horn-blaring traffic, and sped back the way he came.

51

E very member of Steven's small staff at Burn's Home Remodeling owned their own vehicle, but a company car, a white Honda Accord, was kept in the parking lot for emergencies. The Honda was only two years old and due to infrequent use, still in near-new condition.

Eighteen minutes was all it took for Steven to drive back to the office, swap his Silverado for the Honda, then speed across town to Memorial Park. Instead of pulling into the public lot, he parked the Honda a block away and across the street. From this position, without ever leaving the Honda, he could see the park's two entrances, as well as all the street parking nearby. Steven could now secretly observe anyone entering or leaving the park.

Steven checked his watch.

5:57 PM

Now all he had to do was spot one person in particular.

Each time they met at the bench, the stranger appeared only after Steven was seated. That meant the stranger had to be watching from somewhere close. But where?

In the fading daylight, Steven scanned the lamplit park and

the surrounding area. A few joggers, kids playing basketball, two moms pushing strollers, a double-parked FedEx van with its hazards flashing. Nothing out of the ordinary. Steven even had a partial view of the bench beneath the big oak in the middle of the park. Of course, the bench was empty.

This wasn't unexpected. The man who always wore gloves was obsessively cautious. Steven knew he couldn't rely on locating the stranger's hiding spot, so instead he'd wait for the stranger to reveal himself.

Steven's plan was simple. Blow off the meeting. Hide nearby and wait for the stranger to leave... then follow him. Steven's three-ton truck would surely be spotted, but a white Honda was so indistinct it was practically invisible. With any luck the stranger would lead Steven to his home, or place of business, or anywhere that would help identify the man. And if Steven found an opportunity to take the stranger's picture... that would be a grand slam.

Steven checked his watch again.

Six on the dot.

He focused on the parallel-parked vehicles just outside the park. The stranger was probably staked out in a nondescript sedan, just like he was. Unfortunately, the glare of streetlights made it impossible to see inside any of the parked cars.

Steven checked his watch again.

He was now four minutes late for their meeting.

He wondered how long the stranger would wait before leaving. Five minutes? Ten? He was surprised the stranger hadn't driven off already. Steven wished he could speed things up by texting a last minute cancellation, but he had no way of contacting the stranger. His only option was to keep his eyes open, and wait.

Twelve minutes later, at 6:15 PM, Steven became concerned

that something had gone wrong. Was it possible the stranger had somehow spotted him and now knew what he was up to? And if that were true, how would the stranger react?

Steven's breathing grew shallow. Until that moment his focus never left the park area, but now he pivoted his head left and right, glancing out the side windows. He saw nothing but empty streets and shadows. His focus shot back to the line of parked cars outside Memorial Park.

Where was the stranger? He had to be out there, somewhere. Where else would he--

Steven was struck with the desperate need to hear his wife's voice. He snatched up his phone and was about to dial when it vibrated in his hand. A text message appeared.

WHERE ARE YOU?

Steven nearly dropped the phone.

He took a calming breath, then typed: *Sorry. Can't make it. Wife is sick. Can we reschedule?*

He stared at the small screen, waiting. He could feel his throbbing heart in his fingertips.

His phone vibrated again.

I'LL BE IN TOUCH SOON.

Steven peered down the block at the parked cars. He expected to see headlights wink on as one of the cars pulled away. But what happened instead left him puzzled.

The hazard lights on the double-parked FedEx van stopped blinking, and the van began moving.

Steven stared as the white cargo van bearing the FedEx logo accelerated away down the avenue.

Was that a coincidence?

No. Using a FedEx van was smart. The perfect cover. That had to be the stranger.

Steven reached for the ignition key, but froze.

What if I'm wrong?

The van's red tail lights were getting farther and farther away. Becoming harder to distinguish from other traffic.

Steven had to make a decision right now.

52

After following in light traffic for only two miles, and questioning his decision the entire way, Steven was surprised to see the FedEx van suddenly pull over and stop.

Separated by half a block, Steven had just enough time to react by whipping the Honda to the curb and quickly killing the engine and headlights. He felt encouraged when he noticed both sides of this street were dominated by a huge construction project. The site was shut down for the night and there were no nearby buildings or homes to receive a FedEx delivery, so why stop here?

Peering down the dark block at the van, Steven received his answer when the door swung open and the driver climbed out. Instead of a FedEx uniform the man wore a familiar black windbreaker.

Night had fallen and the street was dark, but Steven had no trouble recognizing the stranger.

Steven straightened up in his seat as he continued to watch.

The stranger glanced about to make sure he wasn't being observed, then peeled the FedEx logo off the side of the van.

Steven couldn't help an impressed chuckle.

The van was a counterfeit. The FedEx logos were merely magnetic vinyl signs.

Steven watched in astonishment as the stranger quickly removed two more signs, one from the van's opposite side and one from the hood, then tossed all three into the rear.

An instant later the stranger climbed back behind the wheel of what was now a simple white cargo van, and sped off.

Steven paused to give his quarry a cautious lead, then he restarted the Honda and continued to follow.

53

The white cargo van traveled north on State Route 114 in light traffic. The van stayed in the center lane and never once exceeded the speed limit.

Steven followed in the Honda Accord, at all times maintaining a separation of at least three vehicles.

Over a span of about forty minutes the lights of suburban sprawl gradually gave way to vast stretches of darkness.

Just as Steven began to question if the stranger was intentionally leading him to a remote location, the van's turn signal flashed and it merged off the highway at an exit marked Lake Eliza.

Steven veered toward the ramp but allowed a delivery truck to exit first, to serve as a buffer between his Honda and the van.

Moments later Steven was cruising along Lake Eliza Boulevard, the two-lane main strip of a small lake town. An incongruous combination of charming old shops and garish chain drive-thrus lined the avenue. Steven had never heard of Lake Eliza, and probably never would have, if not led there by his need to unmask the stranger.

The delivery truck still rumbled along between Steven's

Honda and the van, providing much needed cover. Unlike the highway, traffic was sparse on the narrow boulevard, increasing the chance the stranger would notice he was being followed.

The signal light on the van flashed as it turned into a small corner gas station and stopped at a pump.

Steven drove past the station, through the intersection, then pulled over a half block away and killed the engine. He adjusted his rear view mirror until he had a perfect view of the stranger filling the van's gas tank.

A younger man, about 30 and wearing coveralls, exited the station's store and greeted the stranger with a handshake.

Steven noticed the stranger no longer wore his black leather gloves.

The conversation between the two men appeared casual, but the younger man's demeanor was respectful, as if addressing an employer or parent.

Another handshake then the younger man returned to the store. Soon after, the stranger completed filling his tank, then climbed back into the van, and drove out of the station.

Steven ducked low as the white cargo van cruised past the parked Honda and continued along Lake Eliza Boulevard.

For an instant Steven considered abandoning the tail in favor of questioning the gas station attendant. The two men were clearly friends. Even if the attendant didn't know the stranger's address, he would almost certainly know his name. But Steven decided against it. Lake Eliza was a small town, which meant cagey neighbors. The last thing he wanted was for the attendant to tell the stranger someone from out of town had been asking questions about him.

Steven restarted his car and resumed following. The delivery truck was gone, but now an SUV towing a fishing boat advantageously occupied the road between the Honda and the van.

A quarter of a mile later the white van turned right and

disappeared onto a side street. But as Steven neared the corner, beneath a street sign that read Lakemont Drive, he spotted another sign that made him pull over and stop.

NOT A THROUGH STREET

A quick check of the Honda's GPS confirmed what Steven immediately suspected. Lakemont Drive was a residential street that ended in a cul-de-sac. All the neighbors would surely know each other. If Steven continued to follow, the stranger would notice the unfamiliar vehicle instantly.

On the positive side, the GPS showed the distance to the end of the cul-de-sac wasn't far. Meaning, Steven could continue following on foot. He'd never catch up to the stranger to observe which house he went into, but maybe he'd spot the white van parked in the driveway.

Steven locked the Honda and walked briskly into the block. There were no street lamps, only the glow of landscape lighting. It was an affluent neighborhood. Old multistoried houses separated by spacious, well manicured yards. Between the homes, glimpses of a moonlit Eliza Lake could be seen.

Being spotted by one of the stranger's neighbors could prove disastrous, so Steven stuck to the shadows as he crept from house to house. When he was half way into the block, a car sped by. The driver, a woman, showed no sign of noticing him. He waited until the car disappeared into a garage, then continued his search.

Moments later, Steven froze when he saw it.

The largest house in the neighborhood, a three-story rustic, stood at the very center of the cul-de-sac.

The white cargo van was parked in the driveway.

The house was beautiful and so... homey. Steven found it difficult to visualize the stranger residing there. But at the same time, the perfect, everything-just-so appearance of the home seemed to fit.

Steven pulled out his cell phone and snapped quick photos of the house and of the post-mounted mailbox at the curb. A name and address were emblazoned on the side of the box.

WALKER. 224 LAKEMONT DRIVE.

It struck Steven that he now knew the stranger's name and home address. So far his plan had gone by the numbers. All he needed now was a photo of the man himself. A quivering in Steven's gut told him to forget the photo. To quit while he was ahead and hurry home. But the adrenaline coursing through his body urged him to swing for the fences.

I'm already here... and he's so close.

Warm light emanated from the ground floor windows. Closed blinds obscured the view of inside, but Steven could still make out movement. The silhouettes of more than one person.

A family? Did the stranger have a wife? Children?

Heart pounding, Steven crept across the lawn. To reach the nearest window he had to step in a bed of hydrangeas.

He tried to peek around the edge of the blinds but all he could see was a stone fireplace and--

The screech of tires.

Glaring bright light flooded the property.

"Police," a voice boomed behind Steven. "I have a weapon aimed at you. Don't fucking move!"

Steven froze, head swimming with disbelief and rising panic.

"Now raise your hands and turn around. Slow. No sudden moves."

Hands trembling, Steven did as he was told. Suddenly he faced two uniformed officers. Both stood behind the open doors of an idling sheriff's cruiser, pointing sidearms. The cruiser's headlights were off, but the side-mounted spotlight was trained on Steven and the house.

The front door flew open and the stranger hurried out, trailed by a woman and a teenaged boy. He no longer wore the black windbreaker, just the white dress shirt. Shielding his bespectacled eyes from the light, the stranger said to the officers, "Jerome? Bobby? What the hell's going on?"

"Sorry for the disturbance, Judge," the older officer said. "But one of your neighbors spotted this man snooping around your property."

Steven's mind did a backflip.

Did that cop just call him a judge?

Still shielding his eyes, the stranger paused when he finally recognized the man standing on his front lawn.

Steven stopped breathing as the stranger's unreadable eyes bored into him. And what happened next left Steven numb with confusion.

The stranger smiled at him, then began to laugh.

54

The man Steven now knew to be Judge Walker, told the two officers a simple, but perfectly believable lie.

Steven, a contractor, was there to give a kitchen remodeling quote. The front doorbell is sometimes difficult to hear so Steven must've tried knocking on the window.

Without asking a single question, the officers apologized to Steven, said goodnight to everyone, then climbed back into their cruiser and sped off.

Steven wasn't surprised the Judge covered for him. The nature of their connection wasn't something he'd share with the police or his family. But watching the Walker family cheerfully wave goodbye to the departing officers, like a scene from a Hallmark movie, felt like an out-of-body experience.

Steven wanted to get the hell out of there, but he was strangely riveted by this glimpse of the Judge's apparent double life.

"Sorry about that," the Judge said extending a hand to Steven. "So glad you could make it."

The sight of the Judge's ungloved hand caused Steven to hesitate before shaking it. "No problem."

The Judge gestured to his wife and child. "This is Helen, and our son, Willem." Helen wore an apron over a curvy figure. Steven guessed she was about a decade younger than the Judge. Willem, now riveted to his cell phone screen, looked to be about twelve.

Helen, wearing a warm smile, said to Steven, "Believe it or not, the Judge never said a thing about you coming tonight." She frowned at her husband. "And don't say it was a surprise. Just admit it old man. You forgot."

The Judge chuckled and raised a hand as if taking an oath. "I plead the fifth."

Helen turned back to Steven. "I'm still cooking dinner. Will I be in the way?"

Seeing a chance to avoid falling deeper into the hole he dug for himself, Steven said, "It's probably best if I just come back at a more convenient time. No problem, really."

But the Judge surprised him. "Wait. I have a great idea. Stay for dinner, then after, you and I can talk business." He underscored this invitation with what appeared to be a sincere smile.

"Yes," Helen said. "Please stay. There's plenty of food. Hope you're not a vegetarian. We're having meatloaf."

Never looking up from his cell phone, Willem added, "My mom does make a killer meatloaf."

Steven glanced at the house, tempted. The presence of the Judge's family pretty much allayed any concern for his safety. Also, learning more about the Judge's personal life could only help, right? But why would the Judge so eagerly invite him into his home? The answer came instantly. Because now Steven was even more of a threat. The Judge was as anxious as Steven was, maybe more so, to reaffirm their understanding.

Steven met the Judge's eyes. "I really don't mind rescheduling. Are you sure you want to do this now?"

"Absolutely," the Judge said, giving Steven a friendly slap on the shoulder. "The evening hasn't gone as planned, but I have a feeling this might actually be better."

55

"How is it?" Mrs. Walker asked Steven.

Steven swallowed a bite of meatloaf before answering. "Willem was right. Your meatloaf's amazing. The potatoes, the broccoli, the wine, it's all delicious. Thanks again for inviting me."

Steven wasn't merely being polite, her cooking was exceptional. When he first sat down at the dining table he could barely taste his food. Sharing a meal with a man who frequented his nightmares, not to mention that man's family, was just too damn surreal. But after forcing down a few bites, Mrs. Walker's cooking became an irresistible distraction. And from what he'd seen of the house's interior, her homemaking skills were not confined to the oven. The tasteful decor was worthy of a professional designer, and every room, with the exception of the kitchen, was as tidy as a photograph in Architectural Digest.

As if she'd read his thoughts, Mrs. Walker said, "I've been bugging the Judge to remodel forever. He's so picky about contractors. You must be very good at your job."

Steven shrugged. "I do my best to keep my customers happy."

The Judge, who sat at the head of the table, chuckled and

said to his wife, "Our guest is being modest. Burns Home Remodeling has been top-five rated in Southern California two years in a row. Currently they have five open contracts, two municipal projects, and an eight-month waiting list. And Steven accomplished all that while expecting a child. His wife's due any day now."

Steven stared at him, rattled by the accuracy of his information. Clearly the Judge had kept tabs on him and his family.

"Wow," Mrs. Walker said to Steven. "Congratulations." Then suddenly her eyes narrowed. "By any chance do you advertise on TV?"

"No," Steven muttered. "Not really."

Noticing Steven's discomfort, the Judge set down his wine glass and said, "Sorry. Did I misspeak?"

"No," Steven said. "Everything you said was one hundred percent right. When you shop for a contractor you really do your research, huh?"

"Of course. Hard to make a judgment without knowing all the facts. I try to teach that to my son, but all he cares about is screens." The Judge turned to an oblivious Willem, who was riveted to his cell phone. The dinner in front of him, barely touched. The Judge rapped his knuckles hard on the table three times, like banging a gavel.

Willem, getting the message, quickly swapped his phone for a fork and resumed eating.

Steven met Judge Walker's eyes. "So... you're a judge."

The Judge stared a moment, then surprised Steven by shaking his head. "No. I'm a retired Judge."

Mrs. Walker snorted. "A railroaded judge you mean. That whole mess was so damn unfair and--"

The Judge cut her short with a hard stare. "Calm yourself. Please."

She nodded obediently and grabbed her wine glass.

Steven surmised the Judge had been forced off the bench, but why? He was tempted to ask, but didn't want to push. Despite Steven's unexpected visit, the Judge's willingness to keep things civil seemed genuine. Steven didn't want to test his host's patience by doing anything else that might be perceived as maneuvering. Instead he made a mental note to Google Judge Walker later.

"Willem, your father told you to put that down." Mrs. Walker was frowning across the table at her son, who had his smart phone in his hand again.

"I know," Willem said, "but look. It's him." He turned the phone so everyone could see what filled the screen.

It was a photograph of Steven and Nichole embracing at the press conference. The caption read: PASTOR CONFESSES. VICTIM'S FAMILIES REJOICE.

"Oh my God," Mrs. Walker gasped, turning to Steven. "I knew I'd seen you somewhere before. Years ago, when your daughter went missing, we followed the story closely because--" She whimpered and brushed away tears. "I'm sorry." She turned to her husband. "Did you know?"

The Judge reached over and squeezed her hand. "Of course I knew. That's one of the reasons I wanted to do business with him. I was just waiting for the right time to tell you and Willem."

Steven had assumed Mrs. Walker's tears were out of sympathy for him, but the pained emotion in her eyes revealed something deeper.

Willem said to Steven, "The same thing happened to my sister. Her name was Jessica. I was just a baby then, so I don't really remember her that well."

Stunned, Steven turned to Judge Walker. "Your daughter... she was abducted?"

The Judge nodded slowly. He reset his glasses on his nose, then said, "Almost eleven years ago. Happened inside a convenience store. I made the mistake of taking my eyes off of Jessy for two minutes. Never saw her again. Not alive."

Mrs. Walker swiped away more tears. The Judge held her hand tighter and continued. "No arrests were ever made in Jessy's case. But that doesn't matter. Know why?" He leaned forward and pinned Steven with dead certain eyes. "All my years on the bench have taught me one thing. Evil catches up to you. The animal who murdered our daughter has paid severely for his crime. I know it in my heart."

The hairs on the back of Steven's neck stirred.

Mrs. Walker said to Steven, "The Judge has been saying that for years. All I can do is pray and hope that he's right." Then she sighed and put on a big smile. "Ready for dessert?"

After dinner, Steven made a show of touring the kitchen. Although spacious and well maintained, the finishes and high-end appliances were outdated. He listened to Mrs. Walker's surprisingly tasteful ideas, and offered a few of his own. The Judge tagged along but mostly remained quiet, leaving Steven to carry off the charade.

When it was all done, the Judge invited Steven to join him in the study to negotiate. Mrs. Walker offered to bring in coffee later. The Judge thanked her with a kiss on the cheek.

Moments later the Judge led Steven into a large room that looked like a judge's chamber. Wood paneling, shelves of legal text books, framed law degrees, there was even a gavel on a massive wooden desk. The faint aroma of lemon-scented furniture polish lingered in the air.

The Judge shut the door behind them and gestured to a tufted green leather sofa. "Have a seat. Please."

Steven sat as the Judge crossed to a well-stocked bar cabinet. The Judge asked, "Would you like a drink?"

"No thanks," Steven said. "One glass of wine was enough. I have a long drive back."

"Smart." The Judge poured himself a Scotch over ice, then lowered himself into an easy chair across from Steven. He swirled his drink slowly, peering into the glass as if mesmerized by the gentle tinkle of ice cubes. Finally, he took a long sip. After a savoring pause, he leveled a stare on Steven and asked, "Are you wearing a recording device?"

"What?" The question made perfect sense, but still caught Steven off guard. "You mean like a wire?"

The Judge watched him.

"No. Of course not. I never planned on talking to you."

The Judge nodded and extended an open hand. "Your phone, please."

Steven considered refusing, but saw no point in it. He produced his iPhone and placed it on the Judge's palm.

The Judge swiped and tapped at the screen.

"Wait," Steven said. "You need the password. You can't just--"

The iPhone unlocked and the home screen appeared.

Steven's brow tightened. "How'd you do that?"

"As I told you," the Judge said as he continued to flick and tap, "when it comes to computers... I'm a bit of a handyman."

"What are you doing?"

The Judge shut off the phone and placed it screen-down on the coffee table. "Leave it there until we're done."

Recalling the fate of the iPad the Judge had given him years ago, with trepidation Steven asked, "What did you do to my phone?"

"Erased the photos of my house and turned it off. That's all."

"How did you know I took photos?"

"I assumed you didn't drive all this way to peek in my window."

The Judge crossed his legs and settled back in his chair. He took a another sip of Scotch, then continued, "So, tell me... what are your intentions?"

"My intentions?"

"Do you plan to go to the police?"

Steven shook his head. "No. Not at all."

The Judge stared at him.

"I'm telling you the truth."

"Then why follow me?"

"Information."

"Information... to take to the police."

Steven nodded. "Okay, maybe. Just in case. But going to the police never entered my mind until you showed up today. I was just going to let it go."

The Judge cocked his head. "Let go of what, exactly?"

"Come on," Steven said. "You conned me. You took my money and made me an accomplice in the murder of an innocent man."

The Judge gestured for Steven to lower his voice. "Calm, please."

Steven whispered, "Considering what you put me through, I think I'm pretty Goddamned calm."

A razor thin smile creased the Judge's face. He took another sip of Scotch, then said, "Mr. Burns, you are so wrong about so much."

Steven's eyes narrowed. "If you're trying to make me think you didn't really kill that man, you're wasting your time. No way that was faked."

"No. You're correct. In fact I've come to appreciate the man-stopping effectiveness of a proper baseball bat. I keep one in my car, always."

Steven shook his head in disgust.

The Judge set down his drink on the coffee table. "You need to see something." He crossed to a filing cabinet, removed a folder, then returned to his seat. He tossed the folder onto the table. It was as thick as a daily newspaper, with a name written on the cover in black Sharpie.

ROBERT BRODY.

"What's this?" Steven asked. "Who's Robert Brody?"

The Judge picked up his drink and settled back in his seat. "Open it."

After a moment's hesitation, Steven picked up the file and flipped it open. A mug shot was stapled to the inside cover. His heart thudded when he recognized the person in the photo.

It was the man from the chair. The man he watched the Judge pummel to death with a baseball bat.

Off Steven's expression, the Judge said, "That's his police record. Robbery, assault, rape, murder. It's all in there."

Steven rifled the pages, all of which bore the logos of various California police departments. San Diego, San Francisco, Bakersfield, but most were from the LAPD. Steven never read a police report before, but it wasn't difficult to confirm the Judge's list of Robert Brody's offenses. Also included in the folder were crime scene and evidence photos. A gut-stabbed man, a battered woman, a smoldering house, hand guns, knives, a blood-caked hammer. Page after page dripping with senseless violence.

The Judge said, "Makes you wonder, doesn't it? How filth like that could walk around free." He didn't wait for Steven to respond. "Cracks." He mouthed the word like it tasted bad. "The justice system has cracks and far too often shit slips through." He met Steven's eyes. "So you see, I didn't kill an innocent man... I disposed of a piece of human garbage."

Steven watched as the Judge took a long sip of Scotch, as if toasting his own accomplishment. Struck with a thought, Steven flipped through the file again, then said to the Judge, "How do I know this is real? You faked those photos of Luna with that man. Compared to that, faking police records would be easy."

The Judge scowled at the notion. "A moment ago you said you never expected to talk to me. Well... I never expected you to show up on my doorstep. So, why would I have a forged police file lying around?"

Steven knew the Judge was clever, but to believe he created the file on the off chance that Steven would show up one day was a stretch. He tossed the file back onto the coffee table. "Okay. I see your point. But I paid you a hundred thousand dollars to deliver the man who killed my daughter, not some random criminal. You still took advantage of me."

The Judge sighed and shook his head. "You still don't understand." He got up again and crossed to the bar. As he poured himself another round, he continued. "When Jessica went missing, my life fell apart. Career, home, all of it. Only one thing saved me... tracking down the bastard who murdered my girl and making him pay. When you and I first met, you were a wreck. Your business in the toilet. Your wife gone. And I'm guessing suicide was next. But, after our late-night transaction three years ago, you cleared your head and turned it all around." He gestured to Steven with the Scotch bottle. "Now look at you. Business booming. Wife pregnant. Alive and healthy. Sure, I didn't deliver exactly what you paid for... but I did deliver what you desperately needed. And until that pastor got caught... it worked perfectly. In fact... you're my biggest success story." He made a face. "Well... with one minor hiccup." He carried his refreshed drink back across the room and retook his seat. "I tried like hell to find your man, I truly did, but you were getting worse so I made do. I did something I'd never done before." He pointed to the file folder on the coffee table. "I used a substitute." The Judge peered over the top of his glasses at Steven. "Do you see it now, Mr. Burns? I didn't con or take advantage of you... I gave you your life back."

Steven stared back with narrowed eyes. "So wait, you're saying your intention all along was to help me? If that's true, why take my money?"

The Judge shrugged. "I have a family to support. Money's an incentive, but not what drives me. Like I told you when we first met, I help people with justice problems. In the process I also clean up the streets a little. Believe me... even without the money it's very satisfying work."

Steven sank back on the sofa, his mind racing. Was the Judge being sincere or scrambling to keep his con game going? Buying time until he could deal with Steven in a more permanent manner?

"I know it's a lot," the Judge said. "No matter what I say, there's still that seed of doubt. Hopefully we can fix that." He pointed across the room. "There's a briefcase beside my desk. Do you mind?"

Steven crossed the room. He spotted a slim black briefcase on the floor, leaning against the desk. When he picked it up he noticed it wasn't very heavy, maybe four or five pounds. He carried the case over to the Judge, who raised an open hand like a traffic cop.

"No," the Judge said. "That belongs to you."

Steven stared, puzzled, at the briefcase. Then it struck him. Suddenly he knew exactly what was inside. He laid the case on the table and snapped it open.

Two fat bricks of one hundred dollar bills, bound by thick rubberbands.

"That's why I wanted to meet with you," The Judge said. "To explain the mix-up and return your money."

Steven, flooded by disbelief and confusion, remained riveted to the contents of the case. Could he have been so wrong about this man? From the moment he witnessed the Judge commit brutal murder, he lived in fear of the mysterious stranger he so foolishly conspired with. The Judge was a dangerous man, that was certain, but was it possible he'd told the truth from the start? That his extreme measures were used solely to help people failed by the justice system? And if true, who was Steven to Judge? He himself paid for the opportunity to kill in the name of justice for his daughter. Ultimately, he couldn't do it. Now, instead of fear, Steven wondered if he should feel gratitude toward the man who could.

"It's eleven thousand short," the Judge said, gesturing to the briefcase. "That's all I could pull together on short notice. If you want, I'll get you the rest in--"

"I don't want it," Steven said as he shut the briefcase. "None of it. Let's just leave things the way they were."

The Judge sighed. "Not a good idea. One financial crisis and that seed of doubt will still be there; giving you ideas, like the one that brought you here tonight. Take your money, go back to your life, and forget about me."

Steven shook his head. "I can't take it back. It doesn't feel right. You'll never hear from me again, I swear." Steven pushed the case toward him. "Just keep the money. Please."

The Judge's eyes bored into him.

"You can trust me," Steven said. "Don't you see it? I'm perfectly calm."

A knock at the door shattered the moment, followed by Mrs. Walker's cheerful voice. "You two ready for coffee?"

What happened next took Steven by surprise.

Reaching over the briefcase, the Judge extended his hand, along with what looked like a genuinely friendly smile.

Unaccustomed to seeing warmth where there was usually ice, Steven paused before smiling back and shaking the Judge's hand.

The Judge picked up the briefcase, placed it on the floor by his feet, then called out, "Come in."

57

C alm.
    That was what Steven felt as he cruised back toward Flintridge.

Traffic was light, soft rock played on the radio, and the constant thrum of the Honda's engine had a soothing, lulling quality.

Steven's head buzzed as if he was slightly intoxicated, but it wasn't from the Cabernet he drank with dinner. It was a sense of deep relief. Steven wasn't sure he believed everything the Judge told him, but he believed his eyes. The Judge wasn't a monster. He was just a man with a family who'd suffered an unthinkable tragedy. More similar to Steven than different, and with just as much to lose.

As the speeding car put more and more miles between them, Steven's calm grew deeper and deeper. Finally, that dark chapter of his life was truly and forever behind him.

When Steven merged onto Interstate 210, the final stretch of highway before reaching home, an internal alarm sounded. He'd told Nichole he was going to Glendora, which was only a thirty-minute drive at best. That was almost three hours ago. How would he explain why a kitchen quote took so long? While mentally sorting through possible excuses, it struck him that Nichole hadn't texted or called to see what-- "Shit!" Steven suddenly remembered the Judge had turned off his iPhone. He grabbed the device, powered it on, and found his screen filled with text messages and missed call notifications. The first texts were from Nichole, but the last few from Linton. Eyes ticking between the road and his phone, Steven read the most recent text and his heart began to race.

"This can't be happening."

Steven speed-dialed Linton's number and floored the accelerator.

58

S teven wheeled the Honda into the parking lot of Hamilton Memorial Hospital, then rushed in through the main entrance. He hurried across the modern lobby to the reception desk, where a male receptionist greeted him with a smile. "May I help you?"

"I'm here to see Nichole Walker. I think she was admitted about an hour ago."

The receptionist tapped a keyboard then said, "Yes. Are you related?"

"I'm her husband."

"ID, please?"

After scanning Steven's driver's license and handing it back, the receptionist said, "She's in maternity. Fourth floor."

Steven rode the elevator up then pushed through double doors into the maternity ward. There were about a dozen labor-delivery suites, but little activity, and so quiet he could hear the ventilation system.

A grey-haired nurse seated at the nurse's station waved him over. "Let me guess," she said. "You're the missing dad."

Steven winced. "Am I too late?"

She chuckled. "Oh, no. You're fine. But you did cut it close." She pointed across the ward. "Your wife's in LDR Eleven."

When Steven pushed open the door to room 11 he was greeted by the amplified sound of his unborn child's heartbeat. The audio had a squishy, underwater quality, but the rhythm was fast and steady.

Nichole was propped-up in a delivery bed munching ice chips from a plastic cup. A seasoned nurse, whose nametag read MILLER RN, stood bedside with a clipboard checking the array of fetal monitors and IV drips tethered to Nichole's body. Linton and Sharon were seated together on the sofa, both thumbing their smart phones.

Everyone stopped and stared when he entered, but Steven was focused solely on Nichole, whose eyes were a kaleidoscope of emotions. Anger, confusion, relief.

Steven rushed over and kissed her. "I'm so sorry. Are you okay?"

Before Nichole could respond Nurse Miller jumped in. "She's doing wonderfully. Her contractions are about eight minutes apart and she's responding well to the pain meds. I'd say another fifteen minutes before it's time to push. I'll return with the doctor in a few minutes." Then she exited the room.

Nichole leveled a narrow stare on Steven. "So, what happened to you?"

"I'll explain everything later. I promise. Right now, let's just focus on you and the baby."

"That's what I'm doing," Nichole said. "You know my condition. I want to know what could possibly keep you from returning my calls and texts for three hours. And don't say you were on a quote in Glendora. Linton never heard of that job." She turned to Linton. "Right?"

"Whoa," Linton said, raising his hands. "I said I didn't remember."

Sharon rolled her eyes and said to Linton, "Sounds to me like you're just covering for your buddy."

"Exactly," Nichole said, turning back to Steven. "So, were you in Glendora or not?"

Steven sighed. "Can we just talk about this later? Please?"

Nichole crossed her arms. "I've been lying here in pain for hours. The only thing worse was worrying about you. I'd like to know why."

Steven frowned, then turned to Linton and Sharon. "Could I speak to her alone a moment?"

"Of course," Linton said. He and Sharon immediately rose from the sofa. "We'll grab some coffee. We'll get you one too."

The instant the couple exited the room, Nichole turned anxious eyes on Steven. "Now I'm really worried. Why did they have to leave?"

"You'll understand in a second."

"Wait. Does this has something to do with that strange man?"

Steven nodded. "Believe it or not, he's a judge."

"What?"

He told Nichole everything. How Judge Walker contacted him at the press conference. How he followed the Judge home. Meeting the Judge's family. And the stunning fact that the Judge also lost a daughter to an abduction.

Nichole absorbed all this while wincing through the beginning pangs of a contraction. When Steven was done, one detail caused her brow to wrinkle. "Why didn't you take the money?"

"Because he truly believes he did what he did to help me," Steven said. "I figured it best not to make a man like that feel slighted."

"But is that worse than him not trusting you?"

"What do you mean?"

"Think about it. If you offered someone all that money, money that was rightfully theirs, and they turned it down flat...

would you trust that person? Or, would you think they were hiding some--" Suddenly Nichole groaned and grabbed her midsection with both hands.

"What's wrong?" Steven said.

"Contraction. Strong one." Wincing in pain she pointed to the remote control. "Call the nurse. Hurry."

Steven grabbed the remote and pressed the red button labeled 'nurse.' The button lit up and outside the room a soft bell chimed over and over.

Nichole grabbed Steven's hand and squeezed. "This is it. It's time."

Steven squeezed back. "I'll be right here with you. All the way." As he leaned over and kissed her, Nurse Miller and the obstetrician hurried into the room.

59

W hen Nichole gave birth to Luna, it took almost two hours of constant pushing and screaming.

This time was different.

The delivery was swift and far less painful. One moment she was bearing down and squeezing Steven's hand, and the next the doctor was cradling a crying baby.

A girl.

"You did it," Steven said to Nichole. He was grinning and there were tears in his eyes.

"No," Nichole said, her cheeks also wet with tears. "We did it."

They laughed together and shared a salty kiss.

The doctor handed Nichole the baby, bundled in a pink blanket. A new life placed in her hands... as shocking as losing one.

"She's so beautiful," Nichole whispered. She stroked one tiny hand and the newborn clutched her fingertip.

"Whoa," Steven said. "Look at that batter's grip."

Everyone laughed.

Steven extended a pinky and the infant grabbed on with her

other hand. "Look out," Steven said with a chuckle. "She's a switch hitter."

More laughter filled the delivery room as Steven and Nichole's eyes met. Steven whispered, "It's a girl, so, like we agreed, you get to choose her name. Do you have one?"

Nichole nodded hesitantly. "I do. I like Sophia. And for a middle name I was thinking, maybe... Luna. But, Steven, if you feel that's wrong, or weird, that's okay. We can pick another one."

Gazing down at their newborn baby girl, Steven uttered the entire name slowly. "Sophia... Luna... Burns." He paused to let it resonate, then turned to Nichole and smiled. "It's perfect."

60

I t was well after 3:00 AM when Steven was finally able to tear himself away from his wife and newborn and drive himself home. When he entered his front door he was exhausted, but instead of going straight to bed he plopped down on the sofa and turned on his MacBook Pro.

Sophia's delivery was Steven's entire world for hours, but during the drive home Nichole's earlier concerns about the Judge wormed their way back into his thoughts. Steven agreed refusing the money might make the Judge a bit uneasy, but he had trouble believing it would damage their agreement. Still, Nichole's seed of doubt had sprouted into an irresistible need to learn more about the Judge, if only to reinforce his confidence.

Every light in the house was off. Moonlight through curtains cast the living room in shadows.

Steven decided he'd simply google Judge Walker's background, but his laptop was taking an unusual amount of time to boot up. After several minutes the screen remained black, except for that annoying tiny spinning pinwheel. Those endlessly whirling fun colors seemed designed to mock the user's impatience.

From behind Steven came a low, raspy voice. "Some call that the pinwheel of death."

Steven jumped up and spun around, sending his computer crashing to the floor.

A man stood in his living room, just two steps away. Black windbreaker, black leather gloves, thick framed glasses, and stoic features chiseled by darkness.

Judge Walker said to Steven, "After I searched your hard drive I erased it to make sure I didn't miss anything."

Steven's heart hammered. Terrified and at the same time furious. "What the hell are you doing in my house?"

"You visited my home. So, I thought I'd return the gesture." Then the Judge slipped a silenced handgun from his jacket pocket.

"No," Steven gasped.

Instead of taking aim, the Judge held the gun down at his side and raised a gloved hand. "Calm, Mr. Burns. Stay calm. I'm not here to hurt you."

"Then why are you holding that gun?"

"I need to ask you a few... difficult questions. Once I get the answers I expect, my firearm becomes inconsequential."

"And if you don't?"

The Judge shook his head. "Don't go there. Think positive. I'm almost certain you're okay. I just need to be one hundred percent certain. Once we're done, you can go back to being a husband and a new dad." He cracked a slight smile. "Congratulations, by the way. Sophia's a lovely name."

Hearing the Judge utter his child's name made Steven bristle. He started to ask the Judge how he came by this knowledge, but suddenly remembered the Judge's hacking skills. Instead, Steven took a deep settling breath, then asked, "What are these questions? Why couldn't you ask me earlier?"

"You'll understand momentarily," the Judge said. "Now, I need you to turn around and walk to the bathroom."

"What? Why?"

The Judge adjusted his glasses and leveled an icy stare. "I'd rather not point the gun at you. Just do as I ask. Turn and walk to the bathroom. Please."

After a pause, Steven turned and started across the living room.

The Judge followed two paces back.

As Steven moved down a hallway decorated with family photos, he grappled for a reason the Judge would insist on moving to the bathroom. He couldn't think of anything that didn't involve violence.

When the Judge said he wouldn't hurt him, was that a lie?

Steven stopped outside the closed bathroom door. He and Nichole never left the bathroom door closed. That meant the Judge had previously visited the room, but for what reason?

Hesitantly, Steven reached for the doorknob.

"Wait."

Judge Walker, silenced handgun still gripped at his side, now stood just a step away from Steven in the narrow hallway. He went on, "Before you open that door, I want you to prepare yourself. What you'll see will frighten you, but don't jump to any conclusions. And don't make any sudden movements that will force me to use this." He waggled the handgun. "You must remain calm. Understand?"

Steven's mind raced. He couldn't imagine what the Judge could be hiding in the bathroom that would frighten him more than being held at gunpoint.

"Tell me you understand."

Steven nodded stiffly.

"Good. Now open it."

When Steven wrapped his hand around the cold doorknob

he could feel his pounding heart in the palm of his hand. He gave the knob a twist and pushed the door open.

First the smell hit him... then he saw what the Judge had waiting for him inside.

Steven held on tight to that doorknob to stop himself from trying to run.

New trash bag.

That's the smell that hit Steven the instant he pushed open the bathroom door. Like that pungent, chemical, plasticky waft of air that hits you when you snap open a fresh Hefty bag. And once the door was fully open, Steven understood why. The floor, walls, and ceiling were lined with clear plastic. Even the sink and toilet bowl were covered. Only one area remained untouched.

The bathtub.

With the shower curtain removed, the exposed porcelain tub lay cold and bare... like an open grave.

Suddenly Steven had difficulty breathing. The hallway seemed to be closing in on him. He whipped around in the doorway to face the Judge and found himself staring down the barrel of a silencer.

"Calm, Mr. Burns," the Judge said, peering over his pointed gun. "Don't jump to conclusions. Remember? The plastic drop cloth is merely a necessary precaution."

Steven struggled to keep his voice steady. "You mean... in case you don't like my answers?"

"Unfortunately, yes. But as I said, I'm confident you'll do fine. Now, please step into the tub."

Cold sweat prickled Steven's brow. "Please, you don't have to do this. You can trust me. I swear."

The Judge held Steven with what looked like sincere eyes. "If that's true you have absolutely nothing to worry about. You have my word. Okay?"

Steven wanted to believe him, but feared there'd be no questions to answer once he stepped into that tub... just a quick death. But what choice did he have?

Steven nodded. "Okay."

The Judge motioned to the tub with his gun. "Stand in the middle facing me."

Plastic crunched underfoot as Steven crossed to the tub and climbed in.

Only after Steven was positioned, as asked, did the Judge enter the bathroom. He stopped just inside the doorway, face to face with his prisoner, but well out of reach. If Steven tried to lunge, the obstacle of the tub and the distance between them would ensure failure. The Judge was also far enough away to avoid blood splatter.

Watching Judge Walker take this precaution made Steven's body go frigid.

He was now certain he was about to die.

Steven found confirmation in the Judge's eyes. All sincerity and reason had vanished, replaced by two black voids, like the soulless eyes of a mannequin.

Reading Steven's mind, the Judge frowned and said, "I'm truly sorry, but you brought this upon yourself."

"Why? Because I wouldn't take back the money?"

"Actually, I didn't care either way. I simply wanted you to leave believing we were still allies." The Judge shook his head slowly. "No, Mr. Burns, your mistake was following me home.

The moment you showed up at my door you were a dead man. It was just a matter of when."

If Steven thought yelling for help or pleading for his life might've helped, he would've tried. But he knew it was pointless. Instead his shoulders withered with the weight of numbing acceptance. As tears fell from his eyes, he asked, "What about Nichole? My family?"

"Well," the Judge said, his tone eerily casual. "I'd never harm the truly innocent, so Sophia will be fine. But who will ultimately raise her depends on you."

"What does that mean?" Steven snapped. "Nichole has nothing to do with this."

"For the sake of expediency I did lie about letting you live... but I do, in fact, need a question answered. If you refuse to answer this question I will kill you, then go kill your wife. Do you understand?"

No. Steven didn't understand, and he also didn't give a shit. He couldn't imagine a question he wouldn't answer to save his wife and the mother of his child. He said to the Judge, "I'll tell you whatever you want. What's the question?"

The Judge raised a gloved finger. "I warn you. Keep in mind my particular... gift. I cannot be lied to."

Steven faltered. He'd forgotten the Judge's bizarre claim. But now, knowing a career of sorting lies from truth inside a courtroom backed up that claim, made it all too believable. But what did it matter? Why would Steven take stupid chances... especially with Nichole's life on the line.

"I won't lie," Steven said. "I'll do anything you say. Just please leave my family alone."

"Good," the Judge said as he took a single step closer to the tub.

To Steven the rustling plastic was deafening.

Judge Walker adjusted his glasses, fixed on Steven's eyes, then asked his question.

"Did you tell your wife about my family?"

Steven fought back instant panic. It was as if the Judge had reached into his chest, grabbed his heart, and squeezed. The question was impossible to answer. If he told the truth the Judge would kill Nichole. If he lied, the Judge would know and the result would be the same. Time stretched as Steven struggled to conceal any physical sign of his rising horror. He was too afraid to even blink.

Calm. Stay calm.

Steven had no choice. To save Nichole's life he'd have to lie... and somehow make the Judge believe that lie. But how? Then it struck him.

I have to believe the lie... is the truth.

If I believe... he'll believe.

Just stay calm... and tell him the truth.

Only milliseconds had passed when Steven shook his head and said to the Judge, "No. Nichole was busy giving birth. I didn't tell her anything."

The Judge stared at him. Head to toe. Reading him.

Steven stared back. Resolute. Assured. As calm as can be expected for a man who's about to die.

The Judge's eyes narrowed. "Well... this is a first. I can't tell if you're lying or not."

Judge Walker then aimed his gun at Steven and fired.

S teven collapsed to his knees, wailing in pain. He clenched the deep gash in his right thigh. Warm blood oozed through his fingers and splattered the tub.

Splotches of crimson glistened against white porcelain.

"Look at me," the Judge said. He now stood directly over the tub, gun aimed point-blank at Steven's skull. "I'm not heartless, Mr. Burns. I would prefer to spare your wife. So let's try one last time." He pressed the gun barrel against Steven's forehead. "Did you tell your wife about my family?"

Steven's right leg felt as if it were on fire. Trembling, he struggled to focus.

Stay calm.

Believe.

Steven glared the Judge. "I already fucking told you. Nichole doesn't know anything. Now leave her the fuck alone!"

The Judge didn't react... he just studied Steven with unreadable eyes.

"Come on, Sophia. We can do this."

Sophia wailed and squirmed as Nichole tried with growing frustration to get her newborn to latch on to her nipple.

It was just after 3 AM. The hospital room was dark, lit only by ambient light from life monitors. Nichole was sitting-up in bed, maternity gown open to expose one breast, with Sophia held in a cross-cradle position.

Nichole rubbed her nipple against the infant's upper lip, exactly as Nurse Miller had instructed, but over and over again Sophia refused the invitation. Instead, she preferred to suckle her tiny fist or simply turn away.

Seeing Sophia grow more and more agitated, Nichole finally gave in. She closed her gown, then found the remote and pressed the call button.

Nichole's eyes pooled as Sophia kicked and screamed in her arms. She knew breastfeeding could be a challenge, even for second-time moms. Still, she couldn't help feeling she had somehow failed her child.

As Sophia's cries of hunger began to escalate, Nichole thought it odd a nurse still hadn't responded.

She pressed the call button again.

Usually, one press was all it took to get a nurse to her bedside in under two minutes. When there was still no response after her second attempt, Nichole knew something was wrong. Maybe an emergency involving another patient, or hopefully something less dramatic, like a glitch in the call system.

As Sophia continued to cry, Nichole gently laid her in the bedside bassinet and tucked her beneath a pink blanket.

"Shhhhh. Mommy will be right back."

Nichole stepped into a pair of disposable slippers, then padded to the door. After a glance back at her baby, she exited the room.

Where was everyone?

The maternity ward's open foyer appeared deserted, and was oddly quiet. Only Sophia's faint cries, muffled by the room's door, could he heard.

In an emergency there'd be a rush of medical personnel, but every patient room encompassing the ward was closed, and showed no sign of activity.

"Hello? Anyone here?"

Brow furrowed, Nichole started slowly down the hall. She cocked an ear toward each patient room she passed, but heard nothing but her own padded footfalls.

Reaching the nurses' station, she was greeted by a vacant reception counter. Computer monitors flickered before empty swivel chairs. A steaming cup of tea, but no one to drink it.

What the hell is going on?

A flashing red light on a wall panel caught Nichole's eye. The panel consisted of room numbers, like an intercom directory.

The red light flashed beside number II.

Nichole's room.

Seeing that light blink futilely caused the hairs on the back of her neck to stir. Suddenly all she could think about was her baby, alone in that room.

That's when Nichole noticed a strange sound.

A sound that made her breathing seize.

Silence.

Sophia's faint wailing had stopped.

Nichole hurried back down the hall, and pushed into her room. She crossed straight to the bassinet, and froze.

Sophia was gone.

Behind Nichole, a male voice whispered. "There's Momma."

Nichole spun.

A man was seated on the sofa, gently rocking a cooing Sophia in his arms. He was mostly obscured by shadow, but in the faint light Nichole could see he wore glasses.

"Who are you?" Nichole said. "Give me my baby!"

The man raised a gloved hand. "Calm, Mrs. Burns. Please remain calm."

64

Nichole glared at the stranger who continued to gently rock Sophia in his arms. "Don't tell me to be calm," she said. "Give her to me, right now!"

"Sorry," he whispered. "But I really can't."

"What do you mean 'you can't?'"

A voice behind Nichole answered. "He's right. We never hand newborns to a distraught or upset parent. Strict hospital rule."

Nichole sighed when she turned and saw Nurse Miller enter the room. "There you are," Nichole said. "I had trouble nursing so I pushed the button, but no one answered. I went out to the nurses' station and no one was there. Then I come back in here and see some strange man holding my baby."

Nurse Miller smiled. "Benny's a little unusual, that's true. But only because he has the magic touch when it comes to babies... as you can see." She gestured to Benny who was busy entertaining Sophia with goofy faces. To Benny, she said, "It's dark in here. Get up so Mrs. Burns can see you."

Carefully cradling Sophia, Benny rose into better light.

Now Nichole could see Benny wore blue scrubs and a nametag that played peek-a-boo behind the bouncing baby.

BENNY MASON, RN

Benny frowned at Nichole. "Sorry if I frightened you, Mrs. Burns."

"I should apologize as well," Nurse Miller said to Nichole. "We're short staffed tonight. In fact, Benny volunteered to come in from his vacation to help out."

"Good thing I did," Benny said, gazing down at Sophia. "Because I got to meet this little princess."

Sophia cooed happily as if she understood every word, causing everyone to chuckle.

Benny said to Nichole, "You have a very beautiful baby." Then he passed Sophia to her mother.

The instant Nichole pulled Sophia into her arms, the infant began to wail.

Nurse Miller shook her head. "Told you Benny had the magic touch. You know, I have a silly idea that usually helps while nursing."

"Please tell me," Nichole said while bouncing her crying infant. "I'll try anything."

"Tell me... how's your singing voice?"

65

W hen Steven regained consciousness the first thing he noticed was that he was seated in a chair... and immobilized.

Then he peeled open his eyes.

What he saw caused his heart to pound. He tried to cry out but the ball gag and duct tape blocking his mouth reduced the effort to a feeble groan. He jerked and yanked at the leather straps that bound his wrists, ankles, and forehead to the steel chair, but they were too tight.

The windowless storage room was exactly as he remembered. The stark bluish glow of an LED camping lantern the only light. Dust-caked steel shelves, boxes, and miscellaneous debris crammed into every corner. A dank, musky odor so thick he could almost taste it.

And Steven especially remembered that table.

Two paces from where he sat stood a long table draped with a thick tarp. Beneath the tarp, five bulges of various sizes. As Steven tried to make out the deadly shapes beneath the tarp, his heart raced faster.

What about Nichole?

The last thing Steven remembered was the Judge saying, "I believe you," then jabbing a hypodermic into his neck and the world spinning into darkness. Was Nichole okay? He couldn't be sure. He could only hope the Judge kept his word.

Pulsing pain in his right thigh bloomed into consciousness. He strained against the head strap to peer down at his leg and was surprised to see... nothing. No gash in his thigh where the Judge's bullet grazed him; no blood, not even a rip in his pants. Mind still fuzzy, it took a moment before he put it together.

He cleaned me up.

The jeans and polo shirt Steven wore earlier had been replaced by blue khakis and a button-down shirt. And despite the constant pain, he could now distinguish the tightness of bandages around the deep gash in his thigh. While Steven was unconscious the Judge did more than abduct him and strap him into his private execution chair... he also took the time to dress Steven's wound and change his clothing.

He dressed me for the fucking part.

Steven grunted as he jerked and yanked at his restraints. The leather strap around his left wrist felt looser than the right, but just barely. Fueled by hope, he curled his left hand and pulled hard, straining to slip free. But his hand was slightly too big. The edge of the thick strap bit into the fleshy base of his thumb, sending a spike of pain up his left forearm. Steven winced as he tugged on his hand even harder.

The far-off creak of an opening door froze him.

Then he heard approaching footsteps. Two people.

Steven's gaze shot across the room to the steel door. His mouth went dry as the footsteps drew closer and closer, until they paused just outside the room.

A voice, muffled by the door, said, "I'm going to remove the hood now."

Steven immediately recognized that cold, raspy timbre.

A instance of silence followed, then the Judge's voice returned. "Once I open this door there's no turning back. Do you understand?"

Steven could hear his heart thrumming and feel his pulse pushing against the straps around his limbs.

A new voice responded to the Judge. A deeper voice, edged with anger. "Are you kidding? I can't wait to get my hands on this motherfucker. Open it."

Seized by panic, Steven yanked and pulled and bucked in the steel chair like a trapped animal. Only when he heard the mournful squeal of the door swinging open did he finally wither.

Panting and helpless, Steven watched Judge Walker usher his latest client into the room.

66

Steven had never seen so much anger in a human being's eyes. He wondered if that's how he looked three years ago when he first stood face-to-face with the man he believed to be Luna's killer.

The client loomed just two steps away from the steel chair that held Steven prisoner, glaring, with both hands clenched into huge fists. He was big. Easily over six feet tall with the soft, bulky build of a retired linebacker. His graying, short-cropped beard, combined with the faded tattoos peeking beneath his shirt, put him in his fifties.

Judge Walker stood beside the client, his bespectacled eyes also fixed on Steven. His features impossibly expressionless, as if staring at a stranger, not the man he's conspired to murder.

The client took one step forward and said to Steven, "Do you know who I am?" His bass voice cracked with emotion and rage. "You carjacked my wife. Killed the mother of my kids for a Goddamed Lexus. What kind of fucking animal does that?"

Steven struggled against his restraints to shake his head and shout his innocence, but only managed spastic writhing and unintelligible grunts.

The display only increased the client's anger. Never taking his eyes off Steven, he said to the Judge, "What the fuck is he saying? You have to remove that gag."

"Out of the question," the Judge said, waving a gloved hand. "I told you my rules. Besides, it won't go the way you imagine. He'll say anything to save himself."

"That's exactly what I want," the client said, eyes still drilling into Steven. "I want to hear him beg for his fucking life." He turned to face the Judge. "Fuck it. I'll pay more. How much?"

The Judge sighed. "We're wasting time." He moved to the long table and snatched away the drop cloth.

The client's eyes widened. "Shit!"

The obsessively neat display of four lethal weapons, one of which might be the instrument of his murder, caused Steven's stomach to tumble. Three of the items, a large hunting knife, a 9mm handgun, and a handmade garrote, matched the selection offered Steven three years ago. The last item, a three-foot section of pipe lacked the balanced heft of a Louisville Slugger, but the crude weapon could do just as much damage to a man's skull.

Trembling with tension, Steven watched the Judge describe each weapon to the client. The Judge's words and patter were eerily identical to Steven's memory of this moment, as if the Judge had recited this speech hundreds of times.

Once the Judge concluded, he stepped back from the table, rested a hand on the Glock 38 tucked in his belt, then gestured for the client to make his choice.

The big man wasted no time picking up the hunting knife. He adjusted his grip on the handle and tested the blade's weight, then pivoted back to face Steven.

Steven's hands went ice cold when he saw the expression on the client's face... a slight, eager smile of anticipation.

"I suggest you act quickly," the Judge said to the client. "It's best not to overthink it."

The client snorted. "Don't worry about me. I'm going to carve this fucker up, nice and slow." He closed the space between him and Steven and pressed the knife to Steven's throat.

Steven's breathing seized as the blade's razor-sharp edge bit into his skin. Warmth trickled down his neck. The client leaned in so close that Steven could feel his breath as he spoke.

"How's it feel fucker? How's it feel to know you're about to die?"

Steven moaned and strained to shake his head. He winced when the blade suddenly bit deeper.

"What's that?" the client growled. "What the fuck are you saying?"

Steven struggled to mouth the words "It wasn't me" but produced only grunts and drool.

"Fuck this!" With swift brutality, the client used the knife to sever the duct tape and ball gag, then ripped them from Steven's mouth. As Steven hollered in pain the client jammed the blade back to his throat. "Talk," he said. "Beg me for your fucking life."

The Judge was already rushing forward, so Steven had only seconds to act. He scrambled to think of what to say that would expose the Judge and stop the client from killing him.

Suddenly, Steven was struck with an answer so obvious and perfect that it was almost guaranteed to get a reaction.

Ignoring the stiffness in his jaw, Steven met the client's eyes and uttered three words... "He's a Judge."

"SHUT UP!" Judge Walker clubbed Steven's temple with his handgun.

Blinding pain and jarring disorientation dragged Steven toward darkness. Fighting to remain conscious, he blinked his eyes open in time to see the client square off with the Judge.

Pointing the hunting knife, the client said, "You're a Judge? What the fuck is he talking about?"

The Judge sighed and leveled his gun on the client. "Listen

carefully. I need you to calm down and place that knife back on the table, then I'll explain."

"Explain? What the fuck is there to explain?"

"I warned you about this, remember? He'd say anything to save himself. Anything."

The client's eyes narrowed. "But why say that? Why not say you're a cop or even a fed? Saying you're a Judge makes no fucking sense, unless..."

The Judge frowned. "Be smart. There's still a chance to get back to the business at hand. Just put down the knife and allow me to explain."

The client glanced around the room. "What's really going on here? Is this some sort of set up?"

Judge Walker took his time adjusting his glasses, then stared at the man in silence.

"Don't just fucking stand there. Say something."

The Judge shrugged. "What's the point?"

Steven flinched as Judge Walker fired three perfectly grouped shots into the client's heart.

The big man was dead before he hit the floor. Blood began to pool beneath the body.

The Judge shook his head at the corpse, then frowned at Steven. "That's your fault... not mine. And rather pointless considering there was no way for him to save you." Then the Judge raised his gun and aimed point blank at Steven's chest.

Steven stiffened in the steel chair. His heart pounded in his throat. It took every ounce of will to lift his terrified eyes from the gun barrel, and meet the Judge's soulless stare. Steven swallowed into a dry throat, then with quivering voice asked, "Is she okay? Please... tell me she's okay."

Annoyance flashed across the Judge's face. "Mr. Burns, you should know by now that I am a man of my word. Your wife's fine."

Steven exhaled.

The Judge cocked the slide of his Glock 38. "Time to finish this."

Steven took a deep, settling breath, then shut his eyes.

Instead of a gunshot, the tense silence was shattered by the muffled ring of a cell phone.

Steven recognized the shrill ringtone instantly.

That's my phone. But how?

He snapped open his eyes.

The Judge was no longer pointing his gun. He was crossing toward the source of the ringing, a small pile of clothing strewn on the floor in a gloomy corner of the room.

Steven recognized the jeans and polo shirt as his own. The Judge must've dressed him here, not at the house.

He watched the Judge free the still-ringing cell phone from the jeans' back pocket. Face now lit by the phone's ghostly glow, Judge Walker studied the screen for a heartbeat, then turned to Steven and said, "Your wife certainly has interesting timing."

With a gasp, Steven straightened up in the steel chair. He already knew the Judge's answer but if there was any chance at all, he had to ask. "Let me talk to her. Let me say goodbye. Please."

The Judge frowned, tapped the screen, and the ringing stopped.

Steven withered as utter hopelessness rushed back.

The Judge gestured to the corpse on the floor. "Just three words from you forced me to do that. Talking to your wife would've been a mistake. I did you a favor."

As much as it twisted Steven's insides, he knew the Judge was right. In his desperate state, he could easily blurt out the wrong thing to Nichole, giving the Judge a reason to go back on his word and--

A single, harmonic chime lit up Steven's cell phone, drawing the Judge's attention back to the screen.

Instantly recognizing the alert, Steven perked up again. "Please," he pleaded with the Judge. "Just give me this one thing. Please."

For an agonizing moment Judge Walker just stared at him. Finally the Judge shrugged and said, "I fail to see how it could hurt. After all... it's just a voicemail."

67

H ey. It's just a little after six so you're probably still asleep. At least one of us is getting some rest. Sophia likes her milk every two hours on the dot. She's like a little alarm clock. Steven, she's so beautiful. I called to remind you to bring my slippers. I think they're in the bathroom. If not, check under the bed. And my lotion. You know, that pink bottle by the sink. We can't wait to see you. Although visiting hours start at nine, dadas can visit anytime. You do know that, right? Okay, that's it.

Judge Walker stood adjacent to the steel chair, cell phone held high so Steven could clearly hear Nichole's message. As the Judge reached to turn off the phone, the voicemail suddenly continued.

Wait. One more thing. I thought about it and changed my mind. You did the right thing. Accepting money from that creep would've been a mistake. Love you. Bye.

The recording died.

The Judge seemed to move in slow motion as he looked up from the phone and leveled baffled eyes on Steven. "You lied to me?"

Steven broke into a sweat and his entire body began to tremble. "No... Please..."

The Judge cracked the faintest smile. "You did. You lied... and you actually had me fooled. Amazing." Then he dropped the cell phone and crushed it with a single stomp.

"She doesn't know anything," Steven's voice cracked with rising panic. "Not enough to help the police. I swear."

The Judge nodded. "You're probably right. But I can't risk it. Sorry."

Steven watched with widening eyes as the Judge moved to the long table and picked up the garrote. "NO!" Steven cried, writing and yanking at his restraints. "YOU CAN'T! NO!"

"Believe me, Mr. Burns, I'd prefer to make it quick for her, but I can't risk gunfire in a hospital, now can I?" The Judge slipped the crude weapon into his jacket pocket as he crossed back to the steel chair.

Steven pinned the Judge with pleading eyes. "Don't do this. I'm begging you."

The Judge frowned. "I also don't enjoy leaving you here to imagine the worst, but I don't have a choice. If something goes wrong, I'll need you to help me get to your wife later." He sighed. "So, this is where we are."

"Nooo..." Tears streamed down Steven's face. "There has to be a another way. I'll do anything. Money. Whatever you want. Please, please..."

"Calm," the Judge said, raising a hand. "I'm going to help you." Then he pulled the gun from his waist and hammered the butt against Steven's temple.

Steven saw flashes of white light... then the world went black.

68

A throbbing migraine wrenched Steven from unconsciousness.

Blurred shapes and shadows greeted him.

He blinked to clear his vision and wincing pain spiked his left temple. The side of his face felt tacky and he could taste blood in the corner of his mouth.

When Steven tried to move and couldn't, everything came rushing back.

"Nichole!"

He blinked again and again, until finally bringing the room into soft focus. He saw the body on the floor, the hunting knife beside it, his crushed cell phone, and across from him, the long weapons table. He froze on the empty spot once occupied by the garrote.

"NO!"

Steven strained against the head strap to look toward the door. "STOP!" He cried out. "COME BACK!"

Then it struck him. How long had he been unconscious? One minute? An hour? Two? The room was windowless, so he had no way of even guessing.

She could already be dead.

"No, no, no..."

Steven's eyes darted, searching for anything that might indicate how long he'd been unconscious. When his gaze settled on the client's corpse he felt a jolt of hope. The blood pooling beneath the body had slowed... but was still steadily expanding. Either he learned it in biology class, or from some cop show, but Steven felt certain dead bodies didn't bleed out for very long. Five, maybe ten minutes tops.

There's still time.

Three years ago, when Steven was foolish enough to climb into Judge Walker's trunk, the Judge assured him the ride would take forty-two minutes. Steven didn't know the accuracy of that information, but his memory of that terrifying night told him it was close enough. If the drive to the hospital in Flintridge was truly about forty-two minutes long, and Steven was only unconscious for less than ten, that meant he still had about a half hour to get to a phone and warn Nichole.

But first he had to free himself from this fucking chair.

Steven tugged at the leather straps restraining his wrists. The left strap still felt looser than the right. Good. If the Judge had checked the straps before leaving, Steven's only chance of escape might have been discovered.

Steven curled his left hand, drew a deep breath... then pulled as hard as he could.

The leather strap dug into the base of his thumb, and refused to slip over.

Somehow, Steven pulled harder. He groaned through clenched teeth as the skin around his wrist peeled forward, exposing raw white flesh.

"FUUUCK!"

Panting, Steven relaxed his arm. Blood oozed, staining the

leather strap and dripping down the arm of the chair. The pain in his hand throbbed in rhythm with his pounding heart.

Steven glared at the strap that held his left wrist as if his stare alone could burn it to ashes.

Nichole will not die because of a fucking piece of leather.

Steven took another deep breath, squeezed his eyes tight, then yanked his hand back with all the strength he had left. He pulled, and pulled, and pulled, and-

Suddenly his hand squirted free from the strap with a dull, meaty pop.

Bright pain shot up Steven's left arm, causing him to unleash a guttural scream.

When Steven finally opened his eyes, he stared at his trembling, blood-soaked, left hand. His thumb, probably broken, was already swollen to twice its normal size. The pain was unrelenting, as if his hand were being squeezed in a spiked vice. This was more than a match for the constant, stabbing pain in his head.

Steven didn't have time to give a shit.

Grimacing in agony, he reached over and began unbuckling the strap that secured his right hand.

69

W hile Sophia slept in the attached bassinet, Nichole was propped up in her hospital bed, eating scrambled eggs and watching Good Morning America. The news piece was a riveting update on the Forty Acres conspiracy. A year ago, when the story broke about the exposure of a secret society of wealthy black men who kept white slaves, it was headline news for weeks. And, like everyone else in the nation, Steven and Nichole became obsessed with the unbelievable details. They'd even gotten into a few lively racial discussions with Linton and Sharon. These discussions were always friendly, but the level of hateful discourse the conspiracy sparked across the country stunned Nichole. She'd probably never see it, but she hoped Sophia might someday live in a world when people weren't so Goddamn stupid.

As if roused by her mother's thoughts, Sophia began to stir, then erupted into a full throated scream.

"Uh, oh," Nichole said with a chuckle. "Somebody's ready for her breakfast."

As Nichole pushed aside the food tray and reached for the

wailing infant, behind her the door opened and Nurse Miller peeked in. "Everything okay in here?"

Nichole didn't respond; instead she began to sing. Gazing into Sophia's eyes, in a low, soothing tone, Nichole sang the nursery rhyme, Five Little Monkeys.

Entranced by her mother's voice, Sophia's crying subsided.

Nichole continued the song as she began to slowly unbutton the nursing flap at the top of her gown.

Still observing from the doorway, Nurse Miller smiled warmly then exited and shut the door behind her.

70

S teven unbuckled the last leather strap from his left ankle. Every joint aching, he slowly lifted himself from the steel chair. Trembling legs gave out and he went sprawling forward. He landed hard atop the corpse and splashed the pool of blood.

"SHIT!"

Careful not to put weight on his injured left hand, Steven staggered to his feet. He swiped splotches of blood from his face and clothing as he stepped over the corpse and stumbled toward the door. A coppery smell invaded his nostrils. His good hand was now red and sticky.

He felt a jolt of panic as he reached for the rusted doorknob.

What if it's locked?

But the knob turned with a squeak and the door creaked open.

Steven flung himself through the doorway into a narrow hall. Corroded pipes. Peeling walls. That thick, dank smell. LED nook lights on the floor lit the way to a stairway at the far end. Exactly as he remembered from three years ago.

Bracing against the wall with his good hand, Steven pushed

himself down the hall. His limbs grew looser with each step. He moved faster and faster.

The short flight of railless, crumbling, wooden stairs rose to a closed door.

As Steven carefully made his way up, he remembered the creaking and lopsided feel underfoot. He felt another jolt of panic when he paused at the top of the stairs and reached for the doorknob.

The knob wouldn't turn.

"No. Please." He took a breath to calm himself. He reset his sticky grip and twisted harder.

The knob turned with a stiff, grinding crunch and the door squealed open.

Steven stepped into a windowless, three bay garage coated with dust and cobwebs. Shredded tires and rusted auto parts lined the walls. Daylight squeezed in beneath three closed, rolling steel gates. A weathered door that also leaked daylight hid in the far left corner, but it was sealed by a fat padlock.

Steven's ears pricked up at the faint drone of traffic through the closed gates. That meant the highway was close. If his estimation was right, and it had to be, the Judge wouldn't reach Nichole's hospital for another twenty minutes. He should have plenty of time to run to the highway and flag down a car.

The three vehicle bays were empty, but the grimy floor of the center bay was scored by fresh tire tracks.

The way out.

Steven started fast toward the center gate, but something he spotted caused him to freeze.

It was leaned against the base of a steel pillar. A faded cardboard sign about the size of a movie poster. All four corners were missing, undoubtedly the result of being ripped down from a wall. In big bold letters the sign read:

DANGER. MICROBIAL HAZARD. DO NOT ENTER

SCHOOL BUILDING BY ORDER OF THE HEALTH DEPARTMENT.

It wasn't the danger of inhaling toxic mold that got Steven's heart racing. It was the fact that he'd seen a sign just like that before.

School building?

"What the hell?"

Steven rushed to the rusted chain dangling beside the center gate, grabbed on with just his right hand... and pulled. He pulled, and pulled, and pulled as fast as he could.

The rolling steel door squeaked and rattled as it rose, slow and steady. As the gap between the gate and the floor widened, the traffic noise became layered with street sounds. Car horns. Squealing brakes. Barking dogs. Distant voices.

Steven pulled faster.

When the opening reached his waist, he ducked low and slipped out beneath the gate.

Squinting against daylight, Steven jogged up a short ramp and stopped to take in his surroundings.

He lied.

Steven stood on the grounds of Sunset Canyon Elementary, the school Luna used to attend before the mold infestation was discovered. Behind him loomed the boarded-up school building, plastered with warning posters, like the one he found in the garage. Directly ahead, a sprawling, neglected schoolyard encompassed by an overgrown wrought iron fence. And beyond the fence... bustling downtown Flintridge. Buildings, cars, buses, pedestrians.

We never left the city.

The night of the trunk ride, the Judge drove around for the better part of an hour just to confuse him.

Steven sagged with relief. The hospital was just fifteen minutes away. He could easily reach Nichole in time to-

Suddenly his eyes widened and his breathing seized.

The judge could already be there.

Steven exploded into a run.

71

When Emily Hyland began working at the reception desk at Hamilton Memorial ten years ago, the people she typically saw wearing surgical face mask were never doctors. They were always Asian patients, mostly from Japan, but also from other Asian countries. Emily came to learn that in East Asia it's customary for the ill to wear face masks as a courtesy to their fellow citizens.

A few years ago, Emily noticed this neighborly practice had become more widespread, at least in Los Angeles. Now, seeing a non-Asian wearing a surgical mask in public wouldn't make her look twice. It was for this reason that, when a sixtyish Caucasian man carrying an armful of flowers approached her reception desk, the black leather gloves he wore were more conspicuous than the white surgical mask concealing his face.

Brushing aside dirty blonde bangs, Emily greeted him with a professional smile. "Good morning. May I help you?"

The older man smiled slightly beneath the mask. "Good morning. Delivery for a patient. A Mrs. Nichole Burns."

"Wow, I see," Emily said, gawking at the large white and pink bouquet of roses, lilies, carnations, and daisies. "They're beautiful. Somebody's about to wake up to a nice surprise."

The delivery man paused to adjust his glasses then said, "Yes. And as I told you her name is Nichole Burns. I believe she's in the maternity ward."

There was something about the man's energy and deep, scratchy voice that troubled Emily. If she hadn't known he was getting over an illness, she'd think he was a little creepy. Tapping computer keys, she checked the database and found the patient's room number. When she looked up from the computer he was eyeing the security camera over her desk.

Yup, creepy.

Once again, Emily put on her cheery receptionist's smile. "You're right," she said. "Mrs. Burns is in maternity. Room LDR11. Need directions?"

"I can find it. You've been very helpful. Thank you."

Emily stared as the man in the surgical mask strode toward the elevators, his huge, black gloved hands gripping those beautiful flowers. To Emily it almost looked as if he were strangling the poor things.

72

"Could I use your phone for a minute, please. It's an emergency."

The business woman scowled at Steven's battered appearance as she sidestepped him and kept walking.

Steven was now across the street from the shuttered school, on a busy shop-lined sidewalk, drawing stares as he scrambled to intercept early rush hour pedestrians.

He caught up to a woman pushing a stroller. "Miss, could I borrow your-"

"I don't have any money," the woman said, picking up speed.

Steven kept on her heels. "Wait. I just need to borrow your phone. Please. My wife's in danger and--"

"I'm in a rush. I really can't. Sorry." Then she wheeled the stroller away around a corner.

Steven jumped into the path of a portly man texting on his cell phone. "Sir, please listen--

"Fuck off," the man barked, never looking up or breaking stride. As he pushed past Steven he swiped Steven's now swollen and discolored left hand.

Steven winced and drew a sharp breath. He spotted a FedEx

driver exiting a store. Cradling his throbbing hand, he rushed over and said to the driver, "You have to help me, please."

"Jesus," the driver said, gaping at Steven's bloodied clothes. "What happened to you?"

"Forget about me. I'm fine. I need to borrow your phone. Please."

The driver shook his head. "All I carry is my job phone. No personal calls allowed. Sorry."

The driver made to walk away but Steven grabbed his arm. "This is an emergency. I'm sure they'll understand. It'll just take--"

"Okay, okay. Easy." But as the driver reached for his phone a stern voice boomed behind them.

"Sir, is there some sort of problem?"

Steven turned and sighed when he spotted a uniformed police officer standing near the curb. He was young and fit, and looked more like a soldier than a cop. His name tag read Slater.

"Thank God," Steven said rushing toward the officer. "You have to call--"

"Stop right there," Officer Slater said, extending a stiff hand. He placed his other hand purposely on his sidearm.

Steven froze about three paces from the officer. "Sorry. I just need help. My wife's--"

"Now, slowly raise your hands over your head."

Steven's brow fell. "Why? I didn't do anything."

Officer Slater unholstered his weapon, but kept it at his side. "Sir, please obey my instructions. Slowly raise your hands above your head."

Steven glared. "No. You're wasting time. My wife's--"

Slater raised his gun and aimed at Steven. "Sir, I'm not going to tell you again. Stop resisting and put your hands up. Now."

"Just do it," came a voice from the small crowd that had gathered on the sidewalk. "Do what he says," murmured another.

"Okay, okay," Steven said to the officer as he raised his hands. "Now will you listen? There's a man on his way right now to kill my wife. Look, just call Detective Adeel Ahmad and--"

"Shut up," Officer Slater snapped. "Stop talking, keep your hands up, and get down on your knees."

Steven recoiled. "What? Did you even hear what I said?"

Gun still pointed, Slater took a step closer. "I said get down on your fucking knees."

Steven didn't budge. Instead, he countered the officer's raging eyes with a determined stare. Slowly he lowered his hands and said, "Shoot me. Go on. Do it."

Officer Slater blinked. "What?"

"I'm trying to save my wife's life," Steven said through gritted teeth. "Now either help me, or shoot me. Just please do something fast... BECAUSE YOU'RE WASTING FUCKING TIME!"

73

W hile her small but dedicated staff tackled the challenges particular to mornings in a maternity ward, Nurse Miller sat behind the nurses' station reviewing patient charts.

Hospital policy required each nurse to submit detailed updates on each of their assigned patients every four hours. Nurse Miller's least favorite part of being a supervisor was hounding nurses with screaming newborns in their arms to complete their documentation. But the assessments had to be entered, and they had to be right. A patient's life could depend on it.

Nurse Miller spotted the newest and youngest member of her staff passing the nurses' station. She waved her over. "Tonya, may I speak to you a moment?"

Tonya stepped behind the counter wearing a guilty frown. "My documentation's late. I know. Sorry. I'll catch up, I promise."

Nurse Miller smiled. "Good. Also, be aware that Mrs. Clarke is being discharged today, so--"

Nurse Miller sniffed the air. "Do you smell flowers?"

They both turned and saw a man wearing a surgical mask walking past the counter with an armful of beautiful flowers.

"Excuse me," Nurse Miller said. "May I help you?"

The man paused. "Hi. Just making a delivery."

"That's fine. You can just leave those with us."

The man smiled politely beneath his mask. "If you don't mind... I'd rather not. These are pretty pricey, and my boss is a real jerk."

Tonya chuckled.

Nurse Miller asked, "What room?"

The man checked the tag on the flowers. "LDR-11. Nichole Burns?"

Nurse Miller nodded. "She's awake. Just knock first, okay?"

"Sure thing. Thank you."

Nurse Miller and Tonya watched the delivery man continue down the hall.

"Beautiful flowers," Nurse Miller said.

Tonya made a face. "Yeah, but what's with those ugly gloves?"

74

"Three little monkeys jumping on the bed. One fell off and broke his head. Momma called the doctor and the doctor said. No more monkeys jumping on the bed."

As Nichole sang softly she watched her newborn baby girl suckle her nipple. Her little eyes, closed. Her tiny hands cupping mommy's breast. Her rosy cheeks rising and falling with a soft squish, squish. So peaceful... and perfect.

Nichole stroked Sophia's downy hair as she began the next verse.

"Two little monkeys jumping on the bed, one fell off and bumped his head. Mama called the doctor and the doctor said--"

"Sorry," a raspy voice whispered in Nichole's ear.

She gasped.

Black gloved hands flashed her field of view. Then there was a sharp tightness around her throat.

Nichole wheezed for air.

Something thin and cold clamped tighter and tighter against her windpipe.

She couldn't breathe.

Wild panic seized Nichole. It took all she had to resist grabbing for the thing around her throat... but she couldn't drop Sophia.

Ignoring the brutal yanking and tugging at her neck, ignoring her burning lungs... Nichole reached out with trembling hands and gently lowered her baby into the attached bassinet.

The instant she left her mother's hands Sophia burst into screams.

Gagging for air, Nichole reached up and clawed at the wire, but it was too tight. Impossible to work her fingers under.

"Don't fight it," the voice in her ear hissed.

But fueled by Sophia's screams, Nichole kicked, and flailed, and writhed, and bucked...

"I said stop fighting." There was a grunt and the wire jerked tighter.

Nichole whimpered. Spittle flowed from the corners of her mouth. Tears rolled from her bulging eyes.

Another violent jerk of the wire and blood trailed down Nichole's neck.

She began to feel light. The room wavered. Colors muted. Consciousness slipping, her arms fell to her side and her body began to sag.

"That's it," the voice whispered. "Just let go."

Then Nichole heard a voice.

Beneath Sophia's wailing... a faraway, familiar voice called her name.

"Mrs. Burns, the police just called and-- OH MY GOD!"

Suddenly the wire around Nichole's throat was gone and she was flung forward. She slammed to the cold floor gasping to fill her lungs. She blinked her eyes open and saw a terrified Nurse Miller backpedaling to the door... and flowers everywhere.

White and pink flowers were strewn across the floor.

Nichole heard a sharp burst of air. Nurse Miller's head

snapped back and she crumbled to the floor upon bloodstained pink roses.

"NO!" Nichole gasped.

Then she saw him. A man wearing a surgical mask and black gloves, gripping a silenced handgun.

Nichole watched him trample flowers as he stepped over Nurse Miller's body, moved to the door, and peeked out.

Leave, leave, leave.

Nichole's soul sank when, instead of leaving, the man quietly shut the door and locked it.

Sophia's crying intensified, as if she could feel her mother's terror.

The screams of her child hardened Nichole's eyes. She scrambled to her feet, snatched Sophia from the bassinet, and bolted toward the bathroom. Bullets hissed past her ears, stinging walls and shattering equipment. Nichole threw herself into the bathroom, slammed the door behind her, locked it, then dropped to the floor and shielded Sophia with her body.

Bullets pierced the wooden door in rapid succession. Then abruptly the shooting stopped.

Dusted with splinters, Nichole listened intently for retreating footsteps or the sound of a gun being reloaded, but could hear nothing over Sophia's screams and the pounding of her own heart.

75

The sight of so many flashing emergency lights filled Steven with hope, but at the same time paralyzed him with dread.

He sat in the rear of Officer Slater's cruiser as it sped across Hamilton Memorial's parking lot and braked behind the swarm of police vehicles parked out front. Uniformed officers, their weapons out, took cover behind cruisers, while more officers manned barricades at the hospital's exits. Overhead, a police helicopter flew a low search pattern.

Officer Slater killed the engine and glanced back at Steven through the steel mesh barrier. "Sit tight while I--"

"Are you crazy?" Steven said. "My family's in there. I can't just sit here." But when Steven tried to open the back door, the handle wouldn't budge. "Unlock it," he demanded. "Let me out of here."

"Can't do that, sir. You're under arrest, remember? And if you don't settle down, broken hand or no, I'll throw the cuffs on you."

Steven took a calming breath. "Look, I have to know what happened to my wife and baby. Please."

Slater opened his door and climbed out. "Like I said, sit tight and let me go check."

Perched on the edge of his seat, Steven watched Officer Slater cross to a long blue panel truck marked MOBILE COMMAND CENTER and disappear inside. Almost instantly he reappeared accompanied by a familiar face with a gold shield clipped to his breast pocket.

Slater used a key to unlock the cruiser's rear door then stepped aside, allowing Detective Ahmad to pull it open.

Steven immediately jumped out and said to Ahmad, "Please tell me you got here in time. Are they okay?"

Detective Ahmad nodded. "Yes. Your family's fine."

Steven sagged against the cruiser and breathed.

Detective Ahmad continued, "Your wife was injured during the attack, but--"

"What? She was attacked? How bad?"

"Like I said, she's okay. Nothing serious. But it could've easily gone the other way." Detective Ahmad pinned Steven with narrowed eyes. "What you did was very stupid. You're facing accessory to murder at the very least."

Steven sighed and bowed his head. "I know, I know. But right now all I care about is my family. Where are they? Can I see them?"

"Unfortunately, no. They're still inside and the hospital's completely locked down. This is an active shooter situation."

"Wait. He's still in there? With Nichole?" Steven started moving toward the hospital.

"Whoa, whoa," Officer Slater said, cutting Steven off and grabbing his arms.

Steven cringed and clutched his injured hand. "FUCK!"

"Sorry," Slater said. "But let us do our job."

Detective Ahmad said, "Mr. Burns, as we speak your wife and child are surrounded by police, not to mention hospital security.

I assure you they're perfectly safe. Meanwhile we're searching room to room and vetting everyone before they exit. If he's who you say he is... we'll get him." He slipped a 5X7 black and white photo from his inside jacket pocket and showed it to Steven.

The professional headshot struck Steven as surreal. A slightly younger Judge Walker, draped in a judicial robe, seated on the bench with the American flag visible over his shoulder. Most disconcerting was the smile on the Judge's face. The thin, self-satisfied smirk of a man with a dark secret.

Steven nodded. "That's him."

"Every officer in that building has this photo," Detective Ahmad said. "I promise you... we'll get him."

"How long will it take?"

The detective frowned as he tucked the photo back into his jacket. "Hard to tell. Lots of exits. Let me get back to it." He turned to Officer Slater. "Keep him here."

Officer Slater nodded, then reached to reopen the cruiser's rear door.

Steven said to Detective Ahmad, "Please don't make me go back in there. I can't see shit and I feel like I'm suffocating."

Detective Ahmad gave Officer Slater a permissive nod then began to walk away.

Steven called after him, "Walker's smart."

Detective Ahmad glanced back.

"With computers, electronics, locks," Steven continued. "If there's an exit you're assuming he can't use. Check it anyway."

Detective Ahmad nodded and continued toward the command center.

Steven leaned against the cruiser and watched the ordered chaos unfolding outside the hospital's main entrance. He cradled his swollen hand and winced when he tried to flex his fingers.

Officer Slater watched quietly for a moment, then said,

"Ahmad's a straight shooter. He wouldn't bullshit you. If he says they're okay... they're okay."

Steven nodded appreciatively. "Thanks."

"What about you?"

Steven stared, puzzled.

"If I go grab someone to treat that hand, will you be here when I get back?"

Steven smiled. "Deal."

"Alright."

Steven watched Officer Slater traverse the line of emergency vehicles and continue to the hospital entrance.

"Excuse me. Do you know what happened?"

Steven turned to face an elderly woman whose fretful eyes were riveted to the commotion outside the hospital. Behind her, he noticed more people approaching across the parking lot with their necks craned.

Steven was about to lie to the woman about what he knew, when he spotted an individual that seized his attention.

On the far side of the lot a man dressed in pale green scrubs moved against the flow of gawkers, walking away from the hospital. His gait fell somewhere between casual and a leisurely stroll, as if calculated to avoid drawing attention. But something even odder bothered Steven. Despite the noise and mayhem of the emergency scene behind him... the man in scrubs never once glanced back.

He looks so... calm.

A chill slithered along Steven's spine.

"Was there a shooting?" the woman asked. "Did someone get hurt?"

Steven remained riveted to the man in scrubs. Studying his walk, his height, his build. Trying to spot if he wore glasses. The distance and angle made it difficult to tell, but--

I have to get closer.

He glanced back at the besieged hospital. Officer Slater was now talking to another officer at the entrance. No one was watching him.

"Oh, my," the elderly woman said. "Do you think it could be terrorists?"

"Sorry," Steven said as he brushed past her and hurried across the parking lot, after the man in scrubs.

76

Separated by an endless row of parked cars, Steven kept low as he crept closer and closer to the man in green scrubs. Peering over hoods and through car windows while in constant motion, it was still difficult to get a clear look at the man. His size seemed right, but the glasses were wrong. They appeared to be wirerimmed, not the thick black frames the Judge always wore.

He could be using a spare pair as a disguise.

Keeping his head down, Steven picked up the pace. He overshot his quarry by several cars, ducked behind a minivan, then peeked around the rear bumper and waited. The narrow space between the parallel-parked vehicles offered him a perfect view of the opposite walkway. When the man in scrubs passed, Steven would get an unobstructed view of his--

Loud barking erupted behind Steven. He whirled to face an angry terrier pulling at its leash.

An embarrassed middle-aged woman struggled to control the animal. She frowned at Steven. "I'm so sorry," then yanked the yapping dog to her side and continued away.

Steven whipped back to his hiding spot, expecting to see the man in scrubs stroll by... but saw nothing. Carefully, he peeked over nearby cars to check the man's position... and froze.

The man in scrubs was gone.

Fearing the man had already reached his vehicle, Steven stood and scanned the cars in the immediate area. He saw no one climbing into a car, or seated behind the wheel, or even glowing taillights.

Where could he have gone so fast?

A short distance away, a blue full-sized sedan grabbed Steven's attention. Despite being unoccupied and no one nearby, the trunk was wide open. More than likely, someone in a rush to check out the commotion at the hospital, simply forgot to shut their trunk. Still, combined with the man in scrubs' sudden disappearance, it struck Steven as odd.

After glancing around one last time, Steven slipped between parked cars and started across the walkway toward the blue sedan. As he drew closer to the open maw of the trunk, he noticed its dark interior was empty, except for a spare tire and what looked liked small pieces of torn paper. A few steps closer and Steven's brow tightened with puzzlement.

What he thought was torn paper was in fact white and pink flower petals.

Steven continued closer. Only when he stood directly over the open trunk could he see another object laying inside. A familiar, horrific object that caused him to recoil with a gasp.

The cold poke of a gun muzzle against the base of his skull caused Steven to freeze.

The Judge's raspy voice filled his ears. "Move and you're dead."

77

"How the hell are you here right now?" the Judge grumbled in Steven's ear.

He loomed so close that Steven could feel every syllable on the back of his neck. With one finger he poked Steven's swollen hand causing Steven to draw a sharp, grimacing breath.

"Clearly, I keep underestimating you," the Judge went on. "Not anymore." He jabbed Steven's spine with the gun. "Get into the trunk."

Steven didn't move. He couldn't. Not yet. "You're done," Steven said, resisting the urge to turn and face him. "I told the police everything. They have your name. Your address. Your picture. You're secret's already out."

The Judge made an amused sound. "Yes... and if you think I'll let you just walk away--"

"Not me. Nichole. Killing her is pointless now. Give me your word you'll leave her alone and I'll come quietly. Please."

The cacophony of shouts and sirens from the hospital filled the tense silence that followed. Finally, the Judge leaned closer and hissed, "Objection overruled." Then he grabbed Steven's injured hand and squeezed hard.

Steven doubled over, groaning in pain.

The Judge shoved him forward.

Steven tumbled headlong into the trunk. Crashed hard onto his back atop the flower petals.

Framed by the open trunk, the Judge, in pale green scrubs, loomed over him. Silenced handgun gripped at his side. Glaring.

"You've destroyed my family," the Judge said. "So I'm going to destroy yours. Beginning with you..."

The Judge raised the gun to fire...

Using his good hand, Steven grabbed the object beside him and swung out in a wide arc.

A millisecond before the gun exploded, the Louisville Slugger connected.

The Judge clutched his hand and cried out in pain as the gun went sailing across the parking lot.

Steven scrabbled to his knees in the trunk, winced as he gripped the baseball bat with both hands, and swung again.

The Judge's left leg buckled sideways with a wet crack and he crumbled to his knees, screaming.

Steven took his time climbing out of the trunk, his movements now deliberate and focused. Looming over the Judge, he dropped into a batter's stance and cocked the bat for one final swing. His lethal, resolute eyes were targeted on the Judge's bowed head.

Cradling his bleeding hand, glasses gone, the Judge looked up and met Steven's stare with a weak smile. "We both know you can't do it. So just calm down and--"

"You threatened to kill my family!" Steven growled.

The Judge sighed. "I served on the bench for thirty years. I have powerful friends. I'll serve some time, but I will get out.

When I do... you'll see what I said was no threat." His eyes narrowed. "It's a long-term goal."

Steven bristled. Hands trembling, he tightened his grip, hauled back on the bat, and--

"Freeze!"

"Drop it! Now!"

Steven turned.

Detective Ahmad and Officer Slater stood six feet away, pointing guns. More officers were running toward them.

Peering over his gun, Detective Ahmad said to Steven, "Don't be foolish. Your wife and daughter are safe and waiting to see you. Drop the bat. It's over."

Steven shook his head. "No, it isn't over. He said he has connections. He said he'll get out and kill my family. I can't let that happen."

"I understand," Detective Ahmad said. "But if you swing that bat--"

"Don't worry," the Judge called to Ahmad. "He doesn't have the guts to protect his family." He turned to Steven. "Isn't that right, Mr. Burns?"

Steven wheeled back to the Judge, coiled to strike.

"No!" Detective Ahmad shouted. "He saw us coming."

Steven froze. Glanced back at the detective. "What does that mean?"

"Don't you see what he's doing? Swing that bat and the only real witness against him is eliminated. He made that threat because he must've seen us coming. Think about it. Why else would he provoke you into assaulting him."

Steven paused to let that sink in, then turned back to the Judge with uncertain eyes.

"You pathetic coward," the Judge snarled at him. "Not even man enough to fight for your family. That's why Luna's dead. You let her die. You failed her... and now you're failing Sophia and your wife. When I get out I'm going to do them first, so you can feel your failure. Remember you could've saved them. Remember this moment when you're standing over their graves."

For tense beat Steven's eyes burned into him, arms taut, hands wringing the bat handle. Then, his rage was pushed back by a weary frown. Steven said to the Judge, "Looks like you're the one who needs to calm down." Then Steven tossed the baseball bat away, the way a slugger does after hitting a home run.

78

Steven strode beside Detective Ahmad down a deserted hospital corridor. Behind them, Officer Slater followed.

Despite the blue soft splint now wrapped around Steven's left hand, his wrists were handcuffed in front of him. His blood-stained top was gone, replaced by a gift shop T-shirt bearing an embroidered Hamilton Memorial Hospital logo. Steven actually liked the shirt and hoped to keep it as a souvenir.

The entire hospital was still under police lock-down, forcing the trio to circumvent food trolleys, gurneys, and wheelchairs abandoned during the evacuation.

Rounding a corner they approached four uniformed officers standing guard outside a hospital room.

The officers stood a bit straighter as they greeted Detective Ahmad with respectful nods.

Detective Ahmad turned to the oldest and only woman. The sleeves of her uniform bore gold chevrons. "How are they, Sergeant?"

"Both safe and sound," she said with a nod. Then she turned to Steven. "Your wife's a tough lady. Good mom, too."

The other uniforms nodded in agreement.

"Thanks," Steven said.

Detective Ahmad signaled Officer Slater who immediately removed Steven's handcuffs. As Steven rubbed his wrist, Ahmad said to him, "There's still a ton to wrap up here, so take your time." With that he gestured to the door.

Steven stepped forward and grabbed the door knob. He paused to take a deep breath, then opened the door and stepped inside.

79

S teven couldn't remember ever hearing his wife sing so beautifully. Her voice was hoarse and cracked, like every note hurt... yet he'd never heard anything more wonderful.

Nichole, her neck bandaged, was sitting up in the hospital bed, singing softly as she rocked Sophia in her arms.

"Three little monkeys jumping on the bed, one fell off and broke his head..."

The room was similar to Nichole's room in the maternity ward, but much larger and with high-end furnishings. Steven stood just inside the closed door, watching them. Mesmerized by a sight he feared he'd never see again.

Nichole glanced up and beamed when she spotted him. She beckoned him over with a wave of her hand.

As Steven approached he said to her, "I'm so sorry I put you and Sophia through--"

Nichole pressed a finger to her lips, "Shhhh." Then she tugged him closer and kissed him gently. When they parted there were tears in both their eyes. She whispered, "All that matters is that we're all okay." They kissed again, then Nichole carefully transferred the drowsy infant into Steven's arms.

As Steven gazed down at his daughter's peaceful little face, Judge Walker's last words intruded on the moment.

"Remember you could've saved them when you're standing over their graves."

But then Nichole began to sing that silly nursery rhyme again. Steven remembered it was Luna's favorite. Now, undoubtedly, it would someday be her sister's favorite as well.

Steven began to sing along with Nichole, drowning out the Judge's voice along with the cold lingering feeling of the waiting handcuffs.

"...momma called the doctor and the doctor said, no more monkeys jumping on the bed."

80

Four years later, beneath a brooding grey sky, Steven stood over the grave of his daughter with his face buried in his hands.

Navigating around headstones and stepping over grave markers, Linton approached Steven and laid a hand on his shoulder. "Hey, you okay?"

Steven shook his head. "No. It doesn't make sense. I went to prison for nearly three years for conspiracy. Walker's a killer. Worse, a serial killer. How could he get out?"

"Probably some bullshit technicality," Linton said.

Steven threw up his hands. "What am I talking about? Judge Walker did exactly what he threatened to do. He warned me. And right in front of the police. Goddammit!"

Linton grabbed him. "Listen to me. You can't linger on this. It'll mess you up. You have to go on with your life. And don't forget that Sharon and I are here for you. Always."

Steven nodded and embraced his best friend. "Thanks."

"Of course."

Steven felt a tug on his jacket. He looked down and saw an adorable four-year-old girl gazing up at him with big brown eyes. She wore a pretty violet dress with a matching bow, and a puzzled frown on her face. She said to Steven, "Why are you crying, daddy?"

Steven wiped his eyes, crouched down and gave Sophia a warm hug. "I'm okay sweetie. Daddy's just a little sad today, that's all."

"Why? Because it's Luna's birthday?"

"Oh, no. Never. That's something we celebrate."

"Then why are you sad?"

"Well--"

Suddenly Linton came to the rescue. "Come here, you little monkey." He hoisted a giggling Sophia into his arms. "Where's my smooch?"

As Sophia deposited a kiss on Uncle Linton's cheek, Nichole and Sharon arrived at the gravesite, Nichole clutching a bouquet of white daisies.

Sharon gasped playfully at Sophia, "Oooo, you giving out smooches? Can I have some?"

As Sharon joined Linton and Sophia in a group hug, Nichole noticed Steven's clouded eyes. "What's wrong?"

Steven pulled her aside and whispered, "Detective Ahmad just called. Walker's been released."

"What? How?"

Steven could only shake his head.

Nichole shut her eyes and took a calming breath. When she reopened them she put on a smile. "Not today. This is Luna's day. Come on."

They all gathered in front of Luna's headstone, a traditionally shaped grey marble slab with a large carved heart encompassing the inscription.

In loving memory of our beautiful and talented daughter, Luna Burns.

One by one they each laid a flower upon the grave, said happy birthday, and shared loving thoughts.

When it was Sophia's turn, she took a daisy from her mom, stepped forward, and carefully placed it on the ground. In a soft voice she said, "Happy birthday, Luna. We never met but you're still my big sister and I still miss you. I love you."

Sophia returned to her spot between Steven and Nichole and took both their hands. She frowned up at them. "Was that okay?"

"That was perfect, sweetheart," Nichole said, then turned to Steven, "right honey?"

Steven didn't reply. He was riveted to a man about 100 yards away, leaning against a tree, watching them. The man, who wore coveralls, gave Steven a friendly wave, then picked up a shovel and began to dig.

"Something wrong?" Linton asked.

Steven noticed everyone staring at him. He shook his head. "No. I'm fine." He put on a big smile for Sophia. "So, who's ready for some ice cream and cake?"

Sophia's hand shot up, "Me, me, me."

The End

Thank you for reading my latest book. I hope you enjoyed it. Want to get an email when my next title is released? Click here to subscribe to my newsletter for updates on future releases, sales and giveaways: http://eepurl.com/dwf5eL

ABOUT THE AUTHOR

Dwayne Alexander Smith is a screenwriter and author residing in Los Angeles.

His first novel, Forty Acres, won an NAACP Image Award for best literary debut.

When Dwayne isn't writing or spending time with his wife and son, he enjoys playing poker, reading, and watching movies.

Dwayne does not believe in Big Foot, saucers, or ghosts, but he truly wishes they did exist.

MK
cck

Printed in Great Britain
by Amazon